James Rice

The Cambridge Freshman

Or, memoirs of Mr. Golightly

James Rice

The Cambridge Freshman
Or, memoirs of Mr. Golightly

ISBN/EAN: 9783337251789

Printed in Europe, USA, Canada, Australia, Japan

Cover: Foto ©Andreas Hilbeck / pixelio.de

More available books at **www.hansebooks.com**

THE

CAMBRIDGE FRESHMAN;

OR,

MEMOIRS OF MR. GOLIGHTLY.

BY

MARTIN LEGRAND.

With numerous Illustrations by Phiz.

LONDON:
TINSLEY BROTHERS, CATHERINE STREET,
STRAND.

1878.

LONDON:
SWEETING AND CO., PRINTERS,
80, GRAY'S INN ROAD, HOLBORN.

CONTENTS.

THE
CAMBRIDGE FRESHMAN;

OR,

MEMOIRS OF MR. GOLIGHTLY.

CHAPTER I.

AN IMPORTANT CHAPTER, WHICH IMPATIENT READERS MAY SKIP, BUT WHICH THE SENSIBLE WILL CAREFULLY PERUSE.

THE Rector of Oakingham-cum-Pokeington had made up his mind: his son and heir, Mr. Samuel Adolphus Golightly, who had just completed at home a careful preparation for a University career, should be sent to Cambridge; and, with a bound from the general to the particular, the Rector had selected St. Mary's for his college.

To this conclusion the Reverend Mr. Golightly had not jumped with the haste that marks the precipitate man. He had duly deliberated. He had discussed the weighty question with his brother, the Squire, every time he had dined with him— which was once a-week—for about six months past. He had asked the advice of his curate, the Reverend Mr. Morgan, many times; though without, on any single occasion, intending to be in the most remote degree influenced by it. He had consulted his two maiden sisters, the Misses Dorothea and Harriet Golightly, who, when not at Bath, Cheltenham, or Tonbridge, were in the habit of pitching their tent at Oakingham Rectory; and, as they were the happy possessors of large sums safely invested in the Three per Cent. Consols, greater attention was usually paid to their views than was warranted by their intrinsic value when actually arrived at—a process which was often no easy task, and, indeed, on the present occasion was the source of considerable trouble to their brother; as, after much consideration, Miss Harriet declared decidedly in favour of Oxford and Christ Church, while Miss Dorothea provokingly gave her opinion for Cambridge and St. Mary's.

Their unhappy brother tried to reconcile these conflicting opinions, but unfortunately failed; and as his sister Dorothea was ten years the senior of Miss Harriet, and therefore, in the ordinary course of nature, a transfer of her Consols would take place first; and, further, being of the mature age of—now, I know I ought not to mention it, but I shall venture this once—fifty-eight, it was highly improbable that she would become "an unnatural traitor to the interests of her family" by having one of her own. Her opinion—a golden one— turned the scale. For the Rector himself was in favour of Cambridge, thinking it not so fast a place as Oxford; though in this matter, I have heard him declare, he was disagreeably deceived. Mrs. Golightly, as in duty bound, assented. And, lastly, our hero himself, whose illustrious name illuminates the headings of these pages, professed an entire readiness to set out for either place. For his cousin George had often told him that, if the governor and his two dear aunts only came down in a manner suited to the dignity and position of an ancient family, he would be able to make himself as much at home at one university as at the other. But as cousin George—the son of his uncle, the Squire—was then running the course of his *curriculum* at Cambridge, our hero had a slight leaning in favour of that seat of "sound learning and religious education;" and it was, therefore, with great pleasure that he learnt from his father one day, at the dinner table, that momentous decision of the Rector's with which this chapter commenced.

Before entering upon a minute and trustworthy personal description of the various members of the Golightly family, it will be well to say a few words on the Golightlys in general.

Almost everybody will know—at least, everybody who has ever talked for ten minutes to Miss Dorothea Golightly—that the Loamshire Golightlys are a branch—though a younger one, it must be admitted—of the great Tredsoft family; of whom the present Lord Tredsoft, or Tredsofte—or, as it is sometimes written, Treadsoft—is the direct male representative; and, of course, everybody will know tha t Burke says that this family can trace its pedigree to Edmund the Thickheaded, who flourished about four hundred years before the Norman Conquest; and thence to Simon Slyboots, who was surgeon corn-parer to Edmund the Confessor; whence, through a long line of illustrious ancestors, is sprung Adolphus, fourteenth Earl Tredsoft.

It will be sufficient to have shown that the Tredsoft family is one of the oldest and most distinguished in England; for to establish a connection between that particular branch of the Golightlys with which we are concerned and the noble earl whose pedigree we have just sketched is a most difficult nut to crack. However, Miss Dorothea is satisfied that it is quite clear, and not to be disputed. Her case varies a little, according to the state of her memory; but the last time she mentioned the matter it stood thus: "Her own cousin, three times removed, was the grandnephew of the Earl of Tredsoft's half-sister."

It will be a pleasant and instructive little problem, for such of our readers as are genealogists, to solve the relationship subsisting between Mr. Samuel Adolphus Golightly, the hero of this biography, and the Right Honourable Lord Tredsoft, from the data furnished above. Perhaps the arms of our branch of the Golightly family may be of some assistance in the matter. They are thus described in Burke:—

Arms—Two thistle-eaters, aspectant, proper, on field vert; tails borne erect.

Crest—An arm issuant, holding whip flectant.

No worthier member of the family ever bore these arms, in war and peace, than Mr. Samuel Golightly, the grandfather of our hero—and, consequently, the father of the Squire

and the Rector. The tablet to his memory in
Oakingham Church records his virtues to this
day:—" He was a pious man, a faithful friend,
a generous landlord, a kind husband, and a good
father; and for many years a Captain in the
Militia in this county." All of which is, I believe, quite true. He had the good fortune to in-
herit a large estate from his father, and he came
into a handsome property at the death of his
mother. The former, which was entailed, of course
devolved upon his elder son, John, the present
Squire of Oakingham; and the latter he bequeathed
—subject only to the payment of some charitable
legacies—to his younger son, Samuel, who took
orders and the family living at Oakingham-cum-
Pokeington. Thus, the worthy gentleman had the
satisfaction of providing equally well for his two
sons, and also handsomely for his two daughters—
whose names have already been mentioned. Having now made our readers acquainted with the
family history and position of the Golightlys, we
will, in our next chapter, give them a personal introduction to the various members of the family at
the Rectory.

CHAPTER II.

THE GOLIGHTLY FAMILY "AT HOME."

HE worthy Rector had come to the decision with which our first—and last—chapter commenced, on no less remarkable a day than the First of April. On the evening of the Seventeenth of October, in the same year, it was evident, from the stir in the house, that something was about to happen. The fact was, it was Mr. Samuel Adolphus's last evening at home. On the next day he was to leave the home of his ancestors, the bosom of his family, the arms of his mamma, for the first time in his life. That lady was anxious—as mas are on important occasions—the maiden aunts were fidgety, our hero nervous, the cook in tears, the coachman and butler in spirits, and the other members of the establishment in great bustle and confusion. Upon Mr. Golightly, senior, alone did coming events seem not to cast their shadows before; and it was,

perhaps, with rather more than his usual satisfaction with himself and with things in general, that, after having discussed a bottle of his
particular green-seal claret, accompanied by the
hopeful Samuel, he walked into his cheerful
drawing-room.   And while Tuffley, the butler, is
handing round the tea, we will indulge in a
hasty description of the different members of the
family.

Mr. Golightly, senior, was a short, stout gentleman, of middle age.   His hair was of a sandy
gray—apparently undecided whether to remain
the colour it had always been, or to turn gra-
dually to some other; his whiskers, which were
abundant, were of a lighter tint—indeed, they
might almost be called a sandy white; his chin
was clean shaven, and appeared above a white
cravat; his face was right pleasant to behold,
being lighted up with good-humour, benevolence,
and, I may add, with quiet satisfaction.   Em-
pires might fall, kings topple over, the vintage
of Château Margaux fail; but the rector of Oakingham-cum-Pokeington was still the Reverend
Samuel Golightly.

Mrs. Golightly was a lady tall, thin, and languid.
Her hair was auburn, with a tendency to red,
and was worn in ringlets, except on company

days, when, aided by her maid and pads, she raised a superstructure of plaits and bandoline edifying to witness. She had mild blue eyes and an everlasting simper; was a friend to all

THE GOLIGHTLY FAMILY "AT HOME."

the deserving poor persons in the parish, and took a great interest in poultry.

Near her sat Mr. Morgan, who had succeeded

the former curate when it was thought that the youthful Samuel Adolphus required a better stair-case to Parnassus than that gentleman's tuition afforded. From this it will be gathered that he filled the position of curate and tutor. "Simple, grave, sincere," he enjoyed the confidence and returned the affection of all the family. The two maiden aunts, the Misses Harriet and Dorothea, were overcoming their feelings at parting from their favourite nephew by playing at cribbage for red and white counters, at two and sixpence a dozen. Cribbage was a game to which they usually sat down every evening, directly after dinner, and played until bed-time; unless they left the cribbage board to join in a rubber of whist with the Squire and their brother, or Mr. Morgan. They were well-preserved women for their time of life; and Miss Harriet was still really a comely lady. The elder sister's features were stern and angular; but the younger took after her brother, and possessed his benevolent smile and light complexion. Miss Dorothea was a lady of great determination, and had opinions upon most subjects; whereas, on the other hand, Miss Harriet rarely expressed herself very de-cidedly; indeed, her mind, as a rule, was a faint, though faithful, echo of Miss Dorothea's—a feeble dripping, as it were, from the reservoir of sense and virtue that was enclosed in her elder sister. However, with all respect be it said, Miss Harriet could assert herself: when really *up*, her independence amounted to obstinacy. These two ladies were much attached to each other, and rarely quarrelled, except at cards or over the affections of their dear nephew, Samuel. This young gentleman—before whom a brilliant career was just opening—was leaning over the table at which his aunts were sitting. He was tall, like his mamma; and fat, like his papa. His hair was light and wavy. He was considered to have his mamma's eyes and his papa's nose, quite his grandpapa's mouth, and, without doubt, the family chin. Like his mamma, he smiled at almost everything that was said to him, and with all that he said himself; and, altogether, his face, if not indicative of genius, certainly gave early promise of whiskers—and genius and whiskers are not unfrequently to be found united in the same person.

I may add that, when at all excited or taken by surprise, Mr. Samuel had a habit of hammering and stammering a little at certain consonant sounds, which lent an individuality to his utterance, and thence to his character, thereby relieving it from the imputation of tameness. This habit of hammering and stammering, his mamma attributed to a fright he got in his early infant life, through fancying he saw something in the dark; but in this opinion neither his nurse nor Mr. Gubbett, the family surgeon, agreed. Now, Mr. Gubbett was acquainted professionally with a certain Mr. Glibb, who possessed a valuable system or method for the cure of persons afflicted with a stutter; and as he assured the infant Samuel's mamma that Lady Ralph Penthesilea had tried it with great success upon Master Ralph Penthesilea, and as the mention of Lady Ralph Penthesilea's name alone carries great weight with it in the estimation of Mrs. Golightly, it was decided that Mr. Glibb should be at once consulted; and he directed that Master Samuel should be made to pronounce the Queen's English in monosyllables, with his right hand resting upon a table, and carefully putting down a finger upon it at each syllable he spoke. And this may account for his ideas still flowing rather slowly. Whether Mr. Glibb's system, or increasing years and intelligence, produced the desirable result, I do not know; but, within ten years after trying the system, our hero's articulation had greatly improved, and, at the time of which I write, was as nearly perfect as could be expected.

Tuffley having now removed the tea-cups, the Rector endeavoured to resume, in the drawing-room, the important duty he had commenced in the dining-room—namely, putting a final touch to those precepts which were to mould, and that practical advice which was to guide, his son through the snares and pitfalls of an unfeeling and designing world. He stationed himself upon that rostra from which an English Paterfamilias most easily and happily delivers himself of his sentiments—namely, upon his own hearth-rug, with his back to his own fire, and with his hands well supporting his own coat-tails. His son and heir stood beside him in an attitude of rapt attention; but, as his maiden aunts had not quite finished their last game at cribbage, and Mrs. Golightly was refreshing Mr. Morgan's memory of what—as she had often before told him—was her opinion of what a silver-pencilled Hamburg should be when in perfection, the Rector was sensible that his Platonic sentences hardly fell upon the ears of young Samuel with their due weight. In fact, for some few moments, the conversation had been after this sort—our hero standing on a particular square of the carpet, where he must perforce hear all that was said in the room:—

The Rector: "It is my particular wish—I might

almost go the length of saying command—that you should, immediately on your arrival—"

Mrs. Golightly: "Send a pen of fowls to the Birmingham Show."

The Rector: "Call upon an old friend of mine, named Smith. You will be sure to hear people say—"

Miss Dorothea: "Fifteen two, fifteen four, fifteen six, a pair eight, two are ten, and one for his nob."

The Rector (going on from where he had left off): "Where he lives. He always used to say—"

Miss Dorothea: "Come, hand over the counters. You see, this makes me out: twenty-four and seven's a leg."

Now, "seven's a leg" was a little family bit of fun, which the elder sister always rebuked the younger sister for using when she was out of temper, but used herself whenever she was in a good temper—that is, in good luck. The old militia Captain—whose virtues we recorded before —was, amongst other of "the ills that flesh is heir to," a great sufferer from the gout, which he persistently aggravated by immoderate doses of port, doctored up from a recipe upon which he set a high value; and being a great cribbage player— for with the Golightlys cribbage has become quite

an hereditary game, and comes to them as naturally as going to church or going to bed—he used
to alleviate his sufferings, during the attacks of his
enemy, by playing at his favourite game. And it
is a well-authenticated tradition in the family, that
one day—the gout in his left extremity being more
excruciating than usual—he called out, dropping
his cards at the same time in order to seize and
comfort the afflicted member, "twenty-four, and
seven's a *leg*." Thus it arose, then, that, on this
particular evening, Miss Dorothea—his daughter
—finished her game with "twenty-four and seven's
a *leg*." And the conclusion of the game and the
end of Mrs. Golightly's dissertation concerning
prize fowls occurring together, left the Rector at
liberty to continue, without interruption, his last
address to his son, before sending him forth to
fight his battles with the gyps, bedmakers, examiners, friends, foes, and follies of a University
life.

The worthy gentleman had primed himself for
this trying occasion with the "Aphorisms of Lord
Bacon," my Lord Chesterfield's "Letters to his
Son," and rather more than two-thirds of a bottle
of his own claret; and he was retailing to the
hopeful Samuel a curious mixture of the three,
in which, if he had not been the parson, I should

have said, without one moment's hesitation, the last-named slightly predominated. He enjoined upon our hero, in solemn and touching tones, the respective and collective values of industry, punctuality, and early rising upon a man's future success in life.

"These three qualities," said the Rector, "united with mental tranquillity under all circumstances, collectedness of faculties, and imperturbation of feature, mark the great man. Think, my dear Samuel, of the great Bacon, the politic Chesterfield, the—a—the quiet Watts; think of 'How doth—' I mean—a—

> ' Early to bed, and early to rise,
>   Is the way to be healthy, wealthy, and wise.'"

(Before Mr. Adolphus had been at the University long, he was taught to believe it was—

> " The way to be cross and have very sore eyes.")

" And then," pursued the Rector, " my dear boy —I may add," continued his father, with rapidly increasing solemnity of manner and depth of tone, " my *only* boy—think of the example that I have always set you; and think of dear Mr. Morgan, and the precepts he has aided me in inculcating;

and try—do try—to be a man of the world, Adolphus, such as you know I wish to see you—practical, virtuous, steady—an ornament to that station of life in which it has pleased Providence to place you. And," continued the good man, his feelings fast overpowering him, "my last advice is, be cool—be calm—be col—lected!"

This eloquent appeal to the examples and precepts of the living (Mr. Morgan) and the dead (Bacon, Chesterfield, and Watts) was received by the three ladies and the curate with due murmurs of approbation; for in his own family Mr. Golightly was looked upon as a wise and clever man, and out of it as a good but mistaken man; and, therefore, whenever he addressed his family, either from the pulpit in the church or from the pulpit on the hearth, his remarks were received with deference and respect. By our hero alone—such alas! is the callousness of human nature—they were not so highly appreciated; for the fact was, that by frequent repetition his father's opinions and warnings had lost that novelty which is necessary to rivet the attention of a mind disturbed by the prospect of rising an hour earlier than usual next day.

Mrs. Golightly availed herself of this opportunity to send for the butler, to inquire if everything was

c

ready for Mr. Samuel, and if the wine had been packed as she had directed.

It was a source of grief to the good lady that she could not have the melancholy pleasure of starting her son off with cold chicken enough for a week at least, if every meal were luncheon ; for I believe she would have signed the death-warrant of any or all of the finest pullets and cockerels in the poultry-yard with the greatest readiness, in order that her Samuel might think of her and home whilst he ate them, had she not been told by the Rector that such sacrifice on her part was unnecessary, chickens being plentiful and easily procurable from the college kitchens. The astute Aunt Dorothea added a little advice, and expressed a hope that Samuel would learn to play well at whist, a game of which she was an enthusiastic admirer. Miss Harriet, for her part, hoped that he would speedily acquire the art of infusing the tea for himself; and that the elaborate worsted-work tea-pot cover—technically termed, I believe, a tea-cosey—which she had provided for him, would materially assist in the production of that desirable adjunct of the scholar's life, tea. Mr. Morgan intimated that on the morrow it was his intention to present his pupil with a small token of his regard. Miss Dorothea often used to express her wonder at what he did with all his money: a hundred fifty pounds a-year for being a curate and a tutor, and thirty pounds arising from the secure investment of nine hundred and thirty-one pounds six shillings and eightpence in the Three per Cent. Consols! Bless you, Miss Dorothea, that modest hundred and eighty pounds flowed out in as many little rills of beneficence. It gave bread to one, physic to another, and clothing to a third. It was at the command of all the parish, and the only person who really did not have any of it was that good Mr. Morgan himself. What want had he if his neighbour lacked? And Miss Dorothea wondered what he did with his money!

Hark! the jingle of glasses. In comes Tuffley with the tray, and all the family partake of a little negus, to make them sleep—of course, the ladies have it very weak ; and they all of them indulge in an anti-flatulent biscuit a-piece, and then retire for the night.

And Mr. Samuel Adolphus dreamed that he and his cousin George were playing at leap-frog in their caps and gowns in the parish church, and would not let old Bumpy the beadle come in ; and Bumpy was pounding away at the church door with a clothes-prop out of his garden, when—

"Oh! all right, Smith.   Yes—say I am getting up now.   All right!"

For it was Smith the footman, and not Bumpy the beadle; and, instead of the church door, it was our hero's own bed-room door at which the knocking was going on.

CHAPTER III.

IN WHICH MR. GOLIGHTLY STARTS FOR CAMBRIDGE,
IN THE COMPANY OF HIS COUSIN GEORGE AND
THE HONOURABLE JOHN POKYR, AND DULY AR-
RIVES THERE.

IF there was bustle and confusion in the house of Golightly on the night before, what was there on the great day itself? Everybody was trying to do everything at once, and tumbling over everybody else. However, breakfast was got on the table by half-past eight somehow; and the different members of the family came down to partake of it. Mrs. Golightly's eyes looked pinky, and Miss Harriet's were positively red. I believe the former, and I am sure the latter, had let fall a few womanly tears. The Rector was doing his best to keep up appearances, by playing the philosopher at the expense of his feelings. Mr. Samuel had been round to pay a parting visit to various dumb friends—

dogs and horses.   Having performed this duty to
himself and his favourite animals, our hero then ran
in to breakfast; and with difficulty got through
that meal, scalding his mouth with the coffee he was
pouring down his throat to save himself from being
choked with his toast and butter.   And then his
father presented the new gold lever he had always
said he should have to take to the University—
Mr. Samuel had previously worn an antiquated
verge, once the property of the worthy Captain of
militia mentioned in a previous chapter—and Aunt
Harriet's tea-cosey was found to contain several
pieces of peculiar tough printed paper, dated from
the Bank of England, and signed Hy. Dixon,
which were understood to be the joint offering of
the two maiden ladies at the shrine of youth and
virtue.   Mrs. Golightly, his mamma, brought forth
a knitted sofa blanket and a noble pair of slippers,
with foxes' heads, having glass beads for eyes, all
over them.   And good Mr. Morgan placed on the
table a sealed packet, which was understood to
contain a pocket Bible and Keble's " Christian
Year."

At this juncture, Smith, the footman, said, flush-
ing slightly as he spoke—"Would Mr. Samuel be
so good as to step outside a moment?"   And there
was Betty, the cook, who had nursed him in his

infancy, with a packet which struck rather warm through the white paper:—"Would Mr. Samuel please to accept it?" And when opened it was found to be a plum cake, recently baked, and a pot of mixed pickles, with "*Affection's Offering*" scrawled inside the wrapper. And then all the presents, except the gold lever, were hastily taken off to be packed; and the Rector placed the watch in his son's hands, but without the speech he had intended to make—which, everything considered, was quite as well; and our hero said, "Thank you, Fa"—for he was in the habit of calling his father "Fa." And then the roll of wheels outside on the gravel drive was heard, and the carriage drew up at the door, and the luggage was all put in—not forgetting the two hampers of wine, which were carefully stowed away in front.

"Good-bye," said Miss Dorothea; "and never forget you are a Golightly, and that your own cousin, four times removed, is grandnephew to an—"

And "Good-bye," said Aunt Harriet; "and be sure you use your tea-cosey."

"And mind," said Mr. Morgan, "you sometimes read your—"

And the good man blushed as he recollected that had been his present, lest he should seem to be reminding his pupil of that, when all he meant was his good.

"And be sure you take to your new flannels if the weather gets cold," said his mother.

THE FAMILY "SHAY."

And both the Miss Golightlys together said— "Write to us directly you get there."

And as he jumped into the family carriage he

heard his father saying, in becomingly solemn tones, " Be a man of the world."

And his mamma's voice chiming in, " Like your dear Fa."

And he was gone—round to the Hall, to call for his cousin George.

The family returned slowly to the breakfast-room, and sat themselves down in gloomy silence. The first thing that occurred to break it was a remark from Mrs. Golightly to the effect that " there was something very supporting about a glass of sherry;" continuing, that she felt quite "shaken." A glass of sherry was instantly brought her, and was found to afford her some slight relief.

For his part, the Rector took an early opportunity of marching off to his study, where he sat down to peruse Bacon's "Aphorisms" and Lord Chesterfield's celebrated " Letters," with a view to preparing himself, from those brilliant models, for a thorough course of improving epistolary correspondence with his son. His mind, I must say, wandered a little from his authors, and his imagination began to play ; thereby enabling him to picture, in a lively and pleasing manner, all sorts of impossible honours, prizes, and distinctions that were to fall in after-life to the lot of his son—a brilliancy which might be reflected upon him, and brighten his declining years with a resplendent though borrowed lustre. Imagination, too, carried him on, and suggested the possibility of " Letters from the Rector of Oakingham to his Son at the University:" London. The good man hesitated between the several rival publishers; and, finally, composed himself steadily for the study of Bacon.

We are not always best at what we think we excel in. I know the Rector thought his vocation in life should have been the statesman's. The character he most admired was the clever, ready, keen-witted man of the world. I know he always regretted that his brother could never be induced to stand for Fuddleton.

Had *he* had the chance! Ah! poor, dear, simple Rector, you would have been food for the fishes. Yet you want Samuel Adolphus to be a man of the world—of course, on a good, sound, scriptural basis, but still—

I recollect the reverend gentleman whipped all the family off to the Isle of Wight once, at twelve hours' notice, because he had just read in a book from Mudie's that a Sir John Somebody, when he was asked when he should be ready to start for India, replied, " To-morrow."

The Rector seized the idea. Poor Mrs. Golightly begged to go to the seaside. The Rector said " To-morrow," and meant it. This he thought was decision of character, energy on a magnificent scale, and so forth.

Poor man, when he found the only razor he could shave with and all his clean pocket-handkerchiefs were left behind, with half the other things, he was obliged to keep his temper and bear it. Now, when the family leave home, a week's notice is always given, at the sacrifice of energy, decision of character, and sentiment generally.

But to return from the author of his existence to our hero himself.

During the ten minutes' drive from the Rectory to the Hall, he felt the pain of a tender heart and affectionate disposition at leaving the bosom of his family, even for the comparatively short period of seven weeks; but he had no sooner arrived at the door of the Hall, and taken on board his sprightly cousin George, than, speedily recovering his usual flow of spirits, he was able to exchange salutations with his uncle, his aunt, and his cousin Arabella, with some show of composure. Mr. George Golightly's luggage—which was of much smaller dimensions than our hero's—being

safely fixed on the top of the carriage, they
drove off, waving their adieux to their affectionate
relatives.   And it was lucky that the Rectory
carriage was a strong, old-fashioned vehicle, of
the species family coach, and not one of those
elegant equipages which the " admirers of light
carriages " delight to possess, or it never would
have stood a ten miles' journey over such roads
as lay between Oakingham and the railway station at Fuddleton, with such a weight upon it
as it had to carry on this occasion.   However,
the carriage did perform the journey, and did
its work rather better than the horses did theirs;
for if two minutes more had been occupied on
the way, the train would, in all probability, have
started without the distinguished passengers inside.

These two Rectory carriage horses always appeared to know—by a sort of intuition, remarkable but unerring — when they were going to
Fuddleton; and, as it was a journey they did not
in any way approve of, went rather more slowly
than was their wont on other journeys.   Their best
pace was about six miles an hour, but they did not
do the Fuddleton course in much under two hours;
being fat, sleek animals, and better adapted for
"staying" than for the "T.Y.C." business.   "Sprint

races," as Mr. George had often remarked, were not in their line.

The two gentlemen sat on the back seat, with their faces to the horses. With the appearance of Mr. Samuel Adolphus our readers are already acquainted. His cousin, Mr. George, was a smart, good-looking young man, and one of the leaders of fashion in the ancient University of which he was a bright ornament. His manners were dashing, his talk lively, and—without a doubt—his coats were of the latest mode. The Cesarewitch had just been decided, and he was occupied some time in adjusting "his book" upon that event, and making a list, in metallic pencil, at the end, of what he had to draw and to pay over it; and, when he had done that he had to swallow his hebdomadal dose of *Bell's Life—Bell* does not reach Oakingham Park till Monday mornings; so conversation did not take place to any great extent between the two gentlemen during the first part of their journey. I know, at this time, Mr. George Golightly used to consider his cousin Samuel's conversation slow. Every now and then, however, he looked up from his paper to grumble at the pace they were going, and declare in strong language that "he'd be blowed if those old pigs would **ever** get them there within an hour of the time."

And our hero, of course, took the opportunity, every time it offered, of consulting his new watch; and it was not kind of George to say that, "If he had got a smarter ticker than other people, he need not be for ever pulling it in and out of his pocket."

However, Mr. Samuel was used to his cousin's playful way, and made himself as happy as he could with his sandwiches and cherry brandy, and tried to think the "Cambridge Guide" was really interesting reading.

At last they arrived at the station, and as they drove up they were overtaken by a smart drag from Fendre Abbey, Lord Shovelle's seat. In it were two gentlemen, the Honourable John Pokyr—my lord's second son—and a college friend who had been spending some days with him, Mr. Calipash Calipee, a native of India— son of Bobadjee Rumwalla Fustijee Calipee, the well-known converted prince and banker of Madras. They were accompanied by two servants, a smooth-haired terrier, a bulldog, two horses, and a considerable amount of heavy luggage; to say nothing of bundles of whips, sticks, and canes, rugs, and other paraphernalia.

"By jingo!" cried Mr. Pokyr, giving the Indian gentleman what is vulgarly but expressively styled a dig in the ribs. "Why, that's old Golightly and his cousin Samuel in the family shay. Gad, this is a go! Why, we shall go up together."

"We may meet with an accident, and never get there," said Mr. Calipash Calipee, slowly recovering his power of articulate speech.

This gentleman, familiarly known as " the Nigger," was very dark, stout, and melancholy; and had a habit of making his society more agreeable by always reminding his company of the possibility of some catastrophe being at hand.

"Come, get out, and don't fancy we are going to lift you down. You know, you're a leetle too heavy for that business, Nigger. Come along."

" How d'ye do, Golightly?" continued Mr. Pokyr, addressing Mr. George, who was just alighting from the "family shay."

These gentlemen shook hands very cordially.

"And you've got the youthful cousin with you," said the facetious Mr. Pokyr. "Well, Mr. Samuel Adolphus, how have you left your dear mam-mar?"

Mr. Pokyr's style of address was familiar; but then he was a very funny fellow, and had a reputation to keep up.

Mr. George and Mr. Calipee shook hands; or, rather, Mr. George shook Mr. Calipee's hand for him.

It is often a social problem, altogether beyond our province to discuss, which *is* to be the
shaker.

"Come here, Nigger," called out Mr. Pokyr.
"Mr. Calipee — Mr. Golightly.   Needn't look
frightened: he doesn't bite—here, you know, I
mean," added Mr. Pokyr, in a whisper.   "In his
own country all the family are Cannibals.   Know
it for a fact, you know.   Take my oath, and all
that.   'Salmi de baby' is quite a common dish.
Come, now," he added, "don't be alarmed.   Shake
hands, and be friends.   There, then," said he,
suddenly expanding an umbrella in his left hand,
whilst he placed the right above their heads,
after the celebrated photograph of the Bishop of
Oxford.   "Ber-less ye, my children, ber-less ye.
Kiss and be friends."

The porters, who knew him well, thought he *was*
the funniest fellow that ever came to the station;
and all agreed, as they drank his health at the
Railway Arms, after they had started the train
and pocketed a tip, "that he were a rum 'un, he
were, if ever there wor one."   And old Jinks, the
superannuated carriage-wheel greaser, added his
testimony, that "young Muster John were no more
of a man nor his father wor afore him.   He recollected him just such another."

The luggage having been taken over to the up-platform—

" Now, then, any more for Bletchley, Cambridge, Oxford, or London?" called out the ticket-taker, merely as a matter of form; and the bell rang just as Mr. Samuel rushed wildly up to Mr. George, exclaiming—

" Goodness gracious, George, I've left my purse on the p—piano! I—I th—thought I should leave something behind!"

" Just what I thought," said his cousin, considerately. " I suppose I had better take a ticket for you. You can't very well be left behind."

So he did so; and they all four got comfortably into the carriage. Mr. Samuel and Mr. Calipee had managed to monopolize the hot-water pans between them, when the former gentleman found he had left his pocket-handkerchief in the carriage; and the porter was started off for that, and just got to one end of the platform as the train was moving out at the other. So our hero borrowed his cousin's, and made use of it with great vigour, in order to prove that he really wanted his own. The colour was just fading from his physiognomy, after the last of a series of tremendously exciting "blows," when it was painfully recalled by Mr. Pokyr's hand descending with

D

some force upon his leg, accompanying the question—

"And what are you backing **for next** year's Darby, Mr. Samuel Adolphus?"

Our hero was obliged to confess, with a blush of shame upon his countenance, that he "wasn't backing anything at all."

"Pretty innocent," said the Honourable John, producing from the pocket of his overcoat a sporting-looking volume. "Let me lay you the odds against something, then. Must back something, you know. Everybody does that. It is necessary before matriculation!"

"Indeed!" replied our hero.

Now, with his father's advice never to betray an ignorance of everyday matters still fresh in his recollection, I verily believe Mr. Golightly would, on the spur of the moment, so far have accommodated Mr. Pokyr's book as to invest a small sum upon something; but he did not know the name of a horse in the race. This difficulty was unexpectedly overcome by Mr. Pokyr's saying that he could lay against Blue Bell, the Laird, or Catch-him-who-can; and that he had a little more to lay out against Whistler for a "situation," if Mr. Golightly preferred that form of investment.

At this period of his existence, however, the

gentleman to whom this offer was addressed was in happy ignorance of what a "situation" might be; and therefore it was not reasonable to suppose that he would express a decided preference for that method of losing his money.

He was hesitating as to what course should be pursued by one who, from the very outset of his career, desired to be thought a man of the world, when his cousin George interfered to prevent his losing his money to Mr. Pokyr, by showing a way in which he might lose it to him.

"Don't you be in a hurry to back anything, old fellow," said Mr. George, confidentially. "I shall have a book on the race myself, and I'll let you have the market price against anything in the race, and give you a tip besides."

"I'll give you one now, if you don't know anything," said Mr. Pokyr, readily. "And I've been told—" he added, sinking his voice into a whisper —"but you'll keep this quiet?"

Our hero assured him, on his word and honour, he would.

"Well, then, I've been told of an outsider," mentioning an animal whose name he had not had the pleasure of pencilling, "called Dormouse; and they do say he stands a wonderful chance. Had the tip direct from Newmarket, where he is trained.   Now, you can have ten to one against him.   Let me lay you the odds to a 'fiver'—now, do.   Well, then," putting his pencil to the book, "to a sov.   Come, that can't hurt you!   Shall I book it?"

"What has he told you," asked Mr. George.

Forgetting his solemn promise, Mr. Samuel mentioned the name of "Dormouse" with the greatest innocence of manner.

"Didn't you say you would keep that quiet?" demanded Mr. Pokyr, doing his best to suppress a smile and look fierce.

"Keep it quiet!" said George; "it would take some time to make it noisy, wouldn't it?"

"I—I b—beg pardon," said our hero; "I quite forgot.   I did really, now."

"All right, Golightly; never mind, old fellow— done no mischief.   You were just going to tell me to put you down—"

Mr. George winked at Mr. Samuel.   The latter gentleman understood what that wink meant.

"N—no, I—I would rather not, I think; that is, I will consider about it."

Mr. Pokyr expressed his opinion that the Dormouse required no consideration; but Mr. Samuel could not be brought round.

"Well, then, don't you back anything with your

cousin George without just letting me know what
you're at, because he is sure to have you."

"Do not shout so, Pokyr," exclaimed Mr.
Calipee, from his own corner of the carriage,
where he had made himself tolerably comfortable.
"It is quite a moral impossibility to go to sleep
while there is such a row going on."

"Oh," replied Mr. Pokyr, "if you think you are
going to sleep all the way up, you've made a slight
mistake; so you may as well wake up at once, and
save me the trouble of rousing you. Just look at
him, Golightly; never saw such a fellow to sleep in
my life as he is—on my honour, I never did. The
beggar's been staying with us at Fendre for a fortnight, and 'gad he's been asleep nearly all the time
—that is, when not grubbing. And this is just
what he does at the Cutlet of a Saturday; and, in
fact, everywhere else—isn't it, Golightly? Demme,
Calipee, you are always dropping off. Talk to you
at dinner—think you're listening; look at you—
bedad, you're as near asleep as dammit."

The gentleman thus addressed made a silent
defence by opening both his eyes and producing
his cigar case. He selected a weed from it, stuck
it in his mouth, and passed the case to Mr. Pokyr;
who did the same, handing it in turn to Mr.
George and our hero.

The four gentlemen soon succeeded in filling the carriage with what a lady novelist once called "ethereal vapour of the Virginian weed."

"Talking of the Cutlet," said Mr. Pokyr, between the puffs of his Havannah, "what do you say to putting our noble cousin up, Golightly?"

"Oh, ah!" said Mr. George; "of course, if he likes."

"Has your cousin ever told you anything about the Cutlet?" Mr. Pokyr inquired, addressing the hero of this biography.

"Never, that I recollect," replied Mr. Samuel; "but I will not be quite sure."

"Oh, I see!" was Mr. Pokyr's rejoinder, "anxious to avoid blowing his own trumpet, and telling his fond relatives of all his successes."

"Now, Pokyr, don't be a fool!"

The truth was, his family sketches of University life were artfully toned down to meet the exigencies of the case. The high lights in the pictures were subdued; draperies carefully disposed over some parts and removed from others; books, scribbling-paper, and bundles of quill pens carelessly strewn about the immediate foreground; whilst in the middle distance the Little-go was a prominent object, the background being filled in with the B.A. degree. And all the works of this artist are distinguished by a dense atmosphere of "grinding" and green tea.

They were at this period—the end of his first year at college—much admired by his mother and the Squire.

Mr. Samuel Golightly, hearing with pleasure of his cousin's success, which he not unreasonably connected with mathematical and classical literature, inquired, with an intelligent smile lighting up his intelligent features, "if the Cutlet Club was a literary association?" adding, that "such societies, he believed, affected eccentric names. He had heard of a Savage Club."

He had evidently said something rather good, for his cousin looked amused; Mr. Pokyr laughed for a second or so, till stopped by a violent cough; and even the melancholy Mr. Calipee showed his white teeth. You could tell he was laughing, for his fat sides shook perceptibly beneath his sealskin waistcoat.

Directly Mr. Pokyr had overcome his cough, he replied to our hero's query—

"Oh, yes, Golightly. You have about hit the mark this time. We do all we can, in our humble way, at the meetings of the Mutton Cutlet Club, to cultivate and encourage literature, and to extend the circle of the sciences."

"Dear me!" ejaculated Mr. Samuel, with the most marked interest. "Do you?"

"Yes. And although we do not boast a secretary, we have a president, of whom we are proud."

Mr. Golightly proceeded to ask the name of that exalted functionary.

"Why, a man you may know, or, at least, you've heard of him," replied Pokyr.

"Who is it, then?" demanded Mr. Samuel, in a rapture of impatient interest.

"FitzFoodel," said his informant.

"N-not Frederick FitzFoodel?"

"That is the man, I believe; though we all call him Jockey FitzFoodel."

"Really," exclaimed Mr. Samuel, "now, you quite astonish me. Pokyr, I believe you're in fun! You are such a joker."

"It is true enough—is'nt it, Nigger? You were the rejected candidate—you ought to know."

Mr. Calipee bowed his head in token of assent, remarking, in a scarcely audible voice, "that of course, if he was fool enough to stand for anything, he should not be elected—that was not like his luck!"

"Well—but," pursued our hero, "I had no idea that Fr—, that is, I mean that J-Jockey Fitz-Foodel, as you call him, was a lover of literature!"

"Oh, an enthusiastic admirer of some of its branches, I assure you!" (sporting novels and Weatherby's Calendar)—"and a constant patron of others"—(the President of the Mutton Cutlet Club subscribed to *Bell's Life* and " Baily's Magazine").

" I have heard him shout very loud when he is out with the hounds," remarked Mr. Samuel.

" Fine speaker, I must say," rejoined Mr. Pokyr.

"And what do you do at the Cutlet Club?" inquired Mr. Samuel.

" Oh, meet at each other's rooms, drink tea, and spout—I mean, converse upon literary and scientific subjects."

" Delightful!" exclaimed Mr. Golightly, placing the most implicit faith in all the statements made by Mr. Pokyr.

"Then you think you would like to join us?" said the last-named gentleman.

" I am sure I shall be very much pleased if I am elected," answered our hero.

" Oh, you may make sure of that, old fellow, if I put you up, and the Nigger seconds you. They never blackball our men—do they, Nigger? Dam—he's asleep, I believe," added Mr. Pokyr, raising his voice. "Nigger, wake up! You'll second our friend if I propose him—won't you?"

"All right. Delighted, I'm sure," said the Indian, relapsing again into his slumbers.

"I'm sure my Fa will be delighted too!" said Mr. Samuel, with great animation. "He is very fond of books himself. I shall write home and tell—"

"I do not know what makes your cousin laugh, Golightly! There are lots of men who would give their heads to get in, I can tell you. We are pretty select, you know."

Mr. Samuel Golightly said he was sure they were, and he felt highly complimented at the distinguished honour of being a prospective member of the Mutton Cutlet Club.

"You will favour us with a paper on something at an early date?"

Our hero thought that, for the present at least he should be content to be a listener.

"Tell you what, Pokyr," said Mr. George, "I think this is rather slow. Let's do something."

"Well, wake the Nigger, and let us have a mild rubber. You can play whist?" said he, addressing Mr. Samuel.

"A little," replied that gentleman, with as much truth as modesty.

"That is," said Pokyr, "you know the moves—know a spade from a diamond, I mean?"

" Yes—oh, yes. I have often played with my aunts."

" Come on, then," replied Mr. Pokyr, producing

A HAND AT CARDS.

from his pocket a morocco case, containing two packs of cards.

Mr. Calipee having been roused, and a board— which the guard had supplied before they left

Fuddleton—adjusted between the four gentlemen so as to form a card table, they cut for partners. The result was, our hero and Mr. Pokyr *versus* George and Mr. Calipee.

"Your deal, Nigger—you cut the ace, I think. Half-crown points, if agreeable."

"I'm sure to lose, as usual," responded the lugubrious Nigger. "But anything you wish, you know."

Mr. George and our hero made a similar arrangement, after it had been explained that a dollar and five shillings were convertible terms, and, consequently, half-a-dollar was synonymous with two and sixpence.

The first three tricks fell very smoothly to George and Mr. Calipee. At the end of the fifth, Mr. Pokyr asked our hero, in anything but an amiable manner, what in the world he meant by not returning his lead.

Mr. Samuel felt altogether at sea at this sort of whist. He always played for the best, as far as he could see; but had no particular rules of action.

At the end of the game, Mr. Pokyr, being very irate, rated him soundly for fooling away three tricks at the very least; and wanted to know what he meant by leading his Queen of Clubs, when he held ace and two little ones

Mr. Samuel did not clearly know what he meant by it; but wisely held his peace.

At the end of game number two they had gained a double, against a single scored by their opponents.

Mr. Pokyr, acting upon an old-fashioned but almost universally practised rule—"at the end of every losing game, pitch into your partner!"—did so in very strong terms; at the same time, telling Mr. Samuel to mark the game.

Now, our hero always was in the habit of leaving the scoring to his partner. He knew his Aunt Dorothea always did something with the pegs and cribbage board at the end of a game, and that his Fa put a half-crown and a shilling or two on the table; and observing that Mr. Calipee had placed a shilling on the table, he thought he should certainly be safe if he did the same; and was greatly surprised to hear his partner inquire, in angry tones, "What do you mean by that?"

"I thought you asked me to mark for us," he replied.

"You don't call that marking?"

"Y—yes," faintly replied Mr. Samuel.

"Here!" said Pokyr, producing the morocco case from his pocket, and extracting from it a small book with green covers—"here, I'll make

you a present of this. You will find it useful to
you. You don't play much like a book at present,
I must say."

Mr. Golightly thanked him, expressed his anxiety to learn, and placed the little green book in
his pocket.

" This is not very lively—suppose we change it
to a little 'van.'"

Mr. Samuel Golightly was now, for the first
time, initiated into the mysteries of vingt-et-un.
His early efforts were distinguished by frequent
"bursts;" as, in the spirit of a true sportsman, he
took another seven after he had got twenty. Of
this game he afterwards became very fond; and it
cost him something considerable to learn that
eighteen was not a bad number to stand on.

In this agreeable manner the four gentlemen
spent their time till the train stopped at Bletchley.

Here they had to change from the comfort of
the main train into one of the four or five cold,
"seedy," and aged carriages which seem always to
be waiting at Bletchley for Cambridge men.

Both Mr. Samuel and Mr. Calipee felt hungry,
and crossed over to the little refreshment room,
where they found the usual tempting display of
good things for the consumption of railway travel-
lers; the choice lying, as usual, between three

sandwiches under one glass cover, two Queen
cakes under another, a dish of buns, a cylinder
of captain's biscuits, oranges, or Everton toffy.
Under the circumstances, our hero thought it best
to have his flask replenished with cherry brandy,
and leave the other things till another day.

Having crossed to the Cambridge train, they
sent a porter off for the hot-water pans—so often
forgotten until applied for. When they arrived,
the party seated themselves again in the carriage.
The porter who brought the pans and the porter
who moved their luggage hung about the door in
a manner more suggestive of sixpences than any
words. Mr. Samuel perceived, with his usual dis-
crimination, the object of their delay; and, with
the generosity inherent in his nature, gave them
more than they expected, and sent them off. The
engine now gave forth a discordant whistle, and
Mr. Calipee made the remark "We're off." This,
however, was a mistake. The next quarter of an
hour would have hung somewhat heavily on their
hands, had not Mr. Pokyr enlivened them by putting his head out of the carriage window and
"chaffing" a porter in a very diverting manner,
getting the better of the rascal on all points. Such
is the influence of example and cherry brandy, that
when the man whose walk in life is replenishing

the grease-boxes arrived at the carriage from the window of which Mr. Golightly was looking out upon the world at large, our hero determined to improve this opportunity for an excellent joke by asking him "If he ever greased his hair with that yellow pomatum?"

The surly ruffian, evidently missing the point of the joke, replied in the negative; adding that he thought—

"It was some people's heads, and not hairs, as wanted a-greasin'!"

Mr. Samuel was collecting himself for a suitably severe and Johnsonian rejoinder to this remark, when the opportunity for the display of cutting repartee was lost for ever by the train moving out of the station. Nor was his temper improved when Mr. Pokyr exclaimed—

"By Jove! got you there, old fellow. One too many for you as yet, on my honour he is. Look out for that fellow on the return journey, dear boy. Plenty of time to think over a reply."

This, however, I believe, is the last known occasion on which Mr. Golightly so far forgot his dignity as to joke with a railway official.

After having smoked another cigar, the gentlemen again resumed their game at "van," at which lively and exciting amusement they continued to play till the train arrived at the platform at Cambridge.

Mr. Golightly thanked his cousin George for the cash he had lent him; and also found that the chief expenses of a railway journey are not necessarily the tickets.

Here two flies were procured; and Mr. George and the Nigger got into one, whilst our hero and Mr. Pokyr took their seats in the other. The men were instructed to drive to Skimmery, the name by which St. Mary's is commonly known—a college that is described by a well-known historian, in one of his famous essays, as "the finest place of education in the world"—which opinion, I believe, Mr. Samuel Golightly cordially endorses. His first impressions of it we shall leave for our next chapter.

CHAPTER IV.

SKIM. COLL., CAM.

E left our hero in a fly, with his friend, Mr. Pokyr. He looked out, as they drove along, at all the objects of interest by the way, and his companion supplied him with a great deal of information in a very small compass. For instance, he learned that the imposing white brick edifice, with arcades in either wing, which is passed to the right hand of a carriage driving up Trumpington-street, was the official residence of the Vice-Chancellor. This building, however, he afterwards found out, was known as Addenbrooke's Hospital; and as many others of the places he saw during this drive he discovered, at a later period of his residence in Cambridge, to be more commonly called by names quite different from those Mr. Pokyr gave to them, it is useless, as far as practical purposes are concerned, to repeat here the names he first knew them by. Suffice it to say, in justice to Mr. Pokyr's genius, that they were more fanciful than trustworthy. After a drive of fifteen minutes, Mr. Golightly was set down at the gate of the college—his college! Proud reflection! I think, at this moment, had the statue of the founder, which is perched up over the gate, been within reach, Mr. Samuel would have been inclined to embrace it. However, as it was some feet above him, he contented himself by following his luggage and Mr. Pokyr across the great quad, through the Screens, into the Cloister court, where, through his cousin's influence with the Rev. Titus Bloke, the tutor, rooms had been allotted him. He followed his guide up a flight of old oak stairs, and found himself on a landing, on either side of which was a door, and over one of these doors was the name "Pokyr;" and over the other, in newly painted white letters, on a black ground, the name "S. A. Golightly" met his delighted gaze. With a very natural impulse he entered, seated himself upon the green sofa, and was about to indulge in a poetic reverie upon his new abode, when he was rudely awakened to the stern realities of life by the sudden and simultaneous appearance from an inner room of two figures—a man and a woman—his bedmaker and his gyp. The former —a lady advanced in years, and attired in a brown

dress, carrying in her left hand a clothes brush—
was dropping a series of little curtseys, which is a
way bedmakers have of expressing welcome and

PORTRAIT OF MRS. CRIBB.

respect. The latter was scraping and bowing with
a like intention.

"Please, sir—bedmaker, sir; yes, sir;—if you
please, sir," said the lady.

" Gyp, sir—please, sir," said the man.

Our hero smiled benignly upon both.

" Cribb, sir—Mrs. Cribb, sir," said the lady.

" Betsy," said the gyp.

" Which my christenin' name is Elizabeth, sir: wherefore Betsy or Cribb; and either name answered to when called," said Mrs. Cribb.

" Sneek, sir," said the gyp, as he caught Mr. Golightly's eye.

" John," said Mrs. Cribb.

" Yes, sir—John Sneek," assented Mr. Sneek. " And," he continued, addressing his new master, " Cribb and me, sir, 's gyp and bedmaker on this staircase."

" Which we are," put in Mrs. Cribb. " And Sneek, as I said before, the gentleman's cousin to Mr. Golightly below."

" 'Xcuse me, Cribb, but I told you; for Mr. George Golightly says to me, ' Sneek,' says he—"

" Now, what *is* the use, John Sneek, when—"

The person addressed gave a wink, intended for our hero's edification, and pointed expressively over his left shoulder.

" Below you, sir," he continued, pointing down, " ground floor, you've got your cousin—which I never want to see no better master. Above, Mr. Eustace Jones, which we expect will be senior the year arter next, sir; and to your right 'and, sir, the Honble Pokyr."

During this speech Mrs. Cribb stood with her arms akimbo, and her gaze intently fixed on the ceiling.

"Now, don't you hear Muster Eustace Jones a-callin' you?" said the gyp, addressing Mrs. Cribb. "I'm sure we shall do very well without you for a minnit; sha'n't we, sir?" he continued, glancing at our hero.

Mrs. Cribb, being thus compelled to attend to the summons of the gentleman above, reluctantly resigned to her coadjutor, Sneek, the opportunity both desired of having the first "pull" at their new master. Directly she was well clear of the room and her footsteps heard on the stairs, the gyp —who was a man apparently of about forty years of age, with a "corporation" worthy of an alderman, but with legs scarcely adequate to its support; a face the colour of parchment, and slightly pitted with small-pox; two sharp twinkling eyes, one of which was about half an inch higher than the other; a large mouth, half of which nature or habit taught him to dispense with, as he always spoke with the left corner closed and tightly pursed up; and a crop of very short, straight black hair. He was attired in a suit of seedy black, the annual gift of the Fellows, whose clothes Mr. Sneek had declared, any time for the last twenty years, "fitted him to a T." This, however, nobody perceived but himself, or "fitting to a T" is but a bad fit after all—well, this worthy, directly Mrs. Cribb's back was turned, began to speak of her merits as follows:—

"Now, that's just Cribb, that is," he said. "Now, you wouldn't believe it, sir—you wouldn't, indeed —she takes no more notice of a gen'l'm'n a-callin' nor nothink at all. Leaves 'em there, up them stairs, for instance, or down them stairs, as the case might be, you know, sir, a hootin' and shoutin' their very insides out, till I says, 'Now, Cribb, Muster So-and-so's a-callin' of you.'"

" Indeed," said Mr. Samuel Golightly.

" Every word gawspel truth, I assure you, sir You'll find it out afore you've been here long, sir; and that's all about it," said the gyp, pulling a doleful face. " But you'll like to look through your rooms whilst I unpack your traps for you, sir. Three rooms you've got, sir; and most fortunate to get into college in your first term, sir. Yes, sir, this is your keeping-room; and this," continued Mr. Sneek, leading the way, "this here's your study, as Mr. Grantley, as had these rooms last, used to call it—not to say as he studied much hisself though—

which, perhaps, you aint a-goin' to over-fatigue yourself; and, as I frequently say, one readin' man on a staircase is quite enough; and there's no denyin' as Mr. Eustace Jones, as keeps above, is a readin' man—never drinks nothink but green tea and soda water."

"Really!" said our hero—wondering, perhaps, how a man would look after a long course of these two beverages.

" Readin'," exclaimed Mr. Sneek, contempt flashing from every feature of his expressive face— " now, readin' aint the thing for an out-an'-out gen'l'm'n, is it, sir?—like the Honble Pokyr now, for instance, or you, sir, beggin' pardon for what I say; though he keeps a man of his own, which — being gyp on the staircase—aint no pertickler advantage to me. No, not pertickler," added he, with an ironical smirk and suppressed chuckle. " Wine, sir," partly addressing himself to the hampers and partly to their owner. " Let's see: this'll go into the bins in the winders, and then there's that closet, and there's the cupboards in the bookcase."

Mr. Golightly inspected them minutely.

" Keys, sir," replied Sneek, in answer to a query of our hero's. " Yes, there is keys somewhere. I've got a key at home, I know, as fits that far-

thest bin; for sometimes, when there was nothink
in it, it used to be locked. But, lor bless you, sir!"
he added, in a confidential whisper, "keys aint no
use where Cribb is—aint indeed, sir; nothink more
nor ornaments—aint, 'pon my word, sir. You've
no idea of what she is. Ah!" said he, with great
feeling, "my poor wife 'ould be the bedmaker for
this staircase—"

Whatever eulogium was about to follow was
instantly cut short by the appearance of Mr.
Pokyr, of whom the gyp stood in wholesome
dread.

"What lies is that rascal telling now, Golightly?" demanded Pokyr.

Mr. Samuel Adolphus expressed a faint hope that
his gyp was speaking the truth, the whole truth,
et cœtera.

"Don't believe a word he tells you; and come
in and have some dinner in my rooms, as we are
too late for Hall—ready in ten minutes."

With this invitation, Mr. Pokyr left our hero to
complete a hasty toilet.

"He's a funny un, he is," remarked Sneek, as
he unpacked our hero's portmanteau.

Mr. Samuel Golightly was on the point of leaving his own rooms for those of his friend, when he
was met by Mrs. Cribb. The gyp had gone to the

gate for his other luggage. This was Mrs. Cribb's chance. She was equal to the occasion.

"I hope that officious Sneek aint been a purloinin' of my character, sir. But shall you like a cup of tea to-night, sir, if you please?" she asked, in her very blandest tones. "I shall be here again at nine, sir; when, if there's anything else you want, I hope you'll tell me. I've ordered you what groceries you want, sir; and your sheets is as well aired as if I was a-going to sleep in 'em myself. Really me, now!" she exclaimed, as she set her foot among the bottles Sneek had placed upon the floor, "I was almost knocking these here bottles over. John Sneek might have put 'em in a safer place. You're a-going to have 'em put into the bins, I s'pose, sir," Mrs. Cribb continued. "Now, there was keys to them bins when fust Mr. Grantley come into these rooms; but he never wanted to lock up nothink with no keys. But keys—bless you, sir!—keys aint no use where John Sneek is. I've know'd him many years, sir. "Ah!" said she, with evident emotion, "my poor dear husband, which is such a convicted martyr to the rheumaticks, 'ud be the gyp for this staircase. As I've often said to different gentlemen as I've had for masters—which they all thought the same as I did—Sneek's habits is not suitable for such a place, as you'll find out afore you've know'd him long, sir."

Mr. Samuel Golightly was about to soothe Mrs. Cribb's agitated feelings, by expressing an unbounded confidence in the gyp-like capabilities of that "convicted martyr to the rheumaticks," when Mr. Pokyr's servant called him to dinner.

We have stated that Mr. Golightly's friend, Pokyr, "kept"—as the phrase is — in the rooms opposite his own. The dinner was laid for four; and our hero found his cousin, Mr. Calipee, and his host seated when he entered. During the interval between the soup and the fish, he had time to look round Mr. Pokyr's luxuriously furnished apartment.

The room was, like all others on this staircase, panelled throughout with oak. On the walls hung a choice and varied collection of engravings: Herring's "Silks and Satins of the Turf," and "Silks and Satins of the Field," occupying the places of honour on either side of the mantelpiece; above which were ranged pipes of every age and condition, from old to new, and clean to very dirty. Round the glass were stuck letters, "invites," meets of "the Drag," "Cambridge Hariers," Cutlet Club dinners, "Lyceum" suppers, and racing fixtures for the current year. Plants in blossom, from the nurseryman's; and beautiful busts and sculptures from the studio of that celebrated Italian artist, Signor Ariosto Ramingo, whose "Buy a nice image to-day" is so well known, graced the room. A piano, with a case of books on each side, stood between the windows. Mr. Golightly was just admiring, for the third time, the portrait of Miss Menken as the Mazeppa, which hung above it on the wall opposite him, and was vacantly taking his first mouthful of crimped sole, when he was alarmed by terrific cries and violent stamping from the room overhead. He was the more astonished, as the other three gentlemen continued quietly to eat their dinner.

"Gracious heavens!" he exclaimed, starting to his feet. "W-what is being done? What is the matter?"

"Oh," replied his host, "he has got another out. That's all."

"In the name of goodness!" cried Mr. Samuel, preparing to rush to the victim's rescue, "another what? A tooth, a limb—what?"

"No; a problem. It's only Jones. He always does that when he has worked one of his problems out right. We are quite accustomed to it, you see."

The mathematician's yells and stamps of delight were continued for several seconds, and were then succeeded by a dull, rolling noise, accompanied by a great scuffling.

"What is he doing now?" demanded Mr. Samuel, whose nerves had not yet recovered from the shock they had received at first.

"Now," said Mr. Calipee, "he is taking his exercise. He plays at croquet on the carpet. Pleasant for us, isn't it?"

Mr. Golightly could not agree with the native of India on this point.

"Champagne, sir?" said Mr. Pokyr's man.

"Thank you," said our hero.

"How is your wine, Golightly?" inquired Mr. Calipee, at the same time tasting his own.

"Very good, thank you."

"What I am drinking is pretty good, too. As I often tell Pokyr, who drinks a deal of mine, there is nothing more deceptive than wine. This bottle is good," he added, with an air of melancholy resignation; "but who knows what the next may be?"

Such was the Nigger's gloomy way of regarding the future.

In the **room** above them, Mr. Jones was going on with his game of croquet with great spirit.

"Dash the fellow! He's the only drawback to this staircase," said Pokyr.

"If he was not there," said the Nigger, "there would be something else, no doubt. You do not know Tommy Chutney, do you, Golightly?"

"No, not at present," replied our hero, smiling.

"You'll like him," said Calipee. "He comes from Bombay. He's sure to give you a nickname, Tommy is. He called me Nigger before he had known me ten minutes."

A nervous horror crept over Mr. Samuel. He hated nicknames. He hoped it would be some considerable time before he made Mr. Chutney's acquaintance.

"Most of the Cutlet men have got a nickname," continued Calipee. "There's Blaydes, downstairs —Tommy called him Jamaica. Jamaica Blaydes is not bad—is it?"

"Why do they call him J-Jamaica?" asked Mr. Samuel.

"I don't know. Perhaps, because he comes from Jamaica, or something. After dinner, I must call upon him."

"I must look some fellows up after dinner," said Mr. Pokyr. "You will excuse us, I dare say, Golightly?"

Our hero signified his readiness to do so. And, after coffee and a cigar had been discussed, he retired to his own rooms; and, in a few minutes, betook himself to his virtuous couch.

> "Then circumfused around him gentle sleep,
> Lulling the sorrows of his heart to rest,
> O'ercame his senses."

But how long he slept, he never knew; as, from absence of mind, or the newness of his situation, he had forgotten to wind up his watch. He awoke, however, with a start. It was dark as pitch. There was an unearthly boring at his door. He heard a low whisper. Something was being done. His first impulse was to shout "Murder" or "Police." In a second or so the noises had ceased. He sprang out of bed, and made for the door. He tried to open it. Ah! locked—no; here is the key. Why, won't it open? He pulled, he pushed; but the door remained fast as a rock. Horrible thought!—are the colleges haunted? Was this a ghostly freak, or was he at the wrong door? He was in a cold perspiration. But the idea of night-lights relieved him. He found his matches, lighted his candle, examined the door. It was the only door in the room, and therefore he had come in through it. Now it was fast. Leaving his candle burning on the table beside him, he betook himself to bed, but not to sleep. Twice he heard the great college clock strike, with deep-toned knell, before he fell into a light and disturbed slumber, haunted by fearful dreams. He awoke. It was daylight. The candle had burnt down in its socket. He heard the welcome voice of Sneek, his gyp.

"Here's a go! They've been and screwed him in. Ha'-past eight, sir," he called out, "if you'd like to get up. We shall have the door undone in a minnit. You're screwed in, sir."

And, as Sophocles said—only in Greek—

> " The bugbears of the dreamful night,
> Are food for mirth in clear daylight."

Here was the mystery of the night explained. By an instinctive feeling, Mr. Golightly connected Mr. Pokyr with this business, although he never found out for certain the perpetrators of the cruel plot.

He rose, dressed himself with his usual care, and walked downstairs to call upon his cousin. He found Mr. George still in bed. He gave him an account of the pleasing attention which had been paid him in the night. As a truthful chronicler, I cannot say that Mr. George seemed surprised when he heard it. He said, encouragingly—

" Ah, you must expect these little things at first

—just in your Freshman's term, you know. I have been screwed in myself."

"Who should you think did it, now?" asked our hero.

"'Pon my life, I couldn't tell you—couldn't spot the man for certain. It may lie between a dozen."

Mr. Samuel Golightly had his suspicions, but did not pursue the matter further.

"I'll get up," said Mr. George. "Just step outside and shout for Sneek."

Mr. Samuel did so several times, without eliciting any response. At last, after the sixth time of shouting, Mr. Sneek appeared on the landing.

"Comin', sir; comin', directly!"

He followed our hero into his cousin's bed-room.

"Now, what'll you have for breakfast, old fellow? Say the word. What do you like?"

Mr. Samuel felt sure he should like anything that Mr. George liked.

"Come," said that gentleman, "make a choice. What do you say to a 'spread-eagle' and some sausages? "'Spread-eagle' is a fowl sat upon and squashed, you know."

"Anything you like," replied Mr. Samuel.

"All right. Sneek, order a 'spread-eagle,' with mushrooms, and some sausages."

The gyp departed immediately for the kitchens.

"Now, my boy," said George, "amuse yourself in the next room whilst I dress."

Our hero accordingly took a survey of his cousin's quarters. Just at the same moment, Mr. George made his appearance from his bed-room, and the cook entered with the "spread-eagle," and Mr. Sneek followed with the sausages.

"Tea or cawfee shall I make, sir?" said he, addressing Mr. George.

"Which do you say, tea or coffee?"

Our hero expressed a preference for the former.

Tea was accordingly made ; and Mr. Samuel was just taking his second cup, when in walked his friend, Mr. Pokyr, and Mr. Jamaica Blaydes.

"Oh!" said George. "Blaydes, my cousin."

Our hero formally saluted Mr. Blaydes. This gentleman, who kept in the rooms opposite, wore a yellowish waistcoat and trousers, and a blue dressing-gown, with red tassels and cord.

Our hero, to whom the easy familiarity of University life was new, thought this was a singular dress for a morning call.

"You have scarcely been up long enough for me to ask you how you like Cambridge life," said Mr. Blaydes, addressing Mr. Golightly.

"No, scarcely yet; though I feel sure I shall like it very much indeed," he replied.

"I never knew but one man who didn't," said Blaydes; "and in his case want of taste was excusable. He was going to be married directly he had got his degree."

"I suppose he got through all his examinations very fast, then?" said Mr. Samuel.

"Well, yes," replied Blaydes, "as fast as he could. He used to sigh for his Euphemia; say he hated living in college; and quarrel religiously with Mrs. Cribb."

"Quarrel with Mrs. Cribb!" exclaimed our hero. "Why, she seems to be a very friendly old woman. We are quite good friends already."

"She will be better friends with your brandy bottle, my dear Samuel Adolphus," remarked Mr. Pokyr, "as soon as she has made its acquaintance. What are you going to be up to?" he asked.

"Well," replied Mr. Samuel, "I believe we are going—that is, George and I—to purchase a cap and gown for—for me; and to—to call upon the tutor; and George has promised to show me round the University."

"If perfectly agreeable," said Mr. Pokyr, "Blaydes and I will go with you on the latter errand; but I never visit the Reverend Titus Bloke unless I am sent for. So you'll excuse me from joining you in that visit."

" Oh, certainly," replied Mr. Samuel, smiling.

Accordingly, a few minutes afterwards, they all set out from Skimmery together.

" You must change that 'topper' for a 'pot' at once, or you'll be mistaken for a nobleman," said Mr. Pokyr to our hero. He wore a "pot" himself.

Mr. Samuel was debating within himself whether he should or should not like to be mistaken for a nobleman, when his cousin remarked that " This was the place."

They entered a shop on the Parade.

" Cap and gown, sir? Yes," said the obliging shopkeeper. " Skimmery, sir, may I ask?"

Mr. Samuel replied in the affirmative; and was rapidly accommodated with the well-known blue gown and mortar-board.

" 'Pon my word," said Pokyr, " you look quite interesting in them."

" Gentlemen mostly do, sir," said the tailor.

As Mr. Samuel saw himself reflected at full length in the glass before him, he really could not help thinking he did; and wished his Fa and his Aunt Dorothea could see him in them. However, he was not long before he transmitted to Oakingham six album portraits, done in the best style.

"Now you want some bands," said Mr. Pokyr, glancing at George.

"Bands?" said Mr. Samuel, in an inquiring manner.

"Not music, my dear boy—muslin," said Mr. Pokyr.

"Shall you require bands, sir," said the tailor, "at this early—"

Mr. Pokyr looked at the tradesman in a way that quieted his doubts.

And accordingly our hero was supplied with six pairs, nicely starched, and, as the man remarked, "ready for immediate wear."

Mr. Samuel next purchased the requisite "pot" hat; and then, with some slight embarrassment, asked his cousin to lend him some money to pay for them; as, for anything he knew to the contrary, his purse was still "on the piano."

"Pay, my dear fellow," said Pokyr—"that's a thing we never think of here."

"Don't mention it, pray, sir," said the tailor. "Most happy, sir, to open an account."

"You would feel quite offended, Smith, if he offered to pay you, would you not?" demanded Blaydes, who was himself a customer.

"I most certainly should, sir," said the obliging Smith, as he bowed them out of the shop.

The four gentlemen strolled along the Parade.
Like everybody who sees it for the first time, Mr.
Golightly was very much impressed with the chapel
of King's.   They strolled on past Corpus.

"What church is this," he asked, pointing to the
edifice at the corner of Silver-street.

"That," replied Pokyr, "is the 'Varsity church.
You can go to-morrow and hear the sermon, if you
like."

"Who preaches there?"

"All the great swells—four Sundays at a stretch,"
said Pokyr.   "Do you know who it is, Blaydes?"

"I saw it on the Screens as we came through,"
said Mr. Blaydes.   "It's the Archbishop of Dublin,
I think."

"I must confess, I don't often go," Mr. Pokyr
remarked.   "I've only been once; that was when
the Reverend Titus Bloke, B.D., Fellow and Tutor
of Skimmery, was on.   Then I went to his first,
took a front seat in the gallery, just over the pulpit, so that he was obliged to see me; and paid the
greatest attention to him.   But I could not stand
another dose."

"We have enough of him in chapel,' said
Blaydes.

"What time does the sermon begin?" inquired
Mr. Samuel, determined to hear the Archbishop,

and send a full account in his first letter to the Rectory.

"At eleven o'clock," said Pokyr. "Shall you come?"

"Yes. I am sure I should like to do so," was our hero's reply.

"You can't miss your way—all in a straight line from Skimmery. But if you think you can't find it again, if I am up in time, I will come and show you," said Mr. Pokyr.

"Tell you what," said George; "we must go and look up Bloke."

"All right. We will turn back now," said Pokyr.

So they retraced their steps to Skimmery. Here, on going to Mr. Samuel's rooms, they found that the cap and gown had arrived before them. Mr. Sneek was busy putting the wine into the "bins in the winders;" and Mrs. Cribb was there too, either assisting him or looking on.

"Beg your pardon, sir, but I've had a accident with one," said the gyp, holding up a sherry bottle with the neck knocked off, and half the wine gone.

It afterwards struck Mr. Samuel that he did not notice any on the carpet.

"What had we better do with this, sir?" he asked of Mr. George.

" No reason that I see, Sneck, for breaking one;
but, as it is done, you and Mrs. Cribb had better
have that one."

" Thank you, sir!" said Sneck and Mrs. Cribb
together.

" Not as I care about wine," said she; "for,
when I do take anythink, as John Sneck knows, it
is a glass of sperrits."

" I think you are not very particular, Mrs. Cribb,"
George said.

"Which, sir, it would ill become me to be, havin'
been twelve year a helper on this staircase before
bein' relevated to the duties of bedmaker. How
did you sleep, sir?" she said, addressing Mr. Samuel, who at this moment made his appearance,
attired in full academicals; "for, as I said to John
Sneck, the very fust thing in the morning, to have
gone and screwed you in the very fust night, it were
certingly owdacious, to say the least."

" I must say, Mrs. Cribb, I have slept better,"
replied our hero.

" For as far as the sheets went," continued the
bedmaker, "as I said to John Sneck afore you arrived, 'John Sneck,' I said, ' them sheets is aired
as well as if I was a-goin' to sleep in 'em myself,'
which I am always most pertickler; for my poor
husband, which, as John Sneck knows, is a con-

victed martyr to rheumaticks, always is attributed to havin' slep' in a damp bed. And," she added, "if you are a-goin' to call on the tutor, as I come through the quad I see him a-goin' into his rooms, sir."

With Mr. Samuel's first appearance in a cap and gown, we commence a fresh paragraph. At first he felt a little awkward in his new dress; and all the while was very conscious that he had got it on, but withal rather pleased than not. To his credit let it be recorded, that he soon felt quite at home in it; and that his gown was soon as shabby, and his cap as battered and broken, as a young gentleman's of fashion should be; though this was brought about rather by the efforts of his friends than by any exertions of his own. He would himself have preferred a gown as spotless as his character, and a cap with a board well equilateral and rectangular. Mr. Pokyr, however, soon spoilt the corners and cut the tassel of the latter; whilst, at the very first "wine" he went to, he found himself, after a deal of searching for his own, left with the choice of three gowns, which I can only describe as bad, worse, and worst.

He would have bought a new gown, had not his cousin George interfered to prevent this wasteful outlay of the family property.

Having followed his cousin up a short flight of stairs, he found himself opposite a door with a small brass knocker, and above it was inscribed " Mr. Bloke."

Mr. George knocked. A rather weak treble voice was heard to say, " Come in."

They went in, and Mr. Samuel Golightly was in the presence of his tutor.

Was the short gentleman in spectacles, who was advancing to shake hands with him, and nervously asking him " how he did," the same man who had sent the ten thousand and three corrections to Liddell and Scott? It was.

Mr. Samuel felt much more at his ease than he would have done if the great Don had been a man of commanding presence.

" Pray sit down, Mr. Golightly," he said, rubbing his hands together. " Pray be seated. I have had a letter from your father, apprising me of your arrival. He expresses a hope that you will make great progress during your stay here. I am sure I hope so too. You will have to attend chapel every day, and twice on Sunday. You will also attend two lectures every morning: Mr. Bloss will lecture upon Tacitus at ten, and Mr. Summer will lecture upon algebra from eleven to twelve. I hope, at the end of the term, they will both give me a good

account of you. If at any time you require my
advice, you will always be able to see me in a
morning."

Mr. Samuel thanked him; and perceiving that
the interview was ended, rose with his cousin to
go.

" I wish you good morning, gentlemen," said the
tutor; and in came another Freshman, to go through
the same ceremony.

Mr. Bloke had to see a great many people every
day, and consequently was obliged to get rid of
them quickly; and no man could do this with more
perfect politeness.

Mr. Samuel left the room with a most favourable impression of Mr. Bloke, and of tutors and
dons generally.

" Get into a row," said Mr. George, sapiently,
" and then you'll see his teeth !"

Mr. Samuel fervently hoped he should not get
into a row.

" Have you ever got into one, George?" he
asked.

" Well, Bloke has had to send for me once or
twice; but Pokyr's often going."

" Really !" said Mr. Samuel, " is he, George? I
am not surprised. Pokyr is such a joker."

" Ah! but Bloke never says much to him. You

see, they've got political influence, and Bloke means to be a bishop."

There might be something in this. At least, it was generally thought that if anybody else had done half what Pokyr had done, he would have been sent down, and not requested to come back again.

The political influences of the outer world penetrate at times into the oldest colleges in our two ancient and sister Universities.

CHAPTER V.

MR. GOLIGHTLY CONVEYS HIS IMPRESSION OF CAM-
BRIDGE TO HIS FAMILY IN A CIRCULAR LETTER.

PROBABLY there is one thing that nearly
every rightly disposed young gentleman
does very soon after his arrival either at
Cambridge or Oxford—that is, to write an epistle
to his friends at home, containing, according to his
temperament and capacity for polite letter writing,
a more or less flowery description of his first impressions of University life. Our hero—whom the
readers of this biographical memoir will soon know
as a "rightly disposed young gentleman," if they
have not already arrived at that conclusion—proved
no exception to this rule. Having laid in a stock
of note paper, on which the college arms were
neatly stamped in blue and red, with the words
"St. Mary's College, Cambridge," by way of further explanation, in embossed letters underneath,
he was in a position to write home with be-

coming dignity. He had been received into the lap of his Alma Mater on a day of ill-omen for starting on a journey—namely, on a Friday; but, as the college authorities themselves had fixed that day for his reception, this difficulty could only be got over by compliance with the injunction thus issued; Mrs. Golightly having remarked—when her natural sagacity and a consultation of her almanac enabled her to arrive at a conclusion— "That the seventeenth of October in that year certainly fell on a Friday, and above all things she disliked beginning anything on that day; but she supposed her son must go, as that was the day fixed; and all she could say was, she hoped no harm would come of it."

The Rector and Mr. Morgan having reasoned with her, she was pursuaded to take a more hopeful view of the exigency which compelled her son to issue forth from her care on so ill-fated a day.

Now, nothing would have induced any members of the family at Oakingham Rectory to write a letter or sign their names to any document on a Friday, unless under stress of circumstances; as, for instance, in the case of the worthy old militia Captain, of whom it is recorded, in the family archives, that he signed his will on a Friday. But the exigency of his case was peculiar: though perfectly conscious, and, as the phrase is, in full possession of his faculties to the last, his doctors had warned him that it was more than probable that he would not live to see Saturday morning. The patient here remarked, in a voice scarcely above a whisper—but his words were plainly heard by his son, who has often repeated them to the family—"That if his time was come, he must reconcile himself to his fate; but he had always looked upon Friday as an unlucky day, and it seemed likely to keep up its character to the end."

However, the old gentleman's prejudices were not confirmed, as he survived until the Sunday, having signed a codicil to his will on Saturday, by which he devised a certain close of land to the use of the poor of the parish of Oakingham for ever.

The poor had been overlooked in the hurry of preparing his will, for the gallant Captain had a fine, old-fashioned prejudice against making his will, not at all uncommon among the country gentlemen of his day; and he had a saying which was ever in his mouth, if any of his friends broached the subject—none of his children would have done it for the world—which saying was, "that, for his part, he would never bring himself to believe that a man would make a will unless he had a presentiment of something about to happen;

for," he would add, wisely wagging his head, and sipping the old port that so greatly aggravated his complaint, "you recollect poor old Squire Frampton, of Frampton-in-the-Marsh? I well remember one day, at quarter-sessions, he told me, as he stepped out of lawyer Quilpenn's office, on the market-square at Fuddleton, 'Golightly,' says he, 'how d'ye do?' and, pointing over his shoulder and laughing, says he, 'I've just signed my will.' That was Saturday: he was killed in the hunting field on the Monday after was Guy Fawkes's day:" and here the Captain was accustomed to bring his chalky old knuckles down on the dining table with a bang that made the glasses jump. I might feel that an apology was necessary for so long a digression concerning the Captain; but, as the Golightlys are a Conservative family, they have many traditions in which they religiously believe; and with them, for many generations, the rule has been, " as did the father so does the son."

The immediate ancestor of the Rector had, as we have shown, the strongest objection to the performance of any important act on a Friday. The Reverend Samuel Golightly inherited the same prepossession in all its pristine force; for once, after a quarrel with a refractory churchwarden the parish had elected, the parson of Oakingham, though boiling over with rage at a letter he had received from that functionary, and though every finger itched with desire to take pen and ink, and have at him—Bobbleswick his name was—let who might say nay;—the day was Friday: he waited: indignant as he was, he waited. Tuffley took him up tea to his study at a quarter-past eleven, wondering "what could keep the master up, and me up too." As the last stroke of the midnight hour, by Oakingham Church clock, died away into silence, the Rector seized pen, ink, and paper, and annihilated Bobbleswick—in the opinion of his own family: though I grieve to say irony was lost on the churchwarden, who was one of those intelligent, honest Britons who call a spade a spade, and don't know it again as an horticultural and agricultural implement

These prejudices against Fridays in general—derived immediately from his father and grandfather, and more remotely from many generations of Golightlys in succession—so far penetrated the mind of Mr. Samuel Adolphus, our hero, as to prevent his thinking of writing home on that particular Friday on which he first arrived at the University of Cambridge. There were other reasons in the matter, though, which would have produced a similar result in more practical and less ideal

G

minds than that of our hero. In the first place, he had forgotten to bring any note paper with him; secondly, the shops were shut when dinner was over, and he thought of letter writing; and thirdly, the evening mail had gone out. This information was imparted to him by Mr. Sneek.

"The post goes at eight o'clock—leastways, without a nextra stamp, which takes 'em up to ha'-past, sir."

In reply to a query from his new master, Mr. Sneek continued—

"As to note paper and envelopes, most neatly painted with the Cawllege harms, sir, is to be had at most of such shops as commonly sells it, which I would run now and get some, but the shops is closed; not but what I dessay some of 'em would open; but the post is gawn. (A-*comin*', sir"—this observation Mr. Sneek made with the side of his mouth not in common use, thrusting half his head through the doorway.) "Mr. Eustace Jones, sir, have some readin' gentlemen to tea with him, sir. His is allus teas. Inexpensive and satis-fyin'."

Of this mathematical gentleman it might be said, as it was of somebody else, I believe—

"Tea veniente die, tea decedente bibebat;"

which our lady readers will pardon us for rendering thus—

> " Tea he drank with the morning light:
> Tea he drank till late midnight."

Mr. Sneck, the honest and praiseworthy gyp of the staircase, never lost an opportunity of impressing upon the Freshman minds that came under his notice his own notions of the undesirability of their contracting similar habits. After all, cold tea and fragments of tough muffin are poor perquisites for a gyp.

" 'Xcuse me, Mr. Golightly, sir—don't be led into tea or readin', sir ; but be a gentleman of sperrit—'xcuse me, sir—like your cousin, Mr. George—which I don't want no better master— and the Hon'ble Pokyr."

With these words the gyp withdrew, and ascended to the region of tea and the Calculus on the floor above.

At the risk of the imputation being cast upon me of trying to appear learned, after the manner of " Our Own" when representing the interests of England and his paper abroad, by having both Greek and Latin in the same chapter, I shall here remark, that the man who performs the duties and helps himself to something more than the perquisites of an indoor servant out of livery, at the two Universities, is called at each by a different name.

> "At Cambridge 'gyp,' at Oxford 'scout,'
> Collegians call the idle lout
> Who brushes clothes, of errands runs,
> Absorbs their tips, and keeps off duns."

Of the word gyp, I may remark that, upon the authority of a distinguished Oxford scholar, it is not improbably derived from γύψ, or αἰγυπιός, a vulture. This derivation is ingenious and remarkably *apropos*, as the gyp possesses all the voracious qualities of the bird of prey in a very high state of development. And, on a kindred subject, it might be worth the attention of moralists and social philosophers to consider the causes which have combined, in the course of centuries, to make gyps and bedmakers at the Universities, and laundresses appendant and appurtenant to chambers in the several Inns of Court, and some other places, such particularly disagreeable people to have any dealings with. Out of regard for early English wit, it may be suggested that the cleanly title enjoyed by the latter was given them as a pleasing satire upon the state of dirt they have always been found in for many generations past.

The various reasons enumerated above having prevented our hero from addressing his family from his new quarters on the night of his first arrival there, he proceeded to remedy the omission on the day following. He had not forgotten his aunts' injunction at parting, to write to them as soon as he got to Cambridge. Accordingly, on Saturday he spent half an hour in the afternoon in writing to Miss Dorothea and her sister, Miss Harriet; reserving for Monday a circular letter which should —though nominally written to his father—really be addressed to the whole family, including his late tutor, Mr. Morgan.

The letter bearing the words, " St. Mary's Coll., Cam.," underneath the famous arms of that royal and religious foundation, began with—

" My DEAR FA "—when he had got thus far, our hero hardly knew how to go on, such was the effect of the *embarras des richesses* under which he laboured. However, his father's parting advice to be cool, calm, and collected under even the most trying circumstances, came to his mind at the right moment; and, stimulated by the recollection of the parental maxim, he proceeded : " You heard of my safe arrival" (of course, he did not stammer when he wrote—or sang) " in the letter I wrote to Aunt

Dorothea. I must say, I like Cambridge very well, but I feel rather strange. I have not yet found out who screwed me in. I have not been screwed in since; but, as somebody is screwed in every night, I am expecting it again. Now I know all about it, I am not at all afraid; as Sneek, the servant—or gyp, as he is called—can always 'dig me out,' as they call it. Pokyr calls it 'unearthing.' He is a very agreeable fellow, but rather given to practical jokes—things I very much dislike. I am sure, I should never think of playing a practical joke upon anybody. Then why should I be joked? is a question I ask myself. Yesterday morning, having attended the early service in chapel, and breakfasted, I left the college for what I had been told was the University Church ('Varsity Church they call it, as you know). I dressed myself, as George told me, in my cap and gown. I put on bands like those you wear on Sundays—of which I was induced to purchase six pairs (they may be useful to you, and I will bring them when I come home for the vacation)—my lavender kid gloves that Aunt Harriet gave me; and, as the day was showery, I took my green silk umbrella. I noticed that I was stared at as I walked along the streets; and when I arrived at what I had been told was the University

Church, and was trying to open the iron gate—
which, as it was two minutes past eleven, I thought
had probably been closed—I was startled by a loud
laugh. It was Pokyr—who, with a friend named
Blaydes, and an Indian gentleman, Calipee by
name, were laughing very loudly at me. I saw
at once that I was the victim of a hoax. Mr.
Blaydes took off my bands; Mr. Calipee told me
to put my lavender gloves in my pocket; and Mr.
Pokyr said he would take care of my umbrella—
'mushroom' was the term he used. I found my
umbrella was what he meant, as he took it from
me. What he did with it I don't know. I have
not seen it since. It had disappeared a minute
afterwards, for I observed that he was not carrying it. The place was not a church, but the University Printing Press. The architecture is ecclesiastical, and hence my mistake. You will say,
'Do not be imposed upon a second time.' I promise you, I will not. Perhaps, if I had remem-
bered your advice, I might have been more upon
my guard. At the corner of a street we met a
gentleman, De Bootz by name. I mention him
because, as you are fond of genealogical studies,
the arms of his family may interest you. Pokyr
says they are on a field ermine, a boot stagnant,
proper; crest, a spur; and motto, ' *Usque ad finem*

luceat'—'Shine to the last.' Mr. De Bootz was
ahead of us when Pokyr told me this; and Mr.
Blaydes added, 'I believe that man's great great
great grandfather invented blacking.' If so, the
arms are very appropriate, and you won't think
any the worse of him for this. Mr. De Bootz took
us to the back parlour of a small cigar shop in
Brownlow-street, where we found some other gentlemen drinking beer out of a huge flagon. Here
they introduced me to a Miss Bellair—the Brown-
street Venus, as she is called. She seems a very
lively and amiable young lady, and deservedly
popular, as her manners are very agreeable. Her
mother was present also. It is her mother's cigar
shop. After dinner, we had some wine and des-
sert in Pokyr's room. He says he always keeps a
chapel religiously once a-week; so we all went in
surplices, as it was Sunday. Sherry never used to
disagree with me; but I felt very confused, and
rather giddy. However, to keep myself awake, I
read this sentence—which I found on the fly-leaf
of the battered Prayer Book which was in my seat
—ninety-one times during the service, keeping
count of the number of the times. It was as follows:—'Strongbeerium collegianum bibere malum
est justum antequam in chapellam incas.' It is, as
you will perceive, dog Latin; and I felt it was pe-

culiarly applicable to me, and to sherry as well
as beer; accordingly, I shall be very careful in
future. I think it was the heat of the gas and
candles. With kind regards to you all, I will
here close this letter."

Our hero had given a promise many times to the
members of his family, individually and collectively,
that he would faithfully report to them the various
incidents of his life; and, as will be seen, he entered upon this course at once. But he found very
soon that he could not keep it up with advantage
to all parties, and therefore it has happened that
this history is a biography instead of an autobio-
graphy. Mr. Samuel Adolphus had, in the next
few days immediately following his Sunday visit
to the home of the Brown-street Venus, so far improved his opportunities, that he already felt himself very deeply in love. With that rashness and
utter regardlessness of all ulterior consequences
which is characteristic of the first attack of the
great passion, our hero was seated in his easy
chair, turning over in his mind the propriety of at
once laying his virgin heart at the feet of his
bewitching inamorata, and wondering what his
Aunt Dorothea would say when he introduced
Miss Bellair to the party at the Rectory as his

bride, when he was aroused by a timid tap at his door.

"Come in," cried our hero, his heart beating fast and nervously.

A little boy—a precocious little boy he had not the slightest difficulty in recognizing as Mrs. Bellair's errand boy—entered, cap in hand, and presented to Mr. Golightly's notice a tiny, scented, pink note.

He opened it hastily, and devoured the contents —as novelists say. These were as follows:—

"DEAR MR. GOLIGHTLY—I cannot misinterpret your conduct. Your heart is young, tender, warm. You love me. Dare I say, without for an instant seeming to throw aside the veil of woman's modesty —her brightest jewel—that, from the moment I first saw you, I felt that there was something about you I had observed in no one else? Oh! do not, I pray you, put a wrong construction on these innocent words, written without guile at the prompting of Cupid; but the constraint under which we meet in Brown-street is too great for my nerves. So many are round, and my mamma is so very watchful over her daughter's conduct, we can never be alone. Say you will meet me, then, in half an hour, at the Backs, beneath the third elm tree, opposite the gate of St. Mary's. There no one shall hear, but the winds of heaven only be listeners to the words we speak. If I have not mistaken your feelings—come. If I have—which Heaven forbid!—breathe not this confession to mortal ears, as you are a gentleman, and an ornament to that gown you wear.—Ever yours (in a flutter of hope),

"EMILY BELLAIR."

"No. 91, Brown-street."

"Is there an answer, sir, please?" asked the precocious boy. "I was to wait for an answer."

"Who sent you?" demanded Mr. Golightly, in breathless haste. "Who sent you?"

"Missis, sir."

"Wait one instant," said our hero, fumbling in his waistcoat pocket for a shilling, and nearly giving the messenger of Cupid a sovereign by mistake.

Having done this, he retired to his bed-room, and read the missive again and again. He sponged his temples, heated with the delirious whirl of hope and love conflicting in his breast.

Calmer after this operation, he emerged from his bed-chamber; and, addressing the boy as unconcernedly as he could, said—

" The only answer is—Yes!"

He was under the trees at the back of his college for some minutes before the half-hour had elapsed, with the precious pink note still in his hand.

True to her time, the lady came.

How was it, then, that, when the thick veil which had enshrouded her features fell to the ground—how was it that, when Mr. Golightly, on his knees, was vowing eternal love, a cruel gust of wind tore off the cloak and revealed the form, not of Emily Bellair, but the startling truth that the illustrious hero of this history was at the feet of Miss Jane Sneek, daughter of Mr. John Sneek, gyp?

The further account of this surprising matter is too important for the end of a chapter. With it we begin Chapter VI.

CHAPTER VI.

IN the present chapter of this eventful history, our friend and able coadjutor, "Phiz," favours us with the portraiture of Mr. Golightly at the feet of Miss Sneek, the only daughter of the worthy personage who introduced himself as Mr. Sneek, gyp, and whose Christian name of John was at the same time imparted by the communicative Mrs. Cribb.

It remains for us, in accordance with the promise which brought our chapter to a sufficiently exciting conclusion, to commence the present one by clearing up this mysterious substitution of one young lady for another, by a full and complete explanation of what took place both before and after, as well as on the momentous occasion itself.

We will plunge at once *in medias res*—or "begin

in the middle," as the little boy remarked when he bit the rosy-cheeked apple. Our hero, as has before been recounted, was at his post—or rather, tree—some minutes before the time fixed for his meeting with Miss Emily Bellair by the sender of the pink note. He had no particular difficulty in discovering the spot indicated in the billet, as there were only three trees opposite the gate of St. Mary's College which opened on to the Backs, and as those three trees were, though stripped of their leaves by the rough autumnal blasts—there had been a high wind ten days before—unmistakably elms. Indeed, it only required such a knowledge of arithmetical science as will enable a man to count three correctly to discover which of those elms was the third elm. Mr. Golightly possessed the requisite knowledge; and, with characteristic promptitude, began to count the trees. Here he found himself on the horns of a dilemma. Counting from left to right, there stood the third elm. Counting from right to left, *there* stood the third elm. Metaphorically speaking, the trees changed places by the process; for No. 1 became No. 3.

Revolving this matter in his mind, he happily thought of a not very new, and perhaps not very true, classical quotation, which applied to his own **case;** and saying to himself, "under the middle tree you will be safest," he stationed himself under the spreading branches of elm No. 2. The trees being only a few yards apart, he could easily see all three from the spot where he stood.

However, he did not stand still more than a second or two. His feelings were wrought up to fever heat by the missive he held in his hand. Accordingly, he calmed his agitated breast, though only in a slight degree, by pacing up and down the gravel walk in front of the elm trees. In his fond clasp he still enfolded the pink note; and, while he waited for the writer, he read and re-read it several times.

The principal objects that were conspicuous in the scenery by which he was surrounded were the noble trees of stately growth which form the long avenue at the backs of the colleges. And, as he did not know from what point of the compass the fair Miss Bellair would approach their appointed trysting-place, our hero strained his eyes in his efforts to make their vision penetrate farther into the fast-gathering twilight of the autumn afternoon than any lover's eyes, constructed upon the common optical principles, were capable of doing.

At length—for, to the imagination of love, time flew that afternoon with very faltering wing, and

seconds seemed hours, and minutes days and nights
—as Mr. Golightly was very intently gazing in one
direction, his quick ear detected approaching footsteps in that opposite—soft footfalls, but fast. Oh.
thought of rapture! Was it Miss Bellair? He
wheeled round suddenly, in an imposing, military
manner. He rather regretted that he was not in
full academicals, as she had said the gown was an
ornament to him—or stay, that he was an ornament to the gown he wore. Which was it? There
was no time to decide; for there, advancing with a
step and mien worthy—as our hero thought—of
any fabled fairy princess, came a lady down the
walk from the college which he himself had trod-
den, muffled and closely veiled, with a modesty
as charming as it was becoming to the most
graceful and candid of her sex. The lady was
close to him. Mr. Golightly was near-sighted
—a distinction he inherited from his mother: but
there could be no mistake, it was the figure of
Emily Bellair. He felt somewhat embarrassed.
He had never been placed in similar circumstances
before. Somehow, he wished he had had a few
minutes longer to think over some neatly turned
and appropriate poetic speech. His heart went
pit-a-pat with irregular beatings. His throat felt
dry. His voice seemed to have tucked itself away

in as distant a place as it could. His courage, however, did not for one instant fail.

"A-h-m!" said he—"a-h-m!"

Was it possible that, through her thick veil, Miss Bellair did not recognize him? It seemed almost as if this were the case, for she continued her walk, and actually passed him, though at a slower pace.

Equal to this emergency, and breathing an innocent imprecation upon thick veils, Mr. Golightly instantly placed himself at the lady's side. They walked onwards for a few steps in silence.

"A-h-m! a-Miss Bellair—may I venture—that is, may I dare to—t-a-ake the liberty of addressing you as Emily?"

"What does this mean?" said a musical voice, in its softest and most dulcet tones.

Fearing he had proceeded too hastily in the matter, and asked his first question too abruptly, Mr. Golightly continued, in his most captivating manner—

"Pray pardon me, Miss Bellair; but, from the terms of that note which I hold in my hand"— here our hero pressed his hand, with the precious note in it, to his manly heart, in the most approved style of half-hoping, half-doubting lovers. And, except we believe that the language of love rises untaught to the human lips, we may wonder where Mr. Golightly learned these arts.

" What does this mean ? " again the lady asked, with soft accent.

MR. GOLIGHTLY FINDS HIMSELF AT THE FEET OF
MISS JANE SNEEK.

She stopped, and looked, from under her veil, full into our hero's face.

" It m-means," replied the gallant Golightly,

construing her question as a rebuke for his own mistrustfulness, and an intimation from the lady that apology was quite uncalled for—"It means that I am f-fascinated by your—your charms, m-my dear Miss B-bellair."

"Mr. Golightly," said the lady, softly, "there is some mistake."

"Not the l-least mistake in the world," replied Mr. Samuel Adolphus. "My intentions are most honourable. L-let me call you Emily—d-do!"

The lady moved a pace or two forwards; Mr. Golightly placed himself elegantly upon his knees immediately in her path. His right hand covered the button of his coat that was over his heart. His hat and the pink note fell on the gravel path together.

"Em-Emily—you do not refuse me that privilege?"

"I'm generally called Jane, which is my name," the lady was saying, when a sudden gust of wind blew off her veil, and revealed to our much-astonished hero the features of Miss Sneek.

He was completely dumbfoundered—to use a Scotch phrase—by the shock his astonished nerves received. He looked down, abashed, at the gravel, trying to collect his thoughts, and recover his self-possession. When he looked up again, and was about to offer an explanation of his conduct and account satisfactorily for his present attitude, the lady was gone. Miss Sneek had fairly taken to her heels and run.

"Gr-gracious!" said Mr. Golightly, faintly.

He was preparing to rise, and looking about him for his hat and the pink note, when he felt a gentle knock at his back. Startled and alarmed, he looked quickly round, and, to his utter confusion, beheld Mr. Pokyr's tall and athletic figure immediately behind him, with his hands spread over him in an attitude of benediction. At a few paces from Mr. Pokyr were three other gentlemen Mr. Golightly had no difficulty in recognizing as Mr. Calipee, Mr. Jamaica Blaydes, and Mr. De Bootz. One or two others were there, also, with whom he was not personally acquainted.

"Mr. Golightly, sir," said Mr. Pokyr, sternly, "pray explain yourself. What is the meaning of this unseemly attitude?"

Mr. Samuel slowly rose, and stared vacantly around him.

"Put on your hat, sir."

"I-I don't know what I've d-done with my hat," Mr. Golightly replied, placing his hands on his head, to assure himself it was not there.

"Is this your property?" asked Mr. Blaydes,

holding forth to view a pink note, somewhat the worse for wear.

" I-it certainly—that is, it w-was," replied our hero.

" I move that it be read," remarked Calipee, talking as if he were at the Union on a Thursday night.

" Have you any objection, Golightly?" asked Mr. Blaydes.

Our hero was now fairly surrounded by his friends.

" I would really r-rather you would not," said Mr. Golightly, plaintively.

" I think we must read it," said Mr. Pokyr.

Had Mr. Golightly's frame of mind been more calm, he might have perceived that, as his friend Pokyr carried his threat into execution, he did not require to refer much to the document itself: he seemed to know the contents almost by heart. This, however, our hero failed to observe, being, not unnaturally, absorbed in the peculiar circumstances of the situation. The letter was read from beginning to end by Mr. Pokyr—the reader being many times interrupted by the gentlemen above-named, and by several others who had joined them —accidentally, of course. These interruptions consisted chiefly of cheers and congratulations. Under different circumstances, Mr. Golightly would, with his natural politeness, have acknowledged these marks of attention and esteem; as it was, he stood in the midst of the little knot of admirers that surrounded him, simply stupefied.

"All this must be explained," said Mr. Pokyr, when he had finished reading the note. "I must take care of this epistle myself."

"Others are interested," said Mr. Blaydes. "Other men are in love with Miss Bellair."

"They will be jealous, Golightly."

"There is Tommy Chutney, over head and ears in love," said Calipee, mournfully.

"Put your hat on, Golightly," said Pokyr. "It is disgraceful to see you out here without a hat."

"I wish I could," replied the hero of this history, looking appealingly round for his hat, but altogether unsuspicious of foul play.

"There is the dinner bell," said Pokyr. "Come back to your rooms for your cap and gown. Did you come out without your hat?"

"Cer-certainly not," replied Mr. Golightly, more hurt than indignant. "I had it on, of course."

"Where is it, then?"

"Come, that won't do for us, Golightly," said Mr. Blaydes.

" Where did you lunch? and what was the tipple?" asked another of his friends.

" I am pl-placed in an awkward pre-predicament," Mr. Golightly began.

" You are, undoubtedly—especially as it is not improbable the tutor saw you."

" We saw a Don in the distance," cried several voices.

At length, Mr. Golightly was taken under the protection of Pokyr and Blaydes, and, followed by his other friends, was walked off towards his own rooms, which were not many yards distant from the scene of his discomfiture.

" You are a model Freshman," said Blaydes.

Mr. Golightly felt he was not.

" Why did Venus fly from Apollo," asked Pokyr.

" It w-wasn't Miss Bellair," said our hero, apologetically.

" Not Miss Bellair—who then?"

" The gyp's daughter."

" Sneek's?" said Mr. Pokyr, sternly. " Golightly, you are a disgrace to us! What can you see to admire in her?"

" But I don't admire her."

" Then why were you on your knees?" urged Blaydes.

" I will explain all," said our hero, taking refuge

in his own rooms, and heartily wishing he could find some excuse for not going into Hall to dinner.

" Yes, we demand an explanation of this affair," said Mr. Pokyr. " An explanation is the least you can give us."

" Moët with it, I vote," said Mr. Calipee, emerging from his rooms in cap and gown.

During dinner, Mr. Golightly was made the butt of many harmless little pleasantries; and the pink note, and various not very accurate versions of the affair of love, went the round of Mr. Pokyr's set. Our hero retreated as soon as he had swallowed some mouthfuls of dinner: it became apparent to him that he was being rallied upon his late adventure.

He made his way across the quad, and, rushing up his staircase, gained his own rooms, pulling to the door after him—or, as the phrase is, " sporting his oak "—for the sake of privacy. He felt it necessary to be alone, that he might devise some scheme of action worthy of himself and his father's son.

But he was mistaken: he was not the only occupant of his room. Near his fireplace stood Mr. Sneek, in an unusual and defiant posture. The weight of his rather corpulent person was thrown upon his right extremity, while his left ditto was slightly advanced.   One hand was behind his back, the other pulled a curly lock of hair that graced his classic forehead.

"Good hevennin', sir," said Mr. Sneek, taking the initiative in the discussion.

Mr. Golightly forgot his recent interview with Miss Sneek for the moment.

"Evening, Sneek," he said, in answer to the gyp's salutation, and without noticing the tone of mingled injury and defiance in which it was uttered.

"Good heve—nin', sir!" observed Mr. Sneek, with increased emphasis and rising colour.

"You have brought up some coals? The coal-scuttle was empty before dinner, I know," continued Mr. Golightly, glancing rather nervously at the receptacle for his coals.

He recollected his little affair with Mr. Sneek's daughter; and, with an unerring instinct, he felt sure her papa had come with the intention of asking an explanation, or "kicking up a row." Mr. Golightly did not, at this early period of his undergraduate career, know of that speedy way out of almost all Cambridge troubles, where only a "cad's" wounded feelings are in the case. He was ignorant of that healing balm—that salve of boundless

power—that silver key, potent to open every door
as any fairy "open sesame." Had he fortunately
known of this magic talisman, it would have materially relieved his feelings; as it was, he felt considerably embarrassed as he seated himself on the
edge of his sofa.

"There his coals in your box, if you please, sir,"
said Mr. Sneek, giving the curl a pull, and making
a low bow. "Hand there is, likewise, coals in
your gyp-room, sir; hand, I 'ope, as long as you
keep on this staircase, coals—hif required—will
allus be found at 'and. But it is not of coals I
wish to say a word or two, sir—with permission"
—here Mr. Sneek bowed lower than before—
"and not taking no pertickler libbatty, I 'ope,
sir."

The honest man smiled within himself—"tickled
inly with laughter," in fact—when he had brought
this speech to a satisfactory conclusion. He eyed
Mr. Golightly, his master, as a snake might view a
fine plump pigeon before he swallowed him up.
His master devoutly wished that he had not
"sported" his door, but left it open. He wanted
Pokyr or his cousin George to come in, to put the
gyp to flight. But the door was fast, and assistance could not come. This fact was not lost upon
Mr. Sneek.

In turn our hero bowed, as an intimation to Mr. Sneck to proceed.

"The subjeck I should wish to mention, sir—under permission, sir—is delicate to a parent's feelin's."

Here Mr. Sneck sighed heavily — threw the weight of his body on his left leg—which bent and bowed slightly under it—advanced his right foot to the position his left had lately occupied, rolled his eyes about in an alarming manner, and placed the disengaged hand upon the place where his heart might be supposed to be.

"G-go on," said his master, nervously; as one who would say, "I deserve it all."

"My daughter, sir, she says to me, when I was quietly a-taking my pint of buttery beer, usual at tea, she says to me—rushin' in of a sudden, and puttin' her mother into a state as nothin', I assure you, sir, on my word, but six of pale brandy neat got her round again—she says to me, my daughter says—'Father.' 'Well, Jane,' I harnsered. 'Mr. Golightly, the new gentleman on your staircase, have behaved most extraordinary; and father,' she says—with your leave, sir—'I think the gentleman's mad.'"

"M-mad!" ejaculated our hero. "No doubt—no doubt."

"'Mad?' says I. 'Mr. Golightly aint mad, not in the least'—thinkin' the gal was making game on me. 'Well, father,' my daughter says, 'he went right down on his knees.'"

"Too true," sighed Mr. Samuel.

"Now, sir," said Mr. Sneek, with much dignity, "my feelin's as a father—and as a parent—was hurt. 'Jane,' I said, 'your char-*acter* is beyond dispute.' With permission, sir, may I ask the meanin' of this extraordinary conduct on your part towards a innocent and inoffensive young person?"

Mr. Golightly gave his gyp the best explanation he could of the affair.

"'Oaxed is what you've been, sir, and no mistake; but does that pour comfort into a parent's wounded bo-som, or restore a daughter's feelin's?"

After some broad hints from Mr. Sneek, our hero perceived that a tip would put all right. He gave it readily. Mr. Sneek pocketed it with equal readiness. Holding the door ajar, he said—

"Which, sir, you've behaved in the matter like a genelman, and I'm satisfied of your havin' been victimised. I hope I shall always show my gratitude. Shall I shut the door, sir?"

"If you please."

With an expression of delight upon his features, the gyp did as he was directed. He was just humming a favourite air when he was confronted by his daughter. The hum gave place to a long, low whistle.

"Halves, father," said Miss Sneek, holding out her hand, and looking majestically inexorable.

"Halves—what do you mean?"

"I've been a listenin' outside. He's gev you a sovereign. I know he has, so don't deny it, for it's no use."

Mr. Sneek vowed and protested all the way home, but to no purpose. He found himself in the position of one of Byron's heavy fathers, whose strong-minded daughter thus addressed him:—

> "I knew your nature's firmness.
> Know your daughter's too!"

Like that lady, Miss Sneek was not to be put off with promises — to come due at the end of the term. All she vouchsafed by way of reply to her father's eloquent protestations was said in one word—

"Halves."

CHAPTER VII.

IN THIS CHAPTER, OUR HERO MAKES THE ACQUAINT-
ANCE OF A DESCENDANT OF THE IRISH KINGS,
WHO SOUNDS THE BUGLE OF WAR IN HIS EARS.

IT was not at all likely that a gentleman who had always inculcated in the mind of his son and heir the necessity of punctuality and promptitude to success in life, in all its multifarious walks, would long neglect to reply to his son's first letter from the University. Guileless, but not unambitious, the Reverend Samuel Golightly, Rector of Oakingham, had, from his son's earliest years, laid himself out to form his character upon a model after his own heart. This model, as we stated in a former chapter, was a bold admixture of Chesterfield engrafted upon Bacon; and although, as a father, it was the Rector's first wish and darling hope that his son should become a man of the world, after his own peculiar ideal conception of that character in its perfection,

still, as a parson of the Church of England, ortho-
dox, and brimful of belief in all things of authority,
the Reverend Samuel Golightly proposed, within
his heart of hearts, to add to the compound of character above mentioned a third element—namely,
a loyal and pious devotion to Church and Queen.
We have before hinted that Mr. Golightly, senior,
entertained in his full mind, now more pregnant
than ever with great thoughts, the notion that his
son and heir would become early in life a distinguished man, and that some of the superfluous
éclat arising from his doings in the great world of
men might happily be reflected upon his father.
We claim for this notion, on behalf of the genial
Rector of Oakingham-cum-Pokeington, no extraordinary measure of originality. Many fathers
have entertained similar opinions of the genius of
their respective progeny, both male and female:
opinions which have in various instances met with
a greater or less degree of realization, according to
the circumstances of their peculiar cases; for, as I
have often heard the Rector observe, and notably
on occasions when after dinner he tells the tale of
his having been attacked by the favourite bull of
the tenant who farms his glebe land, "Man," he is
in the habit of saying, "is, after all, but the crea-
ture of circumstances. I might not have been

alive now to tell you the story had it not been for Presence of Mind and a green gingham umbrella, which I commonly carry when walking in the fields in bad weather. By the bye, gingham is a fabric which every day is less used among us." For such —if, in this hypercritical age, I may be permitted to make use of an ugly word—is the universality of my friend's mind, that it is no unusual thing for him to drop from metaphysical speculation or polemical discussion to the common objects of everyday life; *exempli gratiâ*, as in the present instance from Presence of Mind to gingham gowns: as he himself observes on such occasions, "One thing very often suggests another." And this many-sidedness —so to speak—of the Rector's mind the better fits him for his duties in the high calling of a country parson; for though in the pulpit he treats often of a Sunday of those holy mysteries of our faith which, to his judgment, the most require exposition and explanation at his hands, yet on the other days of the week he is never unwilling or unready to enter into the most minute details of domestic economy which are necessary to the welfare of his flock. Nevertheless, both in the pulpit and at the cottage door, the Rector ever speaks with the conscious authority of the Church, but with all the kindliness of the truest of friends; and, not to speak too dis-

respectfully, his portliness of figure and almost
episcopal bearing greatly enhance his qualification
for performing the former of these functions to admiration. The sentiments he utters to this day
among his parishioners, when they consult him
upon their worldly affairs, are, as nearly as may be,
the same as those with which he enlightened them
when first he was inducted into the living of Oakingham, upon the nomination of that honoured
gentleman and soldier, his father. And in the
Church his sermons are year after year identically
the same; for, by an ingenious device of overturn-
ing an old oak cabinet with silver inlaid rims, which
is an heirloom in the family, and is believed to be
made of the very Oak which providentially lent its
friendly shelter to King Charles, and is turned to
this reverent use partly on that account, the Rector
contrives to begin on the first Sunday in January of
every year with the sermon he preached on the first
Sunday of the year preceding it. And so he goes
through his stock of sermons *seriatim* and in their
proper order, only writing a new discourse and sub-
stituting it for one of his old ones on such occasions
as he touches upon politics in the pulpit, which are
very rare. These sermons, together with three he
has preached before the honourable the Judges of
Assize at the county town, when his brother, the

I

Squire, was High Sheriff of the county, he intends some day to publish under the title of "Sermons for Special Occasions," by the Reverend Samuel Golightly, M.A., Rector of the parish of Oakingham and rural dean. All these sermons are very sound in their theology, and safe guides against heterodoxy, heresy, and all schism. It has often been remarked that the best sermons preached in the parish are the Sunday afternoon discourses of Mr. Morgan; and the Rector is very ready to give honour where honour is due, and feels no jealousy whatever at his curate's successes.

We have been gossiping sadly in entering upon these family details; but our excuse is that the Golightlys are a family in which the son so commonly takes after the parent, that, in affording this information concerning some traits of the father's character, we are really helping our readers to appreciate the peculiarities of the son's, the afterwards-to-become-famous hero of this history. We have said that Mr. Golightly, senior, hoped to have some little share of his son's honours reflected upon himself. The question which arose was one which, at first sight, does not appear to be very easy of solution—how was the Rector to connect himself with his son? How was the world to know, unless duly advertised of the fact, that the Samuel

Adolphus Golightly, of the University, the Bar, and the Senate, was the son of the Rector of Oakingham? After some days had been devoted to the study of this problem, the reverend gentleman was struck with the happy notion of applying to his copy of Lord Chesterfield's writings for assistance out of his difficulty. He had hardly done more than warmed his feet at his study fire, and read a few favourite passages, when he felt himself the subject of a thrill that vibrated from his toes to his spectacles. Here was the very idea. It had come, like the inspirations of all true genius, unexpectedly and in a moment. In this way it crossed the Rector's mind—

"Why not 'Letters from the Rector of Oakingham-cum-Pokeington to his Son at the University'? Why not? Why, of course. I wonder it never struck me before."

Mr. Golightly rose, divested himself of the loose coat he wore in the study, put on his black swallow-tail, and went down to the drawing-room without more ado, and there intimated his intention to his family, though only in a sort of mysterious whisper —for the idea was as yet very new, and hardly matured in his mind.

"I hope you will not overwork yourself, Samuel, my dear," said his wife; "that is all. I am afraid, if you are so very active in the parish affairs and with Sunday duty too, it is almost too much. I am sure, I wish you had not left off hunting; and I have often said so."

" But, my dear, I weigh nearly sixteen stone, I'm sure."

" But look at Squire Potterton—he weighs nearly twenty, I know."

" I am not Squire Potterton, my dear," said the Rector, quietly.

" I hope, if ever they are printed, it will not be at your own expense, brother," said Miss Dorothea, who was a very careful spinster in all money matters. " Think of that gentleman you once had here as *locum tenens*, when you were away. Poor man, he was always talking of the expense he had been put to over a volume of sermons; and at last he had to give them all away, except the boxful he kept for himself."

" Time will show," said the Rector. There was a triumphant twinkle in his bright eye as he went upstairs again to his study.

This little domestic incident had occurred some months before our hero quitted the bosom of his family to be received in that of Alma Mater. He was spending a week at the Hall with his uncles and cousins at the time The distance between

the Hall and the Rectory was not great enough to
allow his father to begin then. Accordingly, the
first of this remarkable series of letters—which was
begun with the intention of connecting the hidden
talent of the parent with the reputation of the son
—was deferred until the time of which we now
write. In the hands of our professional story-tell-
ers, long letters at frequent intervals between the
heroines and their confidantes are often the most
boring parts of stupid books; therefore, I shall at
once set the not unreasonable apprehensions of my
readers at rest on this score: the Rector's letters
do not appear set out at length as an ingredient
portion of this history. But of these famous pro-
ductions we only have occasion to give one or two,
which may well serve as a sample of the rest: for,
as my friend the Rector says sometimes—and notably of one family in the parish, in which all the
children are much alike in feature and character,
having indeed what in that part of the country
are called Apple Dumpling faces—"*Ab uno disce
omnes;*" making use of his Latin, in which he has
the repute of being a proficient, in such cases as he
finds the vulgar tongue insufficient to express all
the meaning he desires to convey. The noble
Stanhope began to write his letters to Stanhope,
junior, when that envoy-extraordinary in embryo

was in nankeen breeches and a blue coat with gilt buttons, at the early age of five. The Rector of Oakingham felt that, as a system of educational philosophy, his letters would suffer from his first beginning to write them when his son had so nearly arrived at man's estate; but as they had never been separated from each other for more than a few days at a time, and often on such occasions only an adjoining parish divided them, Mr. Golightly the elder held that, up to the period of his son's leaving home, the labour of epistolary correspondence would have been in some degree supererogatory.

The first of these letters is given to the reader just as it reached Mr. Golightly, junior, at St. Mary's, word for word, and without alteration or addition of any sort. "My dear Son," it began— the Rector decided upon this form of commencing his letter after much debating in his own mind, for he was well aware that his illustrious prototype always began his epistles with "My dear Friend;" but the Rector felt that the custom of this age would hold the latter style cold—therefore his decision.

"My dear Son—In these parts, removed alike from the bustle of commercial Marts, the ceaseless intrigues of Courts, and the elevated disputations of those ancient seats of learning and seminaries of sound knowledge and religious education, in one, and not the less distinguished, of which—for their merits are equal—you are now happily located, we are still engaged in the same dull round of ephemeral and hebdomadary duties and pursuits in which you left us. But you, my dear boy, move in a more extended and spacious sphere ; therefore, I beg of you, lose no opportunity of making yourself intimately acquainted with the manifold passions, peculiarities, and desires of Man the microcosm—"

"The phraseology is almost Johnsonian," Mr. Morgan said, knowing that when the Rector, who was reading the letter to him, came to a pause, he expected a compliment.

Mr. Golightly smiled, bowed, and went on—

"Lose, then, no opportunity of mixing with men of all sorts and conditions; for I especially desire you to possess *les manieres d'un honnête homme, et le ton de la parfaitement bonne compagnie*—and this is the surest way to acquire them. I have no doubt the heat of the candles affected you in the college chapel. I have often noticed a change myself when, on a Sunday afternoon in winter, Bumpy—as you always called the beadle when you were a child—lighted the four candles to warm the air a little above the pulpit, and to enable me to see my book. But in the matter of drinking wine, be cautious; leave port to us old fellows, and adhere strictly to the lighter beverages of France and the Rhine. *Vinum Mosellanum est omni tempore sanum.* *Vinum Rhenanum* is probably the same, and *sana mens in sano corpore* the result of drinking sound and light wines. Lastly, remember my advice, and try to be at all times cool, calm, and collected, and to rise equal to any occasion. Timorous minds are much more inclined to deliberate than to resolve. Let not little things disturb your equanimity. *Æquam memento rebus in arduis servare mentem:* be neither transported nor depressed by the incidents of life.

"P.S.—All desire their kindest regards. Have you called yet on Mr. Smith?"

This letter—in the matter of quotation, at all events—was not a bad imitation of the style of the distinguished man whose Letters have handed his fame down to the memory of posterity.

Our hero had just finished the first perusal of this powerful letter, and was somewhat astonished

at the way in which his Fa could "come out" upon
occasion; further, he was just going to reach down
his dictionary, for the purpose of aiding him in
making a rough translation of the several classical
quotations—for the predisposition of our hero's
mind being rather mathematical than classical, he
was not a "dab" at translation at first sight—
when there was a very loud knock at his door, and
:—without waiting for any "Come in," or other
form of polite invitation to enter—in walked Mr.
Pokyr and Mr. Blaydes.

"I think, if I were you, I would advertise for
them," said Mr. Pokyr, in a confidential way.

"Advertise for what?" asked Mr. Golightly, innocently.

"Why, for your hat and your umbrella, of
course," replied his friend, with decision. "You
haven't found them?"

"N-no—I have not—that is, yet," said our hero,
at first despondingly, and then more hopefully of
the recovery of his chattels.

"The question I ask is, where are they?" said
Mr. Pokyr.

"Precisely what I say—where can they have
got to?" continued Mr. Blaydes, in his turn.

"Gentlemen," said Mr. Golightly, with the preoccupied air of one who had exhausted all specula-

tion on the painful subject—"Gentlemen, I have asked myself that question."

"And echo answered 'Where?' I suppose," said Mr. Pokyr. "Golightly, my dear boy, you must advertise for them. It is the usual thing, is it not, Blaydes?"

Mr. Golightly understood Mr. Blaydes to corroborate the statement of their common friend.

"Cambridge is a queer place. You must try to conform to ye manners and ye customs of ye place and period, or you will be thought singular," said Mr. Pokyr.

"I wish to do so—in all things, I'm sure," responded Mr. Golightly—who, so far in his undergraduate career, had found many things new to him. "My Fa—that is, my father—often said to me, 'Do not be a round man in an angular hole'"—his friends laughed—"or stay, I would not be quite sure," our hero proceeded; "perhaps it was 'an angular man in a round hole.' It was one of these two, I'm sure. Yes, it was. My Fa used to say, too, 'At Rome do as Rome does.' He once visited Rome in the Spring, Pokyr. He means, of course—"

"My dear boy, of course we know what your dear Fa means. Don't explain."

"But to come to business," said Mr. Blaydes,

joining Pokyr in interrupting our hero's anecdote of the Rector.

"Ah! business," said the latter.

"Advertisements, you know," said Mr. Blaydes.

"Yes—in what paper?"

"On small handbills, I advise," said Mr. Pokyr.

"I don't know what is customary; in fact, I am not ashamed to confess that I never wrote an advertisement for lost property in my life."

"Perhaps you never lost anything before."

"Oh, yes!—very often—I often forget things—my purse, you recollect, the day I came."

"I recollect—I recollect," said Mr. Pokyr, hastily. "But there is no time to be lost: the bill ought to be printed to-night. I'll get it done for you. Now, let us have pens, ink, and paper."

Our hero produced his desk.

"You dictate—I will write. Fancy you are Napoleon the Great, and I am one of your sixteen secretaries, all writing at once, and dash it off like a man."

"No—you flatter me, Pokyr. I'm not like Napoleon the Great. You don't think so."

"What shall I write?" asked his friend.

"I-I leave it all to you."

Without any trouble or apparent mental effort,
Mr. Pokyr composed the following handbill:—

LOST,

BY A GENTLEMAN OF ST. MARY'S COLLEGE,

A HAT and an UMBRELLA.

☞ THE FINDER WILL BE LIBERALLY REWARDED BY THE OWNER.

APPLY TO THE PORTER AT THE GATE.

"Bravo," said Jamaica Blaydes.

"That seems capital, I think," said the gentleman most intimately concerned.   "Sh-shall I get
them back, do you think?"

"Sure to do it, my dear boy," exclaimed his
friend Pokyr. "A bill like that must be seen.
We'll print fifty of them."

"Cambridge is a very honest place," observed
Mr. Blaydes. "The only reason that you have not
had them back is, in all probability, because the
finders don't know where to take them."

"In-deed," said Mr. Golightly, opening his
eyes.

"Ya-as," said Mr. Pokyr, rising, and—what I
believe is termed—tipping the wink to Mr. Blaydes.

" Please to read it again," said Mr. Golightly, in his usual irresistible way.

" Certainly—with pleasure, I am sure. Charming little bit of composition, isn't it? *You* read it to the gentleman, Blaydes. I don't like reading my own things—never did justice to them in my life."

" Have you written, then, Pokyr? " asked Mr. Golightly, in astonishment.

" Every member of the Cutlet Club writes," was the epigrammatic and only reply of the Honourable John Pokyr.

This was strictly true—they wrote their names in the members' book. But I do not think that, if a duly elected member were unable to do this, he would on that account be refused admission.

Mr. Blaydes, having cleared his throat, and adjusted the collar of his shirt, now read the handbill as set out above.

" There, that will do," said the clever author rising, and shouting across the quad to his servant, who was just then passing—" Smith."

" Yes, sir," touching his hat to his master.

That gentleman, who had flung the window open, dropped the "copy" down to his valet below.

" Tell the fellow to have it done to-night. Print fifty of the first edition."

"One moment before he goes," said our hero, nervously. "What is '*liberally* rewarded?'"

"Handsomely."

"I mean, how much?"

"Oh, they'll take anything you like to give them," said Mr. Pokyr, in his off hand way.

"But I should not like to give very much; and I should be sorry if they felt disappointed, or that I had not acted up to my word," was the scrupulous rejoinder.

"What's your mushroom worth?"

"My umbrella was given me. A guinea, perhaps. Yes, I think it would be a guinea at Fuddleton, you know."

"Oh, say five and twenty bob, out of respect to the donor's feelings. And your 'tile'?"

"Ten and sixpence, I think."

"One fifteen six, then. Well, say you gave somewhere about double the value—three pounds never mind the 'tizzy'—that would be liberally rewarding the finder."

"It would indeed," sighed our hero, apprehensively. "Stay, I would rather not have the bills printed, I think."

"Don't name it; take you a week to write them, if you had Sneek and Cribb to help. They can go down to my tick."

"I don't mean that, exactly. It's the reward. Pray stop your man!"

"He's gone—there by this time. Now we'll help you to drink a glass of your father's capital Madeira."

After dinner that evening, Messieurs Pokyr and Blaydes, accompanied by De Bootz, Browne, and Calipee, strolled into Green's to pass a social hour over the board of green cloth at the game of pool, a diversion at which the players have been likened to the most rascally of pirates, as all their fun consists in " taking lives." Here the gentlemen above named found their friend Fitzfoodel and others of their own particular set already busily employed.

" Where is the Captain to-night? 'Pon my honour, this is the first time I ever came into this room when there was a pool on, and he was not in it."

The speaker was Mr. Pokyr; and he had scarcely uttered his remark when, through the oval pane of glass in the door—on which was painted in white letters, " Please wait for the stroke"—a nose was visible—a very red and pimply nose. It was the Captain's nose.

" Talk of an angel and—" said Mr. Pokyr, as the Captain entered the room.

The Captain was a gentleman of about forty summers. His name was O'Higgins, and he had more than once told most of the people he knew that his family estates were to be found spreading their broad acres over a large part of the West of Ireland. Why he was called the Captain it is difficult to determine, as he had never been in any army. Possibly it had been originally conferred upon him for the reason that the descendant of the ancient Irish kings should have, even in the land of the domineering Saxon, some courtesy title to distinguish him from other men. How it was he came to settle in Cambridge was another inexplicable mystery. Nobody could account for his preference for the flat scenery of the Fen districts over the wild and magnificent landscapes, the castles, mountains, forests, trout streams, and deer parks of his ancestral domain. Another feature in his character was, that he either employed a most negligent person to collect his princely revenues, or his tenants lived rent free; for it is certain that no portion of his extensive rent-roll ever found its way into the pockets of the royally descended owner, the contents of whose capacious pockets generally consisted of pieces of silver known in the profession as billiard sixpences—these being coins that were sixpences once, but, having seen many years of active service, had arrived at an intrinsic value of about three-pence each, and passed current at their nominal worth only as "lives" at pool. Pokyr called them the last of the silver plate of the O'Higgins family; and it was not strange that the silver possessed by the representative of that ancient race should show signs of wear and tear. It is a fact, nevertheless, that how often soever the Captain disposed of them, they always, sooner or later, found their way back to him, as they were honoured nowhere else. For the rest, he was a very tall man and a very stout man, and wore a velveteen coat, and a huge watch chain credulous Freshmen looked upon as gold. Pokyr said the Captain's nose had cost more to colour than all his own meerschaums put together, and that was saying a great deal.

Something of the general character of Timothy Fitzgerald O'Higgins, Esq., of Mount O'Higgins, in the county of Galway, may be learned from another remark of Mr. Pokyr's—namely, that the Captain was " a fellow who smokes his cigars very low; and they have all been given him into the bargain, you know." For this observant young gentleman had often seen the Captain sucking his Havannahs down to the last quarter of an inch,

K

and then reluctantly parting with even such small stumps. From this it will readily be inferred that the Captain had not enjoyed as many of Fortune's smiles as a royal personage ought to receive.

"Late to-night, Captain," said Mr. De Bootz, as the scion of royalty removed his brown velveteen coat, and hung it carefully on its accustomed peg.

"It's late I am," replied Mr. O'Higgins, finding the key of his case, and extracting thence his own private cue.

"Where have you been, Captain, if it's a fair question?" continued his friend, De Bootz.

"I've been to the Union. Chutney took me to hear him speak."

"What was the row?" asked Pokyr.

"Sir, the subject of debate was, 'That the abolition of the practice of Jewelling' (duelling) 'was creditable to English Societee.' Affirmative, Mr. Grenville, of Caius; negative, Mr. Chutney, of St. Mary's; and now," said the Captain, "you know as much as I do myself about it. I won't be the one to catch myself there again in a hurree."

"Why, Captain?"

"Sir, there's a draught in that Strangers' Gal

lerce enough to take a man's head off. And I wanted to join you; for, on me honour as a gentleman, I lost money here last night."

" Oh!" from several players.

" The last ball is yours, sir," said the marker.

" Would Chutney show fight?" asked Pokyr, suddenly, after the Captain had made his first stroke.

" Well, I don't know; but if tark goes for anything in *this* countree, he's the very brath of a boy, and no mistake at arl about it."

After their play was over, Mr. Timothy O'Higgins went, in the company of Mr. Pokyr, to pay a visit to Chutney's rooms.

The result of the interview was that, in the morning, just as our hero was contemplating the nicely browned mutton chop which had been placed upon his breakfast table, he was startled by a most martially executed rat-tat-tat-tat at his door.

" Come in," he cried.

And in walked the Captain.

With his usual politeness, though considerably astonished, our hero rose to inquire the purport of this unexpected visit. Before, however, he could ask any question, the stranger began the conversation.

" Mr. Golightly, I believe?"

That gentleman bowed in acknowledgment of his patronymic.

" Allow me, sir, to interojuice meself—me name is O'Higgins."

" Mr. O-O'Higgins?" said our hero, rather nervously and very inquiringly.

" *The* O'Higgins, sir, is me prawper title; for me fawthers bore it bee-fore me," said the stranger, in an unpleasantly martial way.

" Indeed, sir," said Mr. Golightly to The O'Higgins.

" To be brief, sir, I am the bearer of a message from me friend, Mr. Chutney, which you'll do well to attend to at once, for it won't keep at arl!"

" S-S-Sir!" exclaimed our hero, " I haven't the pleasure of knowing Mr. Chutney, though I have heard my cousin and — and others mention his name."

" Indeed, sir—then ye soon will have," said The O'Higgins, waving his hand *à la militaire;* " for I may tell you, me friend Chutney is not the man to be throifled with; and, as he has favoured ye with his address at the head of this"—here he handed a letter to our greatly astonished hero—" I'll just lave ye to answer it as soon as ye conveniently can. Mr. Chutney will be found at home all the marning."

And with this remark, and a military salute, Mr. Timothy Fitzgerald O'Higgins took his departure.

CHAPTER VIII.

AN INTERMEDIATE CHAPTER BETWEEN THE ONE BEFORE IT AND THE ONE BEHIND IT.

THE society which constitutes the little world within the walls of a college is marked by divisions into large parties and small parties, pretty much after the same fashion as the society in the great world outside. These parties, again, admit of minute subdivisions into cliques or sects, consisting of a more or less limited number of gentlemen whose tastes, habits, and pursuits may be said to be sufficiently alike to give them objects of interest in common. There are political parties, who fight great battles, with much eloquence, in the college debating society—where a promising spirit of rancour is fostered between the sons of Tory fathers and the sons of Whig fathers, tending to maintain the integrity of the line which divides those great sections of the nation, on the existence of which, as we all know, the stability,

prosperity, and happiness of these realms so largely
depend. There are likewise parties in boating
affairs, in cricketing, and athletics ; and tremendous contests take place, once a term or so, when
one party proposes that Mr. A. should be first captain of the boats or president of the athletic club,
while the other promotes the candidature of Mr. B.,
and a battle royal ensues between the supporters of
these gentlemen. There are parties, too, in matters
of more serious concern than those above mentioned
—religious factions, that come out in all their might
and glory at the end of term, when the election to the
offices of precentor and committee-men of the choral
society takes place. Then there are the enthusiastic gentlemen who fit up their gyp-rooms in the
loveliest way conceivable, as little oratories, with
real kneeling-desks in carved oak, and imitation of
stained windows, with shaven-crowned saints, and
brazen candlesticks with charming wax candles in
them, and brazen vases for flowers, and censers for
burning frankincense and myrrh, and incensing the
rosy-cheeked little choir boys, in their short white
surplices, edged with Nottingham lace, and their
purple cassocks made on the most approved pat-
tern. True, this use of their gyp-rooms may make
it a matter of necessity that their cups and saucers
and commons should be kept in what was con-

structed for a coal-box, and their coals in a box ottoman in their bed-rooms ; but of what account are the vanities of this world ?

Arrayed in opposition to them, we find a party of gentlemen who regard all musical services with absolute horror, and in whose eyes any ecclesiastical habiliment more *prononcé* than a Geneva gown is an abomination, and a potent source of mental and moral disquietude. And of all the battles fought to advance party interests, the hottest and liveliest ones are the contests between these extreme divisions, who are in the daily habit of saying very unpleasant and uncomplimentary things the one of the other. Happily, at these choral, but anything but harmonious meetings, there is always present a third party, holding in its hands the balance of power; looking moderately at all things, and at all men in a spirit of charitable consideration.

Again, outside the walls of particular colleges, and drawing their numbers from the whole body of undergraduates, are other clubs and societies, in which the battles of the parties are fought with more or less energy, according to circumstances.

The Lyceum, the Cutlet, the Drag have their members, who form themselves into special sets upon some unascertained but surely operating principle, like Darwin's theory of natural selection. It was to what was known as the "tea drinking" party of the Cutlet Club that Horatio Clive Chutney—more familiarly termed Tommy Chutney—belonged, whose communication, conveyed by the trusty hand of The O'Higgins, had thrown our hero into such a state of nervous and apprehensive expectation in our last chapter. The epithet "tea drinking" may be thought to carry with it its own explanation. Briefly, it arose from the practice or custom of certain refined and rather young lady-like members of the club drinking tea at half-past four o'clock, successively, in each other's rooms; and, in fine weather, airing themselves afterwards on the King's Parade, with flowers in their coats.

Mr. Chutney, though a native of India, was looked upon as a true Briton—for he was of English extraction, though very dark in colour; and it was he who, with something of implied contempt for the darker side of human nature, bestowed the sobriquet of "Nigger" upon our friend, Mr. Calipee.

Chutney had acquired considerable notoriety in the Cutlet Club by the peculiarly happy knack he had of bestowing nicknames upon the honourable members of that society, which stuck to them in spite of their efforts to sink them in oblivion. On this account, Mr. Chutney was looked up to with considerable fear and respect by all those lucky individuals upon whom he had not as yet tried his powers; while, on the other hand, those gentlemen for whom he had acted the part of a second sponsor, as a matter of course, rarely let an opportunity pass of recording the opinion that they "didn't see much in Chutney." Mr. Fitzfoodel, a great rider, he at once dubbed "Jockey;" Mr. Calipee, as before mentioned, carried about everywhere the addition of "Nigger"—like Sneek's traditional suit of black, it fitted to a T. Upon a mighty athlete, whose name was Johnstone, Mr. Chutney conferred the sobriquet of "Jumper," and Jumper Johnstone he is known as to this day. A Quixotic gentleman, of ancient lineage, in whose high-bridged and defiant nose the Indian saw a resemblance to an eagle's beak, he christened "the Bird;" and behold, "Call upon the Bird for a song" was a common demand at the meetings of the club, for the youthful Quixote had a tenor voice. More unpleasant to bear up against were such nicknames as "the Cow," bestowed by this Adam of the Cutlet Club upon a youth who had very large black eyes, a vacant stare, and a most unchristian gait. The vasty deep was laid under contribution by the mother-wit of this bestower of epithets to furnish

one appropriate to a South country gentleman who
had a Somersetshire accent, and one day, after a
club dinner, told the same anecdote about a big
" vish " many more times than sobriety would have
dictated; so he was called, after his story, the "Big
Vish," or " Vish," ever afterwards—though the
point of the tale has not yet been caught. The
" Female Monkey," too, was answered to and politely acknowledged by another Mutton Cutlet—
why, Chutney only knows. And little did poor
Mr. Samuel think, when his cousin, Mr. George,
took him, on that ill-fated Thursday night, to pay
his first visit to the Union, and hear Mr. Chutney
speak, that the debate to which he had listened
with so much interest was so soon to take such a
seriously practical turn. Introduced by his cousin,
he paid his fees, and inscribed the honoured name
of Golightly—preceded by Samuel Adolphus, and
followed by St. Mary's Coll.—in the books of the
Cambridge Union Society; and speedily found himself one of a crowd of young men in the large and
lofty room in which the debate on the practice of
duelling was proceeding, with unflagging vigour,
among both " pros " and " cons."

Mr. Samuel Golightly's intelligent and expressive features sparkled with more than usual animation as he cheered the gentlemen who opposed the

practice as "unworthy of a great, a progressive, and a civilized nation." While following the lead of others, he used his lungs with melodious effect in shouting " No! no!" and " Question," when the opponents of the motion affirmed, with vehement eloquence, that the "abolition of this practice in England had left us without that means of satisfaction in the last resort which one gentleman had had a right, from time immemorial, of demanding from another. Mr. President—in refuting the wholly untenable arguments of the supporters of this motion, we point defiantly and triumphantly to the example of France; and will honourable gentlemen affirm that France is not a civilized country?"

" Yes," cried our hero, boldly, joining his own with other manly voices; for, through the mazes of the logic and rhetoric pressed into their service by the Opposition, let it be recorded that Mr. Samuel distinctly saw the light of day. He little thought how soon he would be called upon to sacrifice his own convictions to other people's notions of honour! All debates come to an end in time; and this one, after raging hotly for above an hour and three-quarters, terminated in a division; the result of which, when announced to the House by the President, appeared to be—for the motion, seventy-two; against it, seventy-one. The result was received with deafening cheers, in which the voice of Mr. Samuel might have been plainly heard by those near him. Mr. Chutney and his party left the House, defeated but not disgraced. They had lost their cause by a very small majority. The victors laughed, of course—"let him laugh who wins"—and the losers consoled themselves with the recollection, pleasant in their memories, of the good fight they had made; while the moderate thinkers were quite content, calling to mind that line—

> "Which country members always cheer at,
> 'Palmam qui meruit ferat!'"

And so the honourable members—both debaters and non-debaters—wended their way, upon their several businesses intent: some to "sap" at Sophocles or Tacitus, some to "grind" Optics or the Calculus for the triposes; more humble men—owning to the possession of that honest thing, the "Poll mind"—to work religiously at those horrible first six books of the immortal Euclid, though hardly from pure inclination—

> "Renouncing every pleasing page
>   From authors of historic use;
> Preferring to the letter'd sage
>   The square of the hypothenuse."

Others, again—and among them our friends Cali-pee, Pokyr, and the members of the Cutlet Club generally—not being of the kind the poet describes when he has in his eye the man—

> " Who sacrifices hours of rest
>   To scan precisely metres Attic;
> Or agitates his anxious breast
>   In solving problems mathematic "—

devoted their energies of an evening to the plea-sures of pool, the wild excitements of unlimited loo, brag, bézique, or blind hookey; thinking that reading at night was a bad thing for their consti-tutions. Others, again, moved off to spend social evenings in their own rooms, in the milder dissi-pation of tea and talk—little coteries gathering themselves together to discuss the next great party *coup*, and plan the destruction of their opponents' schemes. And, after all, it is a happy thing that the academical year is divided into three terms, with good long slices of vacation intervening—for in the recess party animosities are forgotten, and men meet again friends at the beginning of every fresh term—or college society might not be the pleasant thing it is.

It has been said of a great living statesman and

orator, that he is in the habit of calming his mind, after an exciting debate in the House of Commons, by reading for two hours from the English poets before retiring to his virtuous repose—an innocent and commendable practice. Young Chutney, whose mind was excited by his rhetorical efforts, and by the result of the division on the motion he had that night opposed at the Union, was engaged in the operation of calming himself down again to his normal pressure. But he adopted a different method from that mentioned above. He retired to his room; and was sucking vigorously at a very large pipe, and taking sherry cobbler with it, when The O'Higgins and Mr. Pokyr, accompanied by Mr. Calipee, called upon him.

"I congratulate you, me friend, on your illoquence, your logic, and your facts," said the first of these gentlemen, when they entered. "It reminds me strongly of what I have heard before, in another place," continued Mr. O'Higgins, waving his hand grandly. He did not specify the locality; but may be supposed to have referred either to the Rotunda or his own ancestral halls, at some grand gathering of the Chiefs. "I was compelled to lave your handsome edifice as soon as ye had done speaking yourself, for I—"

"Had other fish to fry. Eh, captain?" said Pokyr.

"Me boy, you've hit the mark," replied The O'Higgins, with all the happy candour of his nation; "for, on me word as a gentleman, I lost money in that room last night."

"You've got your losses back, with interest."

"Ah, you're after joking me, Pokyr, you are," said the Captain. "No, I like a man that can tark loike me friend; and bedad, act up to arl he says, on occasion, bedad. And where's the man who'll say that Chutney is not a man of his word?"

And Mr. Timothy O'Higgins looked round him with an air which plainly said, "I should like to see him."

"Awfully sorry I missed the treat, by Jove," said Mr. Pokyr.

"Just like my luck—forgot all about it," observed the fat Calipee.

"Sit down, and have some liquor of some sort," said their host, rising. "I don't think I did badly —in fact, everybody says I did very well."

"And ye mane every word ye said, and there's a clean breast of the matter," volunteered The O'Higgins.

"Of course I do," said poor little Tommy, unsuspectingly falling into the trap that his friends had laid for him.

"And ye'd foight. I knew you would. I said

to me friend Pokyr—let Calipee correct me if I'm wrong, and every word is not the truth—I said, in the billiard room, before them all, 'Me friend Chutney is the man to protect his own honour, and wants nobody's help in the matter—that is, if tark goes for anything in *this* countree.' Didn't I?"

"And what did we say?" asked Messrs. Pokyr and Calipee, in their turn.

"'Deed then, and you said the same as meself," replied The O'Higgins.

Whereupon the three gentlemen seated themselves, and made themselves comfortable at once.

"Let me offer you a cigar," said Chutney.

"Thank you, I prefer a pipe just now," replied Mr. Pokyr.

"No—not that one," he added, as Chutney handed him a mammoth meerschaum.

"Oh!" replied Chutney, "it's the jolliest pipe—"

"Yes," said Pokyr; "but, as I look upon all pipes, more or less, as levers for loosening teeth, I should prefer something smaller."

Chutney's stock of pipes was large. A chibouk was found to suit Mr. Calipee, a meerschaum for Mr. Pokyr; while The O'Higgins was accommodated with a prime Partaga, which he liked so very much that he was without much trouble prevailed upon to put three or four more in his case.

The business of their visit then became apparent.
Nothing was clearer than the fact that Mr. Samuel
Adolphus Golightly had presumed to fall in love
with a lady for whom Mr. Chutney had often
avowed the greatest regard. This was at once
voted insufferably presumptuous in a Freshman.
The same Freshman had likewise made the lady
ridiculous by his attentions; and a great deal more
to the like effect.

At last, The O'Higgins put the question of a
duel to Chutney point blank.

"Now, me dear boy, tell me, are ye the man I
thought you were?" said he. "He's hardly worth
powder and shot, bedad; but honour, Mr. Chutney, is honour—at least, it was when I used to sit
down to me dinner every day in Kildare-street, except when I was dining at the Viceragal Lawdge,
which was often enough, bedad. Teach him a
lesson. Don't kill him, you know; but just wing
him. Bedad, it's manny a man I've winged meself!" said the Captain, "to say niver a word of
thim I've left dead on the field by dozens at a
toime."

Here the Captain took a pull at his brandy and
water.

Both Mr. Pokyr and Mr. Calipee felt it a duty
to take all he said on this subject seriously.

"I would not give a halfpenny for a fellow that preaches what he does not practise—by Jove, I wouldn't," said Mr. Pokyr.

And the result of the visit was, that the three guests persuaded their host—who was an excitable and easily managed youth—to send that note to our hero of which Mr. Timothy Fitzgerald O'Higgins was the bearer.

CHAPTER IX.

IN WHICH SOME SCENES FROM "THE RIVALS" ARE ENACTED OFF THE STAGE.

"'LL just lave ye to answer it as soon as ye conveniently can," and an intimation that Mr. Chutney would be at home all the morning, were, as our readers will recollect, the words of adieu with which The O'Higgins parted from Mr. Samuel Adolphus Golightly on the eventful morning when he placed the "message" of his injured friend in our hero's astonished hand.

Mr. Samuel's amazement at first, when the blustering descendant of the Kings of Erin's green isle burst in upon him and his mutton chop, had been very great. It became still greater when The O'Higgins announced his style and title, and placed the note of a gentleman to whom he was a stranger in his hand. It culminated with The O'H.'s abrupt and most unexpected departure.

" Good gr-r-acious! what can all this be about?"
exclaimed our hero, as he rushed to his window,
and watched the retreating figure of Mr. O'Higgins pacing, with martial stride, across the quad.

" Wh-wh-what does it all mean, I wonder?"

But he did not long give himself up to ignorant
wondering.

It has been said, by many wise and observing
writers, that if a man receives a letter, among a
number of letters, which he well knows to be an
unpleasant letter, he opens all his other packets
first, and makes himself master of their contents.
Then he chips his egg, and swallows a mouthful of
toast or of tea, eyeing all the while the unpleasant
epistle, and at last reluctantly opens that also.

We claim for our hero the merit of a different
course of conduct; at all events, in the present instance, he neglected the chop now cooling in its
own fat on his plate—he did not even stop to sip
his tea; but the bearer of the missive was no sooner
out of sight than he broke the seal, and satisfied
himself as to the nature of its contents. He read,
with rapidly varying expressions of feature, thus:—

" 101, King's Parade, Friday.

" Sir—As you have been pleased to make both
yourself—which is of the slightest possible conse-

quence—and Miss Bellair—which is of importance
—ridiculous, by presuming to think yourself a pre-
tender to her good opinion, and as I am further ad-
vised you have made certain remarks concerning me
of a disparaging character, though you are a Freshman, I suppose you know well enough the satisfaction one gentleman demands of another under such
circumstances as those above stated. Any gentleman you may appoint to arrange preliminaries will
find me, and the friend who carries this message, in
readiness to receive him at any time that is con-
venient to you.—Yours indignantly,

"HORATIO CLIVE CHUTNEY.

"To S. A. Golightly, Esq."

It instantly struck Mr. Golightly, with very unpleasant force, that the "satisfaction one gentleman demands of another" meant fighting, either
with swords, pistols, or larger weapons, as might
be agreed upon; and that the "preliminaries"
mentioned by Mr. Chutney were the prepara-
tions necessary for the hostile meeting. If these
were among the manners and customs of a
University, Mr. Golightly, who was pre-eminently
a man of peace—for though his grandfather had
borne arms, it was only in the militia—began to
wish he had never come there. He recollected, on

the spur of the moment, that he had never drawn a sword from its sheath, or snapped a pistol in his life; for his late grandfather's weapons were kept hanging up at the Hall, where they were looked up to with due veneration and respect. Here was a pretty predicament to be placed in! And what aggravated the matter, our hero not unnaturally felt that he was not in the least at fault, being the most amiable of mortals, and ready, aye ready, at the call of duty, to resign all claim to the hand of Miss Bellair, or any other young lady to whom any other gentleman reasonably considered that he had a prior right. Glancing again at Mr. Chutney's letter, he noticed the day of the week at its head. "Friday" stared him ominously in the face.

" Y-yesterday was Thursday, and—and it—it *is* Friday," he said to himself; and his family prepossession against that ill-fated day recurred to his memory with a vividness increased by present circumstances.

" I'll—I'll go and talk to George about it, and show him the letter," continued our hero, still talking to himself.

Snatching up his cap, he put it on his head, and hurried down the stairs; but his cousin George's door was "sported" very determinedly against assault, and his knocks and gentle kicks remained unanswered.

He stood in the doorway looking on the quad, when Mrs. Cribb came up, with a can in one hand and a pail in the other. Our hero was first made aware of her presence by hearing her voice—

"Beg parden, sir," said his bedmaker, " but if the tooters should see you in your dressin' gownd, a-walkin' about of a mornin', they might objeck, which has been the case before."

"Oh!" said our hero, for the first time thinking of his dress—such was his excitement of mind on the present occasion, though ordinarily the most particular of men. "I have—that is, I want to see my cousin."

"Meaning Mr. Golightly, my staircase ground floor," said Mrs. Cribb. "He's been gone out half an hour ago. I seed him myself, when I was a-pumpin' a can of water Sneek ought to have pumped an hour and a half before, a-goin' across the quad in his boots and ridin' whip, so I think p'r'aps he's gone for a ride or something, sir."

This was bad news, indeed; and Mr. Samuel's face fell accordingly. Just as George could have been of immense service to him, to find him gone— perhaps for the day! What was he to do? "Be cool "—that was clear, but not easy. Then, again, the honour of the family might or might not be at stake, according to the way in which you regarded duelling. But his aunt Dorothea had cautioned him to "remember that he was a Golightly;" and if the honour of the family were lost through him, what would his aunt say? Write to Oakingham-cum-Pokeington? But his mamma would die of anxiety and alarm; and he never could trust his father to keep the affair a secret, for he knew all the family would insist on reading the letter, or go into instant hysterics if they did not. He was in a dilemma—a peculiar dilemma, of a circular sort, with horns all round. Two would have been nothing to deal with. Turning these things over in his mind, he retraced his steps to his own rooms.

"You've gone and let this nice chop get cold, sir. Shall I put it before the fire for a few minutes? It would soon get hot again, with a plate over it."

But her master had not the slightest appetite for chops, hot or cold; and told Mrs. Cribb that such was the case.

"Dear me, now," said that worthy woman, in a tone of the deepest concern, as she cleared away his breakfast things, and gleefully put the chop into her basket, with the breads and butters and other perquisites it contained.

Mr. Golightly retired into the solitude of the little room dignified by the name of study, and there thought. He had not been so engaged more than a few minutes, when he thought he heard a low and hesitating single knock at the door of his keeping-room. He advanced as far as his study door to satisfy himself of the truth of his surmise. The knock was repeated in the same timid fashion. He walked towards the door, and happening at the same time, as he passed his windows, to cast his eyes across the quad, he saw about half a dozen seedy individuals, of different ages and degrees of shabbiness, coming towards the block of buildings in which he resided. It struck him as being an unusual phenomenon; but what with being near-sighted and much preoccupied in mind with the thought of Mr. Chutney's letter, Mr. Golightly failed to observe that each of these persons carried in his hands a hat, and in some cases an umbrella. By this time, the knock at his door was repeated in a louder and more determined tone, and he opened the door to an individual—who held in one hand the bill describing, in most effective type, the loss of a hat and umbrella sustained by a gentleman of St. Mary's College, and in the other hand a battered beaver and a tattered *parapluie.*

Placing the bill in our hero's hand, the bearer

took off his own hat, and, giving his curling fore-
lock a respectful pull, said—

"Mister G'lighty—d'rected here by the porter
at the gate—said as you was the gen'elman as had
lost a Nat and a Numbereller. Beggin' pardon,
sir, is these 'um? They was found—upon my
Dick, they was—a floatin' down the river agen
Maudlin" (Magdalen) "Bridge. Out in the middle
they was, upon my Dick; and great trouble I had
a-reskyin' of 'um."

Mr. Golightly at once admitted that he was the
gentleman who had lost a hat and an umbrella, and
the bill produced referred to his property; but he
indignantly repudiated any connection with the
articles produced. They were both in the last
stage of decay, and must have been thrown into
the river as the best means of getting rid of them;
but as they were quite dry now, and showed no
sign of any recent immersion, our hero slightly
doubted the assertion of the finder, and felt disin-
clined even to believe him on "his Dick"—which
was probably his way of invoking Saint Richard in
short, an oath he made use of with great solemnity
of manner several times over.

This Bargee—as Mr. Pokyr afterwards styled
him—had hardly got to the end of his narrative of
the rescue from a watery grave of the hat and um-

brella he carried, when several other Bargees made
their appearance, and urged their rival claims to
credence; addressing Mr. Golightly with great respect, and each other with a considerable degree of
contempt, and much more appropriate imagery in
the way of language.

" N-no, no, no—none of them are mine," exclaimed Mr. Golightly, whose room was, by this
time, filled with the Bargees, and who did not
know how in the world to get rid of them.

" 'Xcuse me, sir, but this un *is* yourn, and no
mistake about it," cried one, holding up for our
hero's inspection an old drab wide-awake.

" No, I never had such a one."

" Let the gen'elman alone. He knows his own—
in course he do. This un's his; my brother Billy
seed it drop off his head."

And so each Bargee pressed his claims upon Mr.
Golightly, with much volubility.   At last, a man in
a horsey suit of clothes and a bird's-eye neckerchief,
who seemed to have come in with the rest " on
spec," as he apparently had not found *the* identical
hat Mr. Samuel had lost, remarked—

" Well, if none of these hats aint the gentleman's, what I say is, What is he going to
stand ? "

" That's right, Spot," said one.

" Well done, Glanders!" said another. "Go it—that's the ticket."

" 'It 'im agen!"

" Brayvo!" from a great many.

Encouraged by these remarks, Spot Glanders, their spokesman, proceeded—

" You see, sir, you are a gentleman, and these here men have taken a great deal of trouble to restore your property to you; and if the mistake is theirs, it's partly yours as well, for there isn't no description of the hat and the umbrella on the bills."

" Hear, hear!" from all the Bargees.

" And time is time, and money too, to us working men here."

" So it is, Spot."

A happy thought struck Mr. Golightly. He had some silver in his pocket.

He had proceeded to the distribution of several shillings as a recompense for the trouble the Bargees had taken on his account, when Mr. Sneek suddenly appeared on the scene. Placing himself in his favourite attitude in the doorway, and addressing the assembled roughs, the gyp said, with a smile of irony—

" And what are you all here for? Come, clear out."

In vain Spot Glanders remonstrated; in vain the Bargees protested or murmured at the hardness of their fate.

"Clear out, or I'll have you all discommonsed," said Sneck.

Slowly and unwillingly, those who had not been favoured with the shillings left the room; comforting themselves, however, with the reflection, "We've got enough for a gallon or two o' beer among us."

"They're imposin' upon you, sir," said Sneck, as soon as they were gone. "I do hate imposition of any sort, and often I've said so to Cribb, when I've seed her or anybody else a-takin' advantage behind my back."

"They brought what they said were my hats and umbrellas," said our hero, laughing, and forgetting his greater cause of disquiet in the recollection of the Bargee encounter.

"Your 'At and Umbereller," reiterated the gyp, with a satirical sneer—"let them as sent 'em to you give 'em something for comin.' That's what I say."

Here Mr. Sneck gave a flip or two with his duster to the table legs, with an air of conscious rectitude very impressive to witness.

Our hero was again rapt in thought—the duel

in prospective taking up the whole of his attention. He wanted a confidant very badly; and Sneek was certainly a man of sense, and versed in the customs of University life.

He was within an ace of communicating some slight hint of his trouble to honest John Sneek, when Mr. Pokyr called to pay him a visit, and so relieved him of the necessity of unburdening himself to his gyp.

"Good morning, Golightly," said Mr. Pokyr, with a sprightly but innocent air. "I have just looked up your cousin, but I find his door is sported. So I suppose he's out."

"George is out, I believe," responded our hero. "Mrs. Cribb told me she saw him go across the quad an hour ago."

"Early bird. After the little grubs, no doubt. Had anybody here this morning, my dear boy? Looking at you with the philosophical eye of an old hand, I should say your mental equanimity is slightly disturbed. Whose pills do you take?"

"I do not often require medicine, thank you," said our hero, with refreshing innocence. "When we do, we have antibilious pills from Keele's, at Fuddleton. I have had a number of people here this morning—"

"Yerse," said Mr. Sneek, "we *har* had them, as you s——"

Before he had finished his sentence, the gyp observed that Mr. Pokyr was pointing imperatively in the direction of the door; and there was also a dangling, swaying motion of his right foot accompanying it which was not lost upon Sneek, who rapidly made his exit. When he had closed the door behind him, and was out of danger—pointing back with his left thumb over his shoulder, and at the same time winking his eye—he said to himself—

"You are a-havin' him a rum un. All round the 'oop, and no mistake."

"What say, John Sneek?" said Mrs. Cribb, who was in the gyp-room, just packing up her basket for departure.

"What do I say, Betsy Cribb? I say, get out o' the way," was the polite rejoinder. "What 'ave we got there?"

And Sneek proceeded carefully to overhaul Mrs. Cribb's basket, to assure himself that she had got nothing in it that properly belonged to him—conduct the bedmaker resented very indignantly indeed.

"Really, what a funny thing! Kind of them, though, was it not?" Mr. Pokyr said to Mr. Golightly, when he heard of the visit our hero had received from the Bargees.

"I have thought since, do you know, that they must have known that the hats and umbrellas were not mine," replied Mr. Golightly.

"Not a bit of it, my dear boy, I assure you. All of them honest, poor fellows; and, after all, the working classes are very ignorant, you know. How were they to tell what style of hat you wore on a weekday?"

"We for-forgot to describe them."

"Ah, we did. But it was too bad of you to let Sneek turn them all out just as you were 'liberally rewarding' them."

"Was it! Do you think it was?" said our hero, vacantly—not in the least knowing what his queries meant. "Pokyr," he said, abruptly, "read that." And he placed the missive The O'Higgins had brought him an hour before in his friend's hand. "Read that letter. I don't know what in the world to do."

Mr. Pokyr stood with one foot on the window seat, and carefully read the letter.

"There's no doubt about it," he said, shaking his head, ominously. "You see, Chutney is a very excitable fellow."

"Am I—am I *obliged* to accept it?" asked Mr

Samuel, nervously, placing his hands behind his back, and staring at his friend.

"'Pon my honour, I think you are. There seems no other way out of it. Ugly affair—pre-engagement between Miss Bellair and Chutney, seemingly. But 'take a bull by the horns,' you know," he added, cheerfully.

" But—but—but," said our hero, " I *don't* want to take a bull by the horns."

"All over by this time to-morrow. Be a man. I'll telegraph result to our friends at the Rectory. Think all the better of you for behaving like a man of spirit, whatever *may* happen."

"Aunt Dorothea would," said Mr. Samuel, thinking aloud. " But suppose—"

Mr. Pokyr closed his eyes and shook his head.

" Do suppose a case—only suppose it, you know —suppose I did not exactly wish to fight—"

" The only way out of it now, I fear."

" Would not a sort—a sort of apol—"

"Apology? Oh, Chutney is the last man in the world to take any apology. The fact is, he loves a fight—swords *or* pistols."

" The bloodthirsty little wretch," thought Mr. Samuel.

" His speech at the Union was in favour of duels, was it not?" asked Mr. Pokyr. " I was not there."

"It was," said our hero, with a deep-drawn sigh of despair.

"Screw your courage up to the shooting point. It's nothing, after all. Make your will first, and then you will have nothing on your mind."

"But I thought duelling was quite out of date. I'm sure I've heard so."

"Not here. Universities are old-fashioned places. Old manners hang about for ages."

"Good gracious!" exclaimed Mr. Samuel, in great trepidation, "what would my Fa say?"

"Your Fa would say, Fight. He would not see the family honour in the dust."

"But—but I never fired a pistol off in my life," urged Mr. Golightly, faintly.

"Never mind that—easiest thing in the world, I assure you," said Mr. Pokyr, stretching out his hand and imitating the action. "You can stand close together, you know."

"I should like to be some distance off. I do not wish to shoot Chutney."

"And he does not wish to shoot you, my dear fellow. Merely a matter of form, which must be gone through, or your honour is gone. You could not live here, and see yourself pointed at as the man who dared not fight to rescue his own honour! Now, could you?"

" But suppose anything happened?"

" Fire in the air—thus," said Pokyr, aiming with his finger at the ceiling. " Then you can't hurt Chutney, you know."

" I wish George had not gone out," said Mr. Samuel

" Yes, it is a pity. He would have told you as I do. You must accept the challenge."

In the end, Mr. Golightly commissioned Mr. Pokyr to carry his reply to the other side ; and willingly left all preliminary arrangements in his hands.

During the morning, The O'Higgins was busily engaged in keeping up the courage of Mr. Chutney—not an easy task ; and his mind was considerably relieved when Pokyr arrived with the answer of our hero, accepting the gage that had been thrown down.

Those gentlemen at once sat down to arrange between them the place, the time, and the weapons. This being done to their satisfaction, they strolled into the cigar shop of the *teterrima causa belli*—the Brown-street Venus, otherwise Miss Emily Bellair. Giving Mrs. Bellair a nod as they walked through the shop, they passed into the little back parlour, which was styled, on the half-glass door which shut it off from the snuff and tobacco jars, " Cigar

Divan." Here, looking at the morning papers, they found Mr. Blaydes.

"Well, is it a go?" asked the last-named gentleman.

"Right as ninepence," replied Mr. Pokyr. "They are going to fight it out like men."

"Well done," said Blaydes. "I would have given anything to pay that little braggart, Chutney, back in his own coin. Strange we have so soon got the chance. What a pair of nincompoops they both are!"

Mr. Pokyr nodded benignly, by way of reply.

"When is it to be?"

"To-morrow morning, at eight."

"Where?"

"Behind the Ditch on Newmarket Heath."

"Weapons of war?"

"Pistols—be all the saints," ejaculated The O'Higgins.

"Keep it quiet, and don't tell any fellows," said Pokyr, as a caution to Jamaica Blaydes, whose tongue was not that of a discreet man. "We brought the other little affair with Sneek's daughter off very nicely; and this morning his room was full of Bargees from every point of the compass."

"You got in at the finish?"

" No—I was late. Sneck had just sent them all off. Never mind, the duel will be the best fun we have had this year. They are both in a mortal funk of one another; and I'll lay a wager neither hits a haystack at ten paces."

"They are sure to show up? The Heath is a long way to go for nothing, at such an unearthly hour as eight."

" Better go to-night, and sleep there."

" Not a bad notion; but if Bloke knew the reason, he might refuse the *exeat*," replied the wary Blaydes.

" We are going to keep their courage up. The Captain is to stay with Tommy, and I coach Golightly. We've sent George out of the way—that is, he is sported in, and won't open to anybody— which, after all, is as good as being fifty miles away. He says he dares not advise his cousin Samuel to fight, for fear of after-rows."

After drinking a tankard of bitter, which Mrs. Bellair's precocious little boy fetched from the Pig and Whistle opposite, the three friends separated. Mr. Pokyr went off to coach one rival, at St. Mary's; the Captain to the King's Parade, to keep up the pluck of the other.

" I have brought a pistol with me, for you just to get your eye in, Golightly," said Pokyr, who found our hero in a very despondent state, sitting over his fire, with his head between his hands, looking thoughtfully at the embers.

"Thank you—I don't feel very well."

"But, by Jove, you must feel well, or you'll be nothing but a target to-morrow. Think of Muley Moloch, or some fellow, and be well."

"What did Muley Moloch do?"

"Why, made up his mind to be well, and was well."

"I'll—I'll try," said Mr. Samuel, with a faint smile on his wan features.

"Stand up," said Pokyr, in the tone of a drill-sergeant addressing his awkward squad.

Mr. Samuel rose.

"Right about—wheel."

He turned to his instructor, who placed a pistol in his hands.

"It—it—isn't loaded, I hope," ejaculated Mr. Golightly, eyeing the instrument of destruction with manifest dread.

"No—got a cap on, that's all. Now, make ready —stay, you want a mark. Here," said Pokyr, cutting a button from his pantaloons, and taking a pin from his neckerchief, with which he fixed the button to the wall, "aim at that—fancy it's Chutney's nose."

"I can't," said Mr. Samuel—"it seems so wicked to do so."

Mr. Pokyr never left his principal till late that night. They dined together off beefsteak and oyster sauce, Mr. Samuel's appetite for which was not improved by his second's reminding him more than once that he might never taste oysters again.

During the afternoon and evening he fired many caps at the button, and made it shake on the pin several times. There was a very gunpowdery atmosphere in the room when Mrs. Cribb came in.

"They're been lettin' off fireworks or something, John Sneck," she said. "They'll be doin' some mischief, mark my words."

"There's something hup," said Mr. Sneck, rubbing his nose sagaciously. "I'll find it out, though."

With this remark, the gyp bade Mrs. Cribb good night.

Mr. Golightly spent the night without getting one wink of sleep, and the morning found him very feverish and queer. At the early breakfast improvised before the arrival of Mrs. Cribb, he found the knives had crossed themselves, and he spilled the salt. The omens were unpropitious; but our hero rose above omens. Like a certain potentate we read of, who, when the birds were dead against him, kicked the Sacred Chickens, coop and all, into the sea, Mr. Samuel uncrossed the knives, and let the salt lie, in a reckless manner that plainly bade them do their worst.

The drive to the Heath—a good twelve miles— on a cool morning, took out of him what little courage he had left after his sleepless night; and, like Bob Acres's, Mr. Samuel's valour was gone. In vain Mr. Pokyr was facetious—in vain his joke as they passed Quy Church—

"'Ecclesia Quy stat in agris'—nearest church-yard: might bring you there if anything serious occurs. How shaky you look! Have another pull at the brandy flask."

"I don't feel quite myself," replied our hero.

It was plain he did not.

Behind the ditch they found poor Mr. Chutney and the valorous O'Higgins waiting for them.

"The top of the morning to you," said the Captain to Mr. Pokyr.

The place was chosen—the ground was measured—all was ready for the signal to fire—when an unexpected arrival made Mr. Pokyr exclaim—

"One moment, gentlemen—I perceive strangers approaching."

CHAPTER X.

CONSTABLES AND PEACEMAKERS.

" ET us gently retrace our steps," the long-winded Elder observed, when his congregation thought he had just wound up for that occasion; and, at the risk of disappointing our readers, we must address them in the Elder's words. The amiable hero of this history had been a tolerably pliant reed in the skilful hands of Mr. Pokyr. He had screwed up Mr. Samuel's courage to that "sticking point" Lady Macbeth speaks of, and taught him to snap caps on a pistol at an alarming rate—all in the short space of twenty-four hours; and if Mr. Samuel Adolphus Golightly did not reach the soft turf behind the Ditch at Newmarket an accomplished duellist, it was not his second's fault.

It is, perhaps, not in the common order of things that a man should learn the whole art of duelling in the short space of one day, nor digest the knowledge he has acquired in one sleepless night: a great deal must depend upon the courage, nerve, and coolness of the combatant. Unfortunately, Mr. Golightly was well aware of this; and, with the thought, he bade good-bye for ever to such pluck, steadiness, and *sang froid* as he previously boasted. Many people—the writer of this biography among the number—will not be disposed to think the worse of him for this, under the special circumstances of the case; for, after all, fighting is not a Christian thing; and, as our hero's facetious second observed, a few minutes before the encounter—

"Perhaps, my dear Golightly, you'd rather eat Chutney potted, than—pot him heated, by Jove?"

A very faint smile marked Mr. Samuel's recognition of his friend's reprehensible attempt at a joke.

The O'Higgins had before him a task even more difficult in the work of bringing Mr. Chutney "up to the scratch." The Indian gentleman, forgetful of his valorous words, urged a variety of reasons against fighting himself; and it required all the natural and oily eloquence of the first-named gentleman to convince, calm, and reassure him. On the eventful morning, Mr. Chutney felt so ill, that his second had very hard work to persuade him to start. Mr. Chutney felt the most burning desire to fight; but he wished to put in an *ægrotat* that morning, and postpone the hostile meeting until he felt better fitted for the combat. He talked of a surgeon's certificate; and was only finally persuaded to take his seat in the dogcart from Spratt's on the assurance of The O'Higgins that after all, in all human probability, the ride to the Heath would turn out "merely a matter of for-rm—arl glory and no risk, bedad; for that Golightly will never be there—you see if he will."

It was plain Mr. Chutney devoutly hoped that his adversary would not turn up to time.

"We shall have the ride all for nothing, then," he urged.

"Not at arl, me dear sir," returned The O'Higgins. "If Golightly isn't there, isn't it just as good as shooting him, and better besides?"

"But I don't want to go twelve miles for nothing," Chutney objected.

"Certainly not—of course not."

"Could not we find out if he *is* gone?" he pleaded.

"Well, it would not be the right thing exactly. We must go over and find out for ourselves."

"I don't feel at all well," said the principal. "I hate being rattled about in a dogcart. It shakes me to pieces always."

"I'll drive," replied the second. "You must not touch the reins. You are bound to keep your hand steady."

"Oh!" groaned the Indian, "I thought you said Golightly would not be there."

"It's—it's all Lombard-street to a Chancy orange he won't. I'd—I'd bet a hundred pounds to sixpence he isn't—now!" said The O'Higgins, glaring wildly at his poor little victim.

"I've a great mind to take you," he replied.

But after a moment's reflection, feeling that the Captain's hundred was spelled with three ciphers, and that in reality the wager would be sixpence to nothing at all, he did not accept the offer.

"How do you know Golightly will not turn up?" he asked abruptly.

"Well," said the Captain, turning the matter over in his mind, "Pokyr hinted as much to me yesterday morning."

"I never take any notice of what Pokyr says," retorted Chutney. "Besides, he is sure to make Golightly go."

"One man can take a horse to the water," urged the Captain, allegorically, "but ten can't make him drink."

"How do you mean?"

"Why, I mean he'll fire in the air, if he fires at all. *That* I do know."

The dogcart being now in waiting, Mr. Chutney, having put on many wrappers, took his seat gloomily by the Captain's side; and they drove off together.

"What would the Club think of you, you know, if you didn't show up, after everything that has been said?" the Captain observed, after they had driven some distance without a word being spoken on either side.

"Confound the Club—they've none of them ever fought a duel," replied Chutney, irritably.

"Think of all you've said, though, on the subject," said the Captain, in a soothing tone.

"My views—are considerably altered, O'Higgins."

"Bedad, it's manny a man I've winged," observed the Captain, vaguely, by way of keeping up the conversation.

"Where?"

"In all parts of me native countree. Lave an Irishman alone for picking a dacent quarr'l, when the occasion presints itself," said The O'Higgins, bravely.

"I should like a glass of something," said Chutney.

They were passing a roadside inn, just out of Cambridge.

Some time was lost in rapping up the people of the house, who were hardly astir yet.

After a glass of brandy and water, Mr. Chutney felt better. The Captain joined him for company's sake.

"That's yourself, now," he said, as his friend plucked up courage when he found there were no recent marks of wheels on the road. "We're first, at all events," he added.

"I thought you said they would not come!"

"So I did," replied The O'Higgins. "But if they do, sure you'll behave like a man—and a Mutton Cutlet?"

"Hang the Mutton Cutlet!" was the brief response.

Presently, however, Mr. Chutney's spirits grew lighter. At Quy Church the Captain made the same dog-Latin joke which has been recorded of Mr. Pokyr in our last chapter. "Quy Church stands in the fields," and qui-te remote from the village.

"A *qui*-et place enough if anything should happen to Mr. Golightly," said the Captain.

"I hate stupid puns," said Chutney. "Besides, *ecclesia* is not the word for the fabric of a church, and *qui* does not agree with it."

"Bedad! the prawspict of foighting does not agree with you, me boy," the Captain thought, but wisely said nothing.

"We're first on the field, and that's something," he said, when, after an hour's drive, they pulled up at the appointed rendezvous behind the Ditch.

"How long are we *obliged* to wait?" asked the principal, nervously.

"Not more than an hour or two, at most."

"Bound to do it?"

"In honour," replied the second.

Mr. Chutney's face fell.

They inspected the ground; and The O'Higgins paced it in due form.

"Stand with your back so," said the Captain, "is *moy* advice."

"Goodness!" said Mr. Chutney, cheering up suddenly, "you've forgotten to bring any pistols. I left it to you, of course. We can't—"

"Pokyr will provide the weapons," replied the Captain, calmly.

Mr. Chutney took a seat on the grass bank behind him.

"Stay—hark—h'sh!" cried the Captain. "I think I hear wheels—they're coming."

"No?"

"Yes! all right—here they come."

"I don't hear anything," said the principal, hoping almost against hope. "Now I do. *Is* it Pokyr?"

His doubts were speedily set at rest by the arrival of our hero and Mr. Pokyr in another dog-cart.

"The small pistols or the large ones?" said Mr. Pokyr, after he was safely out of the vehicle, producing two cases of weapons.

"Small ones!" cried both the combatants, in a breath.

"Stop, stop, gentlemen—*we* must settle these things," said Pokyr, conferring with The O'Higgins. "Shall we use the large or the small, Captain? Both brace are certain death"—this remark was made in a voice both Mr. Samuel and Mr. Chutney could too plainly hear—"never knew either of them to miss fire."

The ground was measured—the two gentlemen took up their positions. Behind Mr. Chutney was the wide-spreading Heath. Mr. Golightly turned his broad shoulders towards the belt of trees known as the Plantations. A few friends, who had come over unseen by the duellists, looked calmly on; and a stray donkey left his pasture on the Heath to gaze upon the unaccustomed scene.

As we said in our last chapter, the ground had

been duly paced out, and the rivals held the instruments of vengeance in their hands, and were both of them ready to faint with terror.

MR. GOLIGHTLY MAKES HIS DEBUT ON THE FIELD OF BATTLE.

"'One's frit and t'other daren't,' as the street boys say," Mr. Pokyr said to the Captain.

"That's about it, me boy," was The O'Higgins's answer.

" Are we ready ?"

" We're all ready on *this* side—I'll go bail for that," said the Captain.

Just as Mr. Pokyr was about to give the signal to fire, he suddenly exclaimed—

" One moment, gentlemen—I perceive strangers approaching !"

The strangers were those three active, intelligent members of the county constabulary, Officers 33, 55, and 99, who had been out on General Hall's land, on the trail of a wicked young poacher who had long evaded the clutches of the law. They had searched all night in vain ; and now here was game indeed. Nimbly they hopped over the broken railing which separated them by a feeble resistance from the field of battle ; and before Mr. Samuel Adolphus Golightly had time to recollect where he was, or to ascertain who the expected arrivals were, he was safe in the custody of Constable 33. 55 and 99 gave chase to Mr. Chutney, who had very quickly taken to his heels—fearing in his heart that Pokyr would try to square the police, and after all the thing would go on much as if this lucky episode had never occurred. As fright, however, had rather weakened his knees, he was speedily caught by the aforesaid active and zealous members of the county force.

"Give us your gun," said 99, who could not altogether divest his mind of poaching. "What game are you arter?"

"Ah! what's your little game?" demanded 55, backing up his brother officer.

"We—were—going to fight a duel," gasped Chutney, relieved at being safe in custody.

"Oh, oh!" said the policemen, in a gruff duet. "Breach of Queen's peace."

"Unlawful assembly for illegal purposes."

Now, for the first time, Mr. Chutney saw the friends who had come to see him fight.

"Fight a dooel, eh?" said 99. "Give us your gun!" and he took the pistol from Mr. Chutney's unresisting hand.

"You're our prisoner, sir—for the present, at all events."

"I'm—I'm rather glad to hear it."

"Now, raly, sir, you're too flatterin'. You Cambridge gents are full of chaff; but you don't catch us old birds with none on it."

"I'll give you a sov apiece not to let me out of custody till the thing is all settled—"

"By the magistrates at Newmarket—we sha'n't, don't you fear."

"No—by the other side. I don't want to shoot the other gentleman. You see, he's such a bad shot. I should be almost certain to kill him—I should indeed, and I don't want to do it."

"I don't think he would—would he, Grimes?" said 99, holding up the pistol for his brother officer's inspection. "This 'ere aint up to much, sir—it aint loaded."

Mr. Chutney stood in blank amazement. The statement was true enough.

"Then I've been made a perfect fool of!" roared the principal.

"P'raps the stout young gen'elman's aint loaded either," said Inspector Grimes, with a chuckle.

Mr. Chutney groaned deeply. How different would have been his conduct had he but known all before! How bold his front! But now—! He groaned again.

Meanwhile an explanation had taken place between Messrs. Pokyr, Golightly, and O'Higgins, and that active officer, Constable 33; and they appeared to have come to an understanding. Our hero was laughing merrily, and examining the barrel of his pistol in a way he would never have done if it had been loaded.

"We are of opinion," said Sergeant Grimes, after a short consultation with his brother officers, "that shooting with unloaded pistols does not constitute a breach of the peace in the eye of the law."

" No," said 55 and 99.

" Therefore," continued the sergeant, " gentlemen, you are at liberty."

" And at large," said 99 and 55.

" Let us shake hands," said Mr. Samuel to his late opponent.

But poor little Chutney hung down his head in a ridiculous way.   All his fire was gone.

" Gentlemen," said Mr. Pokyr, taking the rivals by the hand, " you have done all that honour needeth.   Therefore, be friends once more.   You met, and you would have fought—though, happily, without injury to each other's limbs—if the police had not stopped you."

" Many fights are stopped by the police," said Sergeant Grimes.

" In this countree, perhaps," growled The O'Higgins.   " But I know where no fights are stopped; and where, bedad, nobody could humbug Timothy Fitzgerald O'Higgins with empty pistols."

This was a sore blow to the Captain, who believed firmly in the *bona fides* of the meeting—if it could be brought about.

" You don't want to fight, Captain?" said Pokyr.

"Not I, bedad. You've stolen a march on me, me boy; and that's the long and short of the matter. So, least said soonest mended. I'm doosid peckish."

While this dialogue was going on between Mr. Pokyr and the Captain, Mr. Chutney and Mr. Golightly had shaken hands and made friends and acquaintances of each other at the same moment. The various friends gathered round them; and even the donkey drew near to witness the general reconciliation.

"Peckish!" cried Chutney, gaining spirits fast. "I am nearly fainting."

Tommy was very careful of the inner man at all times.

"I am hungry," said our hero, who played no indifferent knife and fork himself.

In the end, it was decided to breakfast at Newmarket. The dogcarts were remounted by some of the party, and room was found in the waggonette Mr. Calipee had driven over for the police, who were invited to partake of breakfast at the Green Lion. Once there, everything unpleasant was soon drowned in the clatter of knives and forks, and in the business of eating.

"Well," said Mr. Pokyr, when he received

the bill for the breakfast which the policemen had eaten,—" Well, I should not have thought it possible that they could have done it — that's all!"

CHAPTER XI.

TREATS BOTH OF THE STABLE AND THE UNSTABLE.

HE duel which came to so fortunate and bloodless a conclusion in our last chapter had at least the single merit of being fought on classic ground. That merry prince whom jolly Dick Steele talks of with so much gusto in his *Spectator* paper on "Pleasant Fellows," visited the Heath times enough in his royal coach-and-six, and often cantered over the very spot afterwards made famous as the scene of our hero's duel, while he watched the struggles of his match horses over the four miles and a quarter of the Beacon course. And since his time, the royal example he set of "being the first man at cock-matches, horse-races, balls, and plays," has been emulated by many personages hardly less eminent than King Charles the Second, who all appear to have been as "highly delighted on those occasions" with what they saw and did, as the Merry

Monarch was himself. Although, since the days
of our Prince, of pleasant memory, large tracts of
land abutting on the Heath, that were waste lands
in his time, have been put under cultivation, and
now bear splendid crops of grain, Newmarket
Heath itself is very little changed. Under the
conservative influences of the Dukes of Rutland
and the Jockey Club, the features of this match-
less racecourse and training-ground remain pretty
much the same from generation to generation.
An old and decayed post may occasionally be re-
placed by a new one, or a few pounds of white
paint be laid on the railings near the Stands: but
these changes are not great. There is, however,
one alteration in the aspect of the Heath since the
days of old, when first it became celebrated as a
place of sport, which we must notice: whereas, in
King Charles's time, a dozen horses of his Majesty's, and a few belonging to certain noblemen of
the Court, were almost all the blood-stock of England; now, seven or eight hundred race-horses are
trained at Newmarket; and as Mr. Golightly was
driven along the level mile from what had lately
been the scene of his hostile encounter with Mr.
Chutney, he observed long strings of these animals
at exercise, walking, doing steady canters, or galloping at top speed, in various parts of the Heath,

and giving it a very lively appearance. Our hero, whose spirits had risen very rapidly at the termination of his duel, and the speedy prospect of breakfast, remarked to his friend Mr. Pokyr, who held the ribands, and managed the steed that had brought them from Cambridge with his wonted skill, carefully nursing him for a spurt into the town to finish with—

"Pokyr."

"Golightly."

"What are those horses? What numbers there are about!"

"Long-tailed uns—race-horses," responded his friend.

"What are they doing? What a pace they are going at!" said our hero, with animation, pointing to a long team galloping on the lower ground to their left hand. "They are racing, I believe," he added, involuntarily rising on his legs in the dogcart, at imminent risk of a fall.

"You'll be spilt if you are not careful. Sit down—had you not better?"

"I am very fond of horses, Pokyr," said Mr. Golightly, as he resumed his seat.

"I should think you are—who is not?" replied his friend, giving the horse he drove a cut with the whip.

"Of all things, I should like to go over the stables," said Mr. Samuel, pursuing the subject.

"Well, you can do that if you like, without much trouble, I dare say," said Mr. Pokyr. "Now we'll rattle into the Green Lion. Hold tight now, and see how I shall turn the corner." With that remark, he tooled the dogcart neatly into the yard.

After breakfast had been despatched, the subject of the stables was revived again.

"Capital weeds Kitty keeps," said Mr. Blaydes.

"Yes," replied Mr. Chutney—who, being subdued in spirit, strove to lose himself in his cigar.

"I always like a cigar after breakfast," said Mr. Calipee, "but I never can smoke any but my own; and, unfortunately, I have left my case behind me. I must blame you, Golightly, for bringing me out so early."

Our hero smiled pleasantly, having quite forgiven his friends for their last practical joke, and rapidly recovering himself from its effects.

"What in the world we are to do at Newmarket, if we stop," Mr. Calipee proceeded, "I really don't know."

"Smoke, I suppose," said Pokyr.

"But I have no weeds with me," said Calipee.

"Shouldn't be surprised if the Captain had got one or two of yours with him," suggested Mr. Fitzfoodel, who hitherto had been occupied with his breakfast.

"No, me dear sir, not at all," said Mr. O'Higgins, in self-defence; "for I smoked me last on the way, and very foine seegyars they are."

"Newmarket is the dullest place in the world, except in Meeting-weeks: is it not, Miss Farmer?" said Calipee, addressing the hostess, who looked very fresh and charming in her white and blue piqué morning gown.

"Newmarket dull!—oh, Mr. Calipee, how can you say so?" replied the lively Kitty, standing behind Mr. Calipee's chair, and playfully patting his fat shoulder with her ring-bedizened hand. "You don't think we are dull—now, do you, Mr. Pokyr?"

Thus appealed to, what could that gentleman say but what he did?

"What place could be dull where you are, Kitty?"

"Don't, pray don't begin to be facetious, Mr. Pokyr," replied the lady.

"Never more serious in my life, you know that—so don't pretend you don't," said Mr. Pokyr. "I want to introduce a particular friend of mine to you," he continued.

"Who is zat?" asked Kitty.

Mr. Samuel blushed slightly. He felt his turn was coming.

"Mr. Golightly, a prominent member of the Swelldom of my native county. Stand up, Golightly, and show Miss Farmer how tall you are. We are a fine race of fellows, are we not? This young gentleman's brethren are all taller than he is."

"Don't be silly, Mr. Pokyr. Glad to see you at Newmarket, Mr. Golightly. Golightly!—oh, yes, I know. There is a Mr. Golightly who comes sometimes. Is he your brother?"

"Cousin," replied Mr. Samuel. "My cousin George."

"Ah, I know why you came!" said Kitty, holding up her finger archly. "Too bad of them. Never mind, though; we'll pay them out some day, won't we?"

And Mr. Samuel felt himself a personal friend of the fascinating Miss Farmer all in a moment.

"Well, Mr. Chutney, no mis'ief done. You must come and play at c'oquet on my ground in the summer, and help me in my garden, Mr. Golightly. Such a beautiful present from Mr. Blenkinsop, of St. Mary's, ze other day"—going to the top of the little crooked flight of stairs. "Eliza! —bring up that set of c'oquet things. There—

are not they capital mallets? So kind, was it not?"

"You must show Mr. Golightly all your presents, Kitty," said Mr. Pokyr.

"So I will, some day—some day when you and he ride over together."

"How are you getting on with your Latin, Miss Farmer?" asked Blaydes. "You know, you translated the 'Nunquam Dormio' on *Bell's Life* for me, the last time I was here."

"Oh, jolly!—such fun—I like it. What are you men going to do?"

"Golightly would like to see one of the stables."

"All right," replied their hostess. "I'll write a little note to Mrs. Lawson, and she will ask her husband to show you over the Lodge House lot. After all, it's the best for you to see."

Presently, Kitty came back to say it was all right; and that Mr. Lawson would be ready for them, if they would walk up to the top of the town.

"Well, I'll go," said Pokyr. "Who else will come with us?"

Mr. Blaydes and Mr. Calipee expressed their willingness to be of the party; and, accordingly, it was arranged that those three gentlemen, with

Mr. Samuel, should proceed to Lodge House together.

"Wait one minute," said Kitty. "Sall you men stay to dinner, because we want to know if you do? We have got some very fine pheasants and a hare."

"Poached?" inquired Mr. Blaydes.

"Of course. My own particular private poacher brought them to me late one night this week. I won't say where they came from."

"Well, I suppose we may as well stay," said Mr. Pokyr. "You order the dinner, Calipee, will you?"

The Indian gentleman having settled matters with Miss Farmer to his satisfaction, they were ready to start.

"Will you have any lunce? What time sall we say for dinner?"

"Oh, let us have dinner early," said Pokyr.

"Earlyish, I vote—not too soon," remarked Calipee, whose appetite required coaxing.

"All right. I know. Early dinner—no lunce—glass of serry and a biscuit, or something of that sort. Oh, mamma," said Kitty, speaking to a very nice old lady they met on their way out, "the gentlemen will stay to dinner. You and cook will see about it for them. Good-bye," she said, standing under the tree in front of the quaint, old-fashioned hostelry, and waving her hand after them as they walked down the road towards Lodge House.

"What a very superior sort of person. Quite a lady in her manners," was an observation made by our hero, having reference to Miss Farmer, of the Green Lion, a lady with whose charms many generations of undergraduates have been smitten.

"Downy—very downy—knows it pays. However, it is a jolly place enough to go to," said Mr. Pokyr.

"I like the old lady—old Mrs. Farmer; she's a brick," said Calipee.

"One peculiarity about Miss Farmer I can't make out," said Blaydes. "She never gets any older—always looks the same. Why, my uncle knew her when he was up at St. Mary's, and he says she looked just the same then."

"No doubt lots of fellows' uncles knew her," said Pokyr.

The sun shone brightly on the tile roofs of the red brick houses, and the picturesque little town looked its best, as Mr. Golightly, escorted by his friends, walked through the main street. Mr. Pokyr pointed out to him the mansions of certain of the nobility who maintain an establishment at

Newmarket, to receive them during the six weeks of attendance there, in the course of the sporting year; the coffee-rooms and Moss's gambling saloons, where roulette and hazard were played nightly during the Meeting weeks, by the noblemen and gentlemen frequenting the place, for many years, openly, and without any interruption on the part of the police; but, quite lately, a stop has been put to these practices, from which nobody will suffer in pocket except those wealthy Israelites who keep the bank; though many gentlemen think it is a great shame that there has been any interference with their pursuits, and lose their tempers accordingly. A sort of exemption for Newmarket and Black Hambledon, in Yorkshire, was given by certain Acts of Parliament, in the matter of horse-races to be run at those places, and the stakes that should be contended for; and other concessions were made to these favoured spots. But it must be very many years since there were races of any note at Black Hambledon, though Newmarket maintains its ancient *prestige*. And it was a vague tradition among the Newmarket people that they had a right, by royal charter, to gamble in the "Meeting weeks," though the strong arm of the law put down the tables in all other parts of England. Certainly, the practice was in favour of this assumption, as every little inn had its roulette table, if it chose to set one up; and hazard was openly played at several places besides the palatial edifices constructed for that special purpose by the Messrs. Moss.

Passing the police station, they saw their three friends, Constables 33, 57, and 99, who touched their hats with great respect to our hero and his friends as they walked by.

Mr. Calipee said he could not go by the Rutland without having a glass of dry sherry; so they walked into the bar, and refreshed themselves. Faintness was a failing of the Indian gentleman's when taking walking exercise.

After going a couple of hundred yards farther, they arrived at Lodge House—a good residence, standing in a garden, very neatly kept, with the great square of stabling stretching at the back of it. Rapping at the door of the house, they were ushered into a large and well-appointed dining-room, where Mr. Lawson gave them sherry and biscuits before taking them over his establishment. The general elegance — we might almost say splendour—of the appointments in the house of the trainer astonished our hero, who was not prepared to find so much luxury and refinement in the domestic arrangements of a *ci-devant* jockey.

They found Lawson a very good sort of fellow. He had a string of ninety horses under his charge.

"And they take up the most of my time, gentlemen."

Lawson wore a suit of dark iron-gray cloth, with a neatly folded white neckerchief, in which was stuck a small gold horseshoe pin, scarcely perceptible at first sight. Mr. Golightly thought Lawson looked more like the Reverend Mr. Bingley, of Fuddleton, than like a professional trainer of racehorses.

"Well, gentlemen—all ready?" asked Lawson, after passing his decanter of capital sherry round again.

Our four friends having signified their readiness to proceed, headed by Lawson, they walked round the house into the great yard, enclosed on three sides by long rows of well-built stables, and on the fourth opening on the portion of the Heath at the back of the town, extensively used as a training-ground.

"We will begin here, gentlemen," said their guide, throwing open a door to his right.

In this stable was a long row of stalls, occupied

by about twenty animals, with thin legs and long tails, which looked very much alike in their clothing; but all of which—in their constitutions, habits, and propensities—were evidently well known to Lawson.

" Don't stand too near that little filly—kicks hard," he said.

Walking up to another splendid animal—with a skin like satin, bright eye, sound legs, and good temper—Lawson pulled the cloths off.

" There, gentlemen—there's one that's what we call wound up : going to run next week in a big handicap."

" Will it win?" asked Mr. Samuel, quite delighted with the horses, and not knowing that trainers never give tips.

" Don't know, sir; might do—might not."

" What is his name?" inquired our hero.

" Mare, sir," said Lawson, with a slight smile. " Her name's Corisande. Belongs to the Duke of B——."

In another stable they saw a Cesarewitch and a Derby winner. Stripping the latter, and giving him a friendly thump, which he acknowledged by frisking about in his loose box, Lawson said—

" Now, gentlemen, you may do what you like

with him.. He's more like a lamb than a horse—
and always was."

Accordingly, accepting this invitation, our hero
and Mr. Calipee stepped into the box, and made
friends with the celebrated horse who inhabited it.

Having gone the round of the establishment,
from the "aged" division to the unruly yearlings
just being "backed" and "broke," our party tipped
the head lad and the head lad's deputy, and then
wished Mr. Lawson good morning, and thanked
him for his kindness in showing them round the
Lodge House establishment. They walked quietly
back to the Green Lion, meeting on their way several strings of horses coming from exercise on the
Heath; and passing in the High-street the loi-
terers, grooms, jockeys, stable-lads, and touts, who
are always to be seen hanging about. They then
managed to while away the time until dinner was
ready; and having done ample justice to that meal,
started on the return journey, which was much
more agreeable to two of the party than the ride
over to the Heath in the morning. The Captain,
not feeling very well, was relegated to Mr. Calipee
and the waggonette, which started a few minutes
in advance of the dogcarts, but was speedily passed
by those vehicles of lighter draught. Under the
able guidance of our friend, Mr. Pokyr, his division

led the way, closely followed, however, by the dogcart driven by Mr. Blaydes. The waggonette overtook them at Bottisham, where they pulled up for
a few minutes; but after that nothing more was

THE RETURN HOME.

seen of it. The two dogcarts drove into Cambridge
in good style; and at the gate of St. Mary's, the
men from the livery stable were awaiting their re-

turn. Our party, having got down, crossed the quad, and following Mr. Pokyr's lead, went with him to his rooms. Here, however, all was darkness—neither fire nor lights awaited them.

"Mrs. Cribb is tight, I expect," said Mr. Pokyr, calmly; "and my rascal is out of the way."

"No candles—no liquor, apparently," said Mr. Blaydes.

"No," replied his friend Pokyr, at the same time giving a loud and resonant "Tally ho! Gone away!—

> 'Rise, Porson, from thy grave, and halloo,
> 'Tis ουδε τοζε, ουδε ταλλω.'

However, we'll find them. Come on, Golightly, your door is unsported."

In our hero's rooms, a singular scene presented itself. Mr. Sneck, who early in the day had smelt gunpowder, observed to Mr. George Golightly that he thought "there was something up—perhaps gone to a pigeon match."

Mr. George, however, let out a hint of the real state of affairs.

"Cribb," said Mr. Sneck to that personage in the gyp-room, "there's somethink hawful in the wind."

"John Sneck," exclaimed the excitable bedmaker, "in the name of Goodness, what—and no gammon?"

"Mr. Samwell G'lightly is a fightin' a dooel."

"A fightin' what?"

"A dooel—he'll never come back alive!"

"Ha' mercy on us! John Sneek, there's a bottle of pale brandy in his cupboard, or I think I should faint."

"Which cupboard, Betsy?"

"The right 'and one, as the tea and shuggar's kep' in."

An hour afterwards, Mr. Sneek and Mrs. Cribb were seated before Mr. Golightly's fire. There was not much of the pale brandy left; but there was some. This, however, was not in the bottle, but in two tumblers on the table. One Mr. Sneek considered his, the other Mrs. Cribb called hers.

"Which pistols and fire-arms I can't abear, John Sneek."

"No more can't I, Cribb."

"It was providential there was some brandy, or I-should-ha'-fainted—I know I should."

"I'm going up to Eustace Jones's," observed Mr. Sneek. "You'd better come. His bed aint made."

"I shall sit here a minnit longer, John Sneek. I havn't got over the shock."

" I don't think you have, Betsy," the gyp remarked to himself; " and they'll be back soon."

Half an hour after this, Mr. Sneek just looked in
at his old acquaintance.

" Come, Betsy, wake up," he said, shaking the
old lady soundly by the shoulder.

" I-doe-care-f-no-b'y," was Mrs. Cribb's answer.
" Le'-me 'lone."

" All right—I'll let you alone, Betsy—I will.
P'raps you'll be sent off—which you richly deserve,
for this and other things—to say nothink of coals
taken out of College every day in your basket; and
then my poor wife, who'd be just the bedmaker for
this staircase, might get the place, Betsy; so J. S.
—meaning John Sneek—*will* let you alone, since
you pertickler request it."

But Betsy snored in innocence and unsuspicion.

" Come on, let's try your rooms, Golightly," cried
Mr. Pokyr, leading the way across the passage from
his own rooms to those of his friend.

" Hallo!—all in the dark here? No, the fire's
not quite out. We'll make it go. Shout for Sneek.
Where is your colza oil kept? We'll put some on
the fire."

" In the gyp-room, I think," said our hero, mildly.

" Pass the lamp, then; let us have some out of

that. Hal-lo! who's this?" Mr. Pokyr said, as he stumbled over Mr. Golightly's easy chair. "Good gad! it's old mother Cribb asleep; or—— Damme! why, she's as tight as a drum! Now, old lady," he said, as he lifted Mrs. Cribb up in the chair, and set her on Mr. Samuel's dining-table—"now, old lady —come, wake up, and tell us all about it."

CHAPTER XII.

IN WHICH OUR HERO MAKES THE ACQUAINTANCE OF THE REVEREND PORSON PLUNKETT, M.A.

IN our last chapter we left that respectable old personage, Mrs. Elizabeth Cribb, elevated in several respects: the athletic Mr. Pokyr having placed her and Mr. Golightly's leather-covered easy chair, in which she was quietly taking a snooze, on the table together. Mr. Calipee, making a great effort to be of service, produced some wax vestas from his waistcoat pocket; and striking one on the heel of his boot successfully, lighted the four candles on Mr. Golightly's mantelpiece, while Mr. Blaydes poured the contents of our hero's moderator lamp on the smouldering embers of his fire, and, by dint of giving it a few vigorous and well-directed pokes, soon produced a blaze. Both fire and lights being thus satisfactorily procured at the same moment, the whole party of gentlemen gathered round the table, with the twofold intention of more minutely scrutinizing Mrs. Cribb's appearance than had been possible in the dark, and also of hearing what reply she would make to Mr. Pokyr's request that she would " wake up, and tell them all about it."   Our hero, who was as yet unfamiliar with the habits of bedmakers and the easy freedom of their ways, was considerably astonished at finding Mrs. Cribb in such a state ; and, judging from the way he stared at her, seemed hardly able to believe the evidence of his senses.   The other gentlemen were amused, and not by any means amazed; for they had on several previous occasions, during their acade-mical career, seen Mrs. Cribb in a condition very similar to the one in which she presented herself on the present occasion.

" I expect some day she will set the place on fire, and herself too," sagely observed Mr. Blaydes.

"Spontaneous combustion much more likely," suggested Mr. Chutney.

" She would burn like a brandy cask," said Blaydes.

" It is really wonderful, when we think of it," remarked Mr. Calipee, in his lugubrious way, " that there never are any fires in the colleges.   I have many things I should not like to lose—and they are not insured," he added.

" Come, Cribb, old lady," cried Mr. Pokyr, push-

ing the chair forward and pulling it back briskly a
few times, " wake up—wake up ! "

And he gave Mr. Golightly's chair a persistent
wriggle that was calculated to leave its mark on his
mahogany as long as it was a table.

" 'Ere's the tooter a-comin'," shouted Mr. Blaydes,
imitating the bedmaker's accents. " The old girl
is frightened to death at Bloke."

" Here's Bloke—Bl-oke ! " cried the whole of the
party in chorus.

Whether the name of the tutor, of whom she
stood in awe, had a magic influence upon her sleepy
ears, or whether the continued wriggling at the
chair kept up by Mr. Pokyr made repose under
the circumstances impossible, is uncertain; but
at this juncture of affairs, Mrs. Cribb slowly
opened first one eye and then the other, at
the same time rubbing both with her grimy
knuckles.

" Sneek—John Sneek," she murmured, softly,
relapsing into unconsciousness again.

" Two tumblers and an empty bottle," said Mr.
Pokyr. "They have both been at your brandy, my
boy."

And he shook the chair more vigorously than
before. Again Mrs. Cribb unclosed her eyelids in
a dreamy way.

" Where-ram I?" she inquired, vacantly staring about her.

" You're all right," replied several of her auditors.

" Righ-as-a-trivet. I'm-all-right—evenin'?"

"WAKE UP, OLD LADY."

" Oh, yes—you are out for the evening, Cribb. There's no mistake about that, I think."

The worthy old lady evidently caught at the

idea, and having a voice much in request as a means of enlivening the bedmakers' tea parties and *soirées*, burst out into melody, leaning on the elbow of the chair for support—

"I'm a Chickaleary Cove, with my one, two, three."

Here, in an effort to mark time with her foot, she broke down, and collapsed again into the chair.

" Not a doubt about it," said Mr. Pokyr.

This musical attempt of Mrs. Cribb's was received with loud cries of " Sing !" and " Encore !"

In the midst of the noise, Mr. Sneek stuck in his honest physiognomy at the door.

"De-ar me !" he observed, pulling a suitably long face at the spectacle his coadjutor in the work of the staircase presented. " Now, what's she bin a-doin' of? Forgettin' herself again, I see. Better let me take care of her, Mr. Pokyr, sir; though there'll never—though I say it myself—be no proper bedmaker on this staircase till my poor wife has Cribb's place—that there won't, gen'lmen. What a state she have been and made herself in!"

Mrs. Cribb having again become so drowsy that it was tolerably evident there was no more fun to be got out of her, Mr. Pokyr lifted her down again in the chair, and she was handed over to Mr. Sneek's care; who, assisted by her husband—who had come to look for her—conducted her to her abode, No. 7, St. Mary's-row, just outside the college gates.

"Such," said Mr. Pokyr, giving our hero one of those hearty pats on the shoulder for which he is justly famous—"such, my dear Golightly, are bed-makers."

"Are they never discharged on account of—" Mr. Samuel began.

"Well, I don't think such a crime, for instance, as—well, say manslaughter—would be looked over; but anything short of that they may do, and still enjoy their places for life, and—"

"Retire on a pension afterwards," interposed Mr. Jamaica Blaydes.

"I think, Golightly, if I were you," said Mr. Calipee, in an energetic manner, "I should fumigate that arm-chair before I sat down in it again. I have some pastiles and also toilet vinegar in my rooms, which are at your service."

"Thank you," said Mr. Samuel, gratefully. "Which had I better use, do you think?"

"Both," said Mr. Pokyr; "for, to my certain knowledge, Cribb never washes her gown more than once a-term."

"And that makes three times a-year, you know," said Blaydes.

P

"I am rather hungry after all this," said Mr. Calipee. "There is some supper in my rooms, I believe."

The invitation of the Indian gentleman was cheerfully accepted by all the party; and before long they were joined by The O'Higgins, our hero's cousin George, and some others of their acquaintance. A very pleasant evening was spent, of which Mr. Samuel Golightly and Mr. Chutney were very properly made the heroes, considering the bold front they had both shown in the early part of the day. Their healths were drunk several times, in bumpers, before the evening was over.

Our hero was aroused next morning by Mr. Sneck's knocks at his bed-room door.

"Ha'-past nine, sir," said Mr. Sneck.

"Come in, Sneck," said his master, who did not feel quite himself; but whether this arose from the excitement consequent on fighting a duel, or from events subsequent to his engagement with Mr. Chutney, we are unable to state.

"Give me some soda-water, Sneck," said Mr. Samuel

"B'ilers require water quite nat'ral," the gyp observed to himself, as he fetched the effervescent and reviving beverage from the gyp-room.

"Ha'-past nine, sir!" he said, as he handed Mr. Samuel the tumbler. "I'll see about breakfast."

"All right, Sneck," said our hero, as he swallowed the bubbling and fizzing soda. "All right. I am going to get up at once."

"Now," said Mr. Golightly to himself, when the gyp had taken his departure, meditatively contemplating his plump fingers, "I know I slept in my ring for something, but what it was I really cannot remember."

All of a sudden, the truth flashed upon his mind. He had to attend the classical lecture of the Reverend Mr. Plunkett at ten o'clock. He hastily took his tub, dressed; and, just as Sneck appeared with breakfast from the kitchens, our hero, in his cap and gown, was ready to sally forth to the lecture.

"I must go to lecture," said he to the gyp. "There is the clock striking."

"Take a cup of cawfee fust, sir, do," said Mr. Sneck. "Can't wait? Well, then, I'll keep the things hot. Mr. Plunkett's lecture, fust staircase, New Quad, right 'and."

With this remark, Mr. Sneck made a profound bow to his master, and proceeded to place the coffee-pot and poached eggs in the fender.

Mr. Samuel, feeling rather feverish and considerably nervous, took his seat at the table with several

others of the Freshmen of his year, who, like himself, were that morning about to make their first
acquaintance with their classical lecturer. Mr.
Golightly had previously attended one or two lectures on mathematical subjects, such as Euclid and
algebra, where he had seen remarkable things done
with a black board and a piece of chalk, and had
been considerably mystified, and, it must be confessed, not in the least enlightened thereby. It
had been the opinion of the Rector of Oakingham
that his son's genius tended rather towards mathematics than classics; and at home, with Mr. Morgan to demonstrate the props of Euclid by cutting
them out in note paper, and carefully piecing them
together step by step, they were pleasant things
enough; and Mr. Samuel undoubtedly entered the
University with clear notions of what an angle was.
But this early knowledge the college lecturer soon
dispelled; and our hero was reluctantly compelled
to behave with regard to props in general as one
does with riddles—give them up. Mr. Samuel
Golightly's experiences of mathematical lectures
were a confused and ill-digested mixture of black
boards, a lump of chalk—which was always falling
on the floor—and a gentleman in spectacles, with a
duster in his hand—anything but the "draughts of
spring water" spoken of by the author of " Day

Dreams of a Schoolmaster," who found out that "the first lessons in geometry and algebra" he received at college "were as draughts of spring water to lips dry with heat and cracked with sand."

Though Mr. Samuel Golightly's lips, on the occasion of his first visit to Mr. Plunkett's rooms, were not literally "cracked with sand," they were, in sober truth, very dry; and when the reverend lecturer made his appearance, with unmistakable signs of eggs for breakfast on his face, our hero felt absolutely unwell. He had a new ordeal to go through; and having devoted the evening before to conviviality, had not read the chapter previously.

"What is your n-name, sir?" asked Mr. Porson Plunkett, who, like Mr. Samuel, stammered slightly.

"Go-go-golightly," said our hero, nervously.

"Have I n-not had you here bef-fore, sir?"

"N-no, sir."

"The n-name of Golightly is in my class-book. What are your initials?"

"S-S-S. A., sir," replied Mr. Samuel.

"Have you three names beginning with S?" asked the lecturer, hardly certain that our hero was not an impertinent and hardened Freshman, trying to take him off for the amusement of the class.

"N-no, sir," said our hero, much confused by the

very short and angry manner of Mr. Porson Plunkett. " I st-st-ammer."

" I p-perceive you do," was the reply. " Now, Mr. Smith, begin."

Mr. Smith, who was quite a swell classic, rattled off a sentence or two fluently enough. Some of the gentlemen present looked at their books, the while evidently calculating the " bit " that it would come to their turn to construe. Others looked about them quite unconcernedly, being well up in the subject; and one melancholy-looking individual took out his pocket-knife, and began to make little paper boxes, of the kind known as fly-traps, with great energy, crushing them up and throwing them under the table as fast as he made them—a pastime he pursued with a great display of perseverance and energy during the whole time the lecture lasted. Mr. Golightly must be placed among the number first mentioned. With his usual sagacity, he had hit upon his own particular " bit " to a nicety. When his turn came, looking at him with unpleasant directness, the Reverend Porson Plunkett said—

" Mr. Golightly."

We may mention that the subject of their studies was the work of the famous Latin historian. Our classical readers will, doubtless, at once recognize

the following well-known passage, which Mr. Golightly read; and non-classical readers will not be
much the worse off if they do not, as we propose
to append a rendering of the same in the vulgar
tongue :—

"'Imperator ater tigris duxit copias suas in Campum Martium et aggĕrem—'"

"'Aggĕrem'—if you please. Thank you," said
the lecturer, tartly.

Blushing slightly as he corrected himself, Mr.
Samuel went on—

"'—Aggĕrem viae tres cohortes obtinuerunt.'"

Reading the Latin—with the exception of the
quantities, at which he was not very good—was, of
course, mere child's play to Mr. Golightly. Putting
the English to it was the difficulty that next arose.
Our hero proceeded to construe; a query first occurring to his mind—"Did it begin with the first
word?" However, he took "Imperator" first, and
risked the consequences.

"'Imperator—'"

"Well?"

"'The Emperor,'" said Mr. Samuel, boldly—
for him. He did not mean it, but he spoke his
thoughts aloud—"What comes next?"

The gentleman near him, who was quite a swell,
answered him in a whisper, "'ater tigris.'"

"'Ater tigris.'"

There was an awkward pause on the part of our hero. He felt it would not do to call the Emperor a black tiger exactly. There was a slight titter all round the table, and Mr. Porson Plunkett said—

"Well!" accompanying that monosyllable with an expressive smile.

"'The buttons in black,'" whispered our hero's prompter; and "'Buttons in black,'" Mr. Golightly said.

A general laugh followed, in which our hero joined himself.

"Jokes are quite out of place here, sir!" said the lecturer, who was very fond of making them himself when opportunities arose, but very angry with anybody else who did so; therein resembling, in a smaller degree, several eminent judges on the bench at the present time.

"Mr. Popham," said Mr. Plunkett, "will you go on?"

Mr. Popham was a singularly stupid-looking young man who sat near Mr. Samuel, and apparently shared his ignorance of the author they were reading, and also his terror of classical lecturers in general.

"'The Emperor,'" proceeded Mr. Popham, timidly

—feeling that to be the only safe spot in the ground he had to traverse.

"'Ater tigris,'" said Mr. Porson Plunkett.

"'A black tiger,'" ejaculated Mr. Popham, quite

THE REVEREND PORSON PLUNKETT'S LECTURE.

defiantly, driven to bay, and heartily wishing the Emperor was down the tiger's throat.

"Well," observed Mr. Plunkett, "let us say 'a

fierce tiger ;' or, as we might render it in English, ' a very tiger.' "

" ' Duxit copias suas '—' led his forces,' " continued poor Mr. Popham, all in a breath; and then, after a momentary pause, he went on timidly, feeling he was on treacherous ground again, " ' In Campum Martium—' "

" Yes—that is here. You have the same reading that we have, I suppose ? "

" ' In Campum Martium,' " repeated Mr. Popham slowly, and in a terrible fright at the frowns of Mr. Porson Plunkett and the smiles of his fellow undergraduates.

" Well—we got as far as that before, you know."

" Well," continued Mr. Popham, drawing a long breath of relief, " 'against the Field Marshal.' "

This reading by the light of nature was the signal for quite a roar.

" Hush, gentlemen, please ! " said Mr. Plunkett. " Will you, Mr. Golightly, complete the translation of the sentence ? "

Thus called upon, Mr. Samuel Adolphus was compelled to proceed, which he did as follows :—

" ' Et aggerem viae tres cohortes obtinuerunt.' "

" You need not have troubled to read us the Latin again."

" 'And three cohorts took possession of the public road.' "

" Can't you give ' aggerem ' a more literal meaning ? "

Our hero looked nervously at his book.

" Mr. Popham ? "

" ' Public road,' " said Mr. Popham.

" We have had ' *public* ' before. Can you not suggest a more literal meaning ? "

" ' Public,' " said Mr. Popham, with stupid tenacity.

" Dear me, Mr. Popham, you'll ask me in a moment to believe that ' a-agger domus ' was a public-house by the side of the road ! "

This smart sally of the Reverend Mr. Plunkett's was received with a laugh, which he did not see the least necessity for repressing.

Neither Mr. Golightly nor Mr. Popham was called upon to construe again that morning ; and each enjoyed the proceedings all the more for that reason. After the lecture was over, Mr. Popham made advances of a friendly kind to our hero. They were partners in misfortune.

" Will you eat some breakfast in my rooms ? " asked Mr. Samuel, blandly.

" Thank you, I will—I have not breakfasted, as I was rather late this morning."

"I was late too," remarked Mr. Samuel.

And, over their coffee and eggs, both gentlemen resolved never again to fall into the clutches of the Reverend Porson Plunkett, M.A., without devoting half an hour beforehand to looking up the matter they would be called upon to expound in so public a manner.

Our hero was giving his friend, Mr. Popham, a succinct but graphic account of the extraordinary condition in which he had found his bedmaker, Mrs. Cribb, on the occasion of his return from Newmarket—at the same time carefully suppressing in his narrative any evidence of his reason for going there—when his gyp put in an appearance to remove the breakfast things.

"Cribb is not here this mornin', sir," said Mr. Sneek, bustling about and blowing heavily. "All the work of the staircase left to me. Now, my wife—"

"Mrs. Cribb was in a disgraceful state last night," said Mr. Golightly; "and I hope I shall never see her so again."

"I hope not, sir; but what we heard upset us both, sir—dooel," said the gyp, knowingly. "Delighted to see you safe back, sir, I was. But Betsy *is* apt to forget herself, it can't be denied."

"I hope she will never do so again."

" Mine seems a good sort of bedmaker," observed Mr. Popham.

" Beg pardon, sir," said Mr. Sneek, with great

"YOUR 'UMBLE SERVANT, GENTLEMEN."

alacrity; " are you the new gentleman on letter X staircase ? "

" I am," said Mr. Popham.

" Bedmaker on that staircase most exemplary

woman—first cousin of my own, sir! Beg your pardon, sir," said the gyp to Mr. Samuel; "rare job with Cribb last night, gettin' her home. I did it, though," he added, with an air of merit unquestionable.

"Yes," said our hero, not precisely apprehending the drift of his gyp's remarks on this score.

"Heavy job it was, sir, I assure you: I wouldn't tell you a story about it. Ha'-past eleven, sir—buttery's open. Pint of ale wouldn't hurt me—it wouldn't."

Mr. Samuel at once gave Mr. Sneek the requisite order for a quart of buttery beer, on a slip of paper.

"Thank you, sir. Your 'umble servant, gentlemen," Mr. Sneek said, as Mr. Golightly and Mr. Popham sallied forth, leaving Mr. Sneek with leisure on his hands to convert his order into "college"—an opportunity he availed himself of without one second's delay.

CHAPTER XIII.

FAME, trumpet-tongued, soon spreads the report of bold deeds, both in large societies and small ones. So it was with Mr. Golightly, at St. Mary's; but whether it arose from the story of his having fought a duel being told abroad, or from his connection with so unimpeachably correct a set as that in which Mr. Pokyr shone as the leader of *ton*, our hero soon became quite a man of mark in his college. For several days after his encounter with Mr. Chutney, on returning to his rooms of an afternoon or coming in from lecture in a morning, Mr. Samuel was wont to find the letter-box, if his outer door was sported, or his table, if it was open, covered by cards left for him by gentlemen, not only of his own standing in the University, but of the years above him. These marks of consideration were left upon him,

not only by gentlemen who—from their proposing
to themselves no more serious affair in their stay at
the University than consisted in getting over the
various obstacles between them and a "poll" degree—might be supposed to have plenty of leisure on their hands, but also among his callers
were men of quite a different class. Mr. Eustace
Jones, the future senior wrangler, dropped quietly
downstairs from his calculus and green tea, and,
timidly knocking at our hero's door, fidgeted
nervously on the extreme edge of a cane-bottomed
chair for precisely five minutes by his own watch,
and then ran up to his own rooms to make up, as
fast as possible, for the time he had thus sacrificed
to the demands of politeness. Mr. Golightly expressed himself much pleased with the opportunity
thus afforded him of making the acquaintance of
so distinguished a mathematician. He could not,
however, as he contemplated the pale face, and
nervous, absent manner of his visitor, help thinking that he should not care particularly to count
this extraordinary genius among his intimate acquaintance.

A reading man of another stamp was the Lord
Ernest Beauhoo, who "ground like a fiend," as
Mr. Pokyr, who was a distant cousin of Lord
Ernest's, expressed it.

His lordship, a solemn young prig, of rather limited classical attainments, was working away at Plato, at Cambridge, previous to enlightening his country from the floor of the House of Commons. A nice little pocket borough, appendant to the family of Beauhoo, awaited his lordship's coming of age: a Cabinet minister filling the dignified position of warming-pan in the borough of Calm, pending the approaching majority of Lord Ernest Beauhoo. And then, oh, faithful electors of Calm! —blue fire and Beauhoo for ever! However, when this legislator in embryo called upon Mr. Samuel Golightly, he found that gentleman out; so he slipped the Beauhoo pasteboard, with the Beauhoo crest on it, into the letter in the sported door.

On the occasion of the first influx into his rooms of a heavy batch of cards, our hero, having placed them carefully on his table, proceeded to call upon his cousin, Mr. George, and asked him to explain the meaning of this suddenly revealed desire of everybody in the college to make his acquaintance.

"Well," said Mr. George, in reply to the query of Mr. Samuel, "it is the usual thing here—only you have more men of the years above you on the list of your callers than is common. You ought to feel honoured, I am sure."

"I do," said Mr. Samuel, with some show of proper gratitude. "My Fa—"

"Well, never mind Uncle Sam just now," protested Mr. George, who did not reverence the oracle of the parsonage so much as his father, the Squire, did.

" My Fa," proceeded Mr. Samuel, however, with becoming filial veneration, nothing daunted, and determined to finish his observation, "wishes me to make the acquaintance of as large a number of men of my own age as possible, while I am here. As I have often heard him say, 'The proper study for mankind is man '—"

"Original and apropos," interrupted Mr. George.

" And," continued our hero, " I am willing to do so, since these gentleman seek my acquaintance."

" Of course you are. What did you come here for ? Enjoy the place as much as you can."

" What am I to do," asked Mr. Samuel.

" You must return their calls. If they are out, leave a pasteboard. If they are in, stay five minutes, and don't refuse a glass of sherry. If you don't know where they keep, ask Sneek to take you round to their rooms—which he will do for a trifling consideration and kind treatment."

Our hero laughed at his cousin's advice, and determined to follow it out to the letter, with the

single exception of not retaining the services of
Mr. Sneek for the occasion.

"Come up to Pokyr's," said Mr. George, abruptly.

"Right," said Mr. Samuel, who was fast rubbing
off his country rust, and acquiring the manners of
his friends.

"COME in," cried the voice of Mr. Pokyr, in
reply to Mr. George's knock—with a long-drawn
out and emphatic "come:"—the tone of an injured
man, who, having got out his books for an hour's
grind, is disagreeably surprised to find five or six
friends have chosen that particular hour for a call.

Mr. Pokyr's dictionaries were open on his table;
but he was not turning over their pages, pregnant
with meaning, but standing with his back to the
fire, talking to Mr. Calipee, Mr. Fitzfoodel, and
several other gentlemen, who were enjoying his society and his cigars at the same time.

"Hallo! at work?" said Mr. George.

"I hope we are not disturbing you," said Mr.
Samuel.

"Ah! about time I did work, I think, with the
'Little Go' before me, and not a word about the
subjects within the range of my knowledge at present. But you do not disturb me exactly. Calipee
began that an hour ago; and when once he is well

seated in my easy chair, he does not again move in a hurry—do you, Nigger?"

"He is going out for a ride with us," said the Nigger, by way of explanation.

"I beg to inform Mr. Samuel Adolphus Golightly of his election as a member of the Mutton Cutlet Club," said Mr. Pokyr, with due form.

"Oh!" said our hero, smiling with complete satisfaction. "Thank you."

"Our meetings are Saturday nights—our club-room is at the Green Dragon. This is Saturday, and I will therefore take you with me, introduce you to the club, administer the usual oaths, and make a Mutton Cutlet of you," said Mr. Pokyr.

"I shall be ready," said Mr. Samuel.

"I hear that they are going to put up Smith," said Mr. Calipee.

"And who is Smith?" asked Mr. Calipee.

"Smith is legion!" said Mr. George.

"Smith is not a bad sort of a fellow," said Mr. Pokyr. "Comes from our county—rides well, and good cattle, with the Loamshire hounds."

"Let us look him out," said one of Mr. Pokyr's friends, strolling up to his host's bookcase, and taking down Burke.

"Need not trouble to look there," said Mr. Fitz-foodel; "find it all—whole affair of family history

—in Smiles's 'Self-Help.' Got Smiles, Pokyr? Save a deal of trouble—assure you."

"I do not possess a copy of the work in question," replied Mr. Pokyr.

"I hope he won't get elected. I hate all those fellows—they spoil the club," said Fitzfoodel, plaintively.

"Well, he'll have my vote," said Pokyr, who was president of this aristocratic and exclusive club.

"And mine," said Mr. George. "I like a fellow who rides well, and is a good sort of fellow besides."

"I hate parvenus," exclaimed Mr. Fitzfoodel, representing the landed interest.

"By the bye," said Mr. Pokyr, giving our hero a tap on the shoulder, "you must join the Drag, Golightly."

"The Drag?" said Mr. Samuel.

"Hounds, herrings, and aniseed—you know," said his friend, imitating the action of a jockey.

"But I don't ride very well," said our hero, apologetically.

"You ride well enough. You must have a quiet horse from Spratt's, and you'll do as well as the best of us."

"Must join," said everybody.

Our hero, with characteristic amiability, consented to become a contributing member to the University of Cambridge Drag Hunt.

" Somebody coming upstairs. Another visitor, Pokyr," said Calipee.

" A dun," said Mr. Pokyr, as a feeble single knock fell on their ears. " Let him knock again," he said, putting a cap on one of his pistols. " I'm ready for him."

" Pray, don't shoot!" said Mr. Samuel.

" They deserve it."

As he spoke, the door opened. In walked Mr. Pokyr's laundress. Bang went the pistol.

" Ha ! you've just escaped it," he cried, pointing to a hole in the ceiling, which truth compels us to state was there before.

" You'll frighten me to death some day, sir, please, sir," said the laundress.

" You have had a lucky escape," said Mr. Pokyr, tossing his laundress a shilling.

" Good morning, sir, and thank you, sir," replied that official, evidently not reluctant to be shot at again, then or another day.

" The horses is at the gate, sir," said Mr. Pokyr's man.

Accordingly, Mr. George Golightly went for a ride with his friends, while our hero spent the afternoon in returning some of the calls he had on his list.

The evening came, and with it his introduction to the Mutton Cutlet Club: an event which, shortly after its occurrence, our hero described in a letter to his father. Prudently reserving any account he might have to give of his encounter with Mr. Chutney for a verbal relation, in case he found his cousin, Mr. George, had mentioned it to any members of his family, Mr. Samuel confined himself on the present occasion to an account of his first dinner with the club, at the Green Dragon. After premising that he was personally in a state of perfect salubriousness, and mentioning some other minor topics, Mr. Samuel said:—

"On Saturday last, I was introduced by Mr. Pokyr to the Mutton Cutlet Club, having previ ously been elected a member, and paid my entrance fees and yearly subscription. I had been led by Mr. Pokyr to suppose that, notwithstanding its curious title, the Mutton Cutlet Club was an association of gentlemen of the University for literary discussion, the reading of papers, and for debates thereupon. But on entering the club room—which is the large room at the Green Dragon, an inn with the name of which, at all events, you are acquainted —I found a long table laid for dinner, some sixteen or twenty covers being laid. However, before dinner began, the secretary of the club produced a silver gridiron, on which I was sworn, in a sort of humorous oath, to do many things, of which these

MR. GOLIGHTLY IS MADE A MEMBER OF THE MUTTON
CUTLET CLUB.

are some of those I recollect—' Never to drink beer if I could get claret, unless I liked beer better;' 'Never to drink claret when I could get port un-

less I liked claret better;' 'Never to dine anywhere
except at the table of the Mutton Cutlet Club on a
Saturday night, unless I had a better place to go
to;' 'To submit to all the fines of the club, as

MR. GOLIGHTLY SINGS A SONG.

levied by order of the president;' 'To sing a song
when called on or pay the fine;' and many like
promises. Dinner being served, I sat near Mr.

Pokyr, who occupied the chair. We had soup first; and there is a legend in the club, which is of an-cient standing, that every dish contains mutton in some form; but I did not detect it in the soup. We had, afterwards, mutton cutlets in various ways —*en papillotes* I chose, recollecting those we used to have in Paris—and other things followed in due course. The wine was very good, and after dinner the fun became very general. Cigars were placed on the table; and the room, though large, was soon filled with smoke, as everybody seemed to smoke. All the members of the club sing, and I was much alarmed when it came to my turn to sing a song, as I only know the one I once sang when we were playing forfeits last Christmas at the Hall, and Arabella imposed a song on me. The words are so simple, that a great deal depends on the way it is sung. I think I sang it well, as it was received with much applause; and being encored, I was obliged to sing it again. It is—

'Did you ever, ever, ever see a Whale?
Did you ever, ever, ever see a Whale?
Did you ever, ever, ever see a Whale?
No, I never, never, never—
No, I never, never, never saw a Whale;
But I've often, often, often—
But I've often, often, often seen a Cow!'

Which is quite true. The words of all the verses

are just the same. I sang a great many, I know
Pokyr said it was a capital song—the melody being
very pretty, and the words simple yet interesting.
Afterwards, to finish up with, we had a Dutch
chorus. Everybody sang a verse of some different
song, as a solo. This went round the table; and
at last the chorus was made by all singing together
their own verses to their own tunes. The effect
was beyond description. I never heard such an
unearthly noise in my life. Pokyr says they always 'finish up with a row.'

"Altogether, I like the Cutlet Club very much."

With these interesting details of the doings at
the club, and his very kind wishes to all the members of the family, our hero closed his second epistle
from the University to his father at Oakingham-
cum-Pokeington.

Mrs. Cribb, on her restoration to health, appeared
for several days in her Sunday attire, by way of re-
habilitating her general character, which might be
supposed to have suffered somewhat from her recent
indisposition.

She appeared, in the portrait on page 52, in the
Sunday dress referred to. The engraving is faithfully copied from her *carte de visite*, which she is in

the habit of presenting to her masters when they leave college, and in return for which she will take kindly to a "tip." She gave one to Mr. Golightly on the occasion of his leaving St. Mary's, observing—

"And, sir, when I were at the photographer's, and see all them pillars and statues and fountains, I said to the young man as was going to take it— 'Young man, bein' a servant, could I be accommodated with a brush to 'old in my 'ands to show the same?"

Which accounts for the clothes brush to be seen in the left hand of Mrs. Cribb, in the faithful likeness which was previously given to our readers.

CHAPTER XIV.

SHOWS HOW POOR LITTLE MR. POPHAM HAS A NAR-
ROW ESCAPE OF BEING EATEN OF DOGS; AND
HOW HIS FRIEND, MR. SAMUEL GOLIGHTLY, COMES
BOLDLY TO THE RESCUE.

PURSUANT to that good resolution which
was announced in a previous chapter, both
Mr. Popham and our hero—who were now
the best of friends, and had several times breakfasted together, besides giving each other invitations for the coming vacation—attended Mr. Porson
Plunkett's classical lectures with undeviating punctuality. This of itself was a step towards softening
the heart of any lecturer; but, besides this, the two
gentlemen regularly conned over the subject-matter
of an evening, sitting together and giving each other
a helping hand—which, certainly, both wanted;
and it would be a difficult point to decide which
of the two required it the more.

"Popham," said Mr. Golightly, on one of these

occasions, as they sat in our hero's rooms, expending the midnight oil over their Livy, taking occasional sips of black coffee—at making which, in a patent percolator, Mr. Samuel had become, with a little practice, quite a proficient—by way of refreshment for the inner man, and dipping into the abstruse mysteries contained in the pages of White and Riddell, and Dr. Smith's grammar.

"Popham."

"Golightly," said Mr. Popham, in reply, looking up from the dictionary in which he had for ten minutes past been digging desperately for a word which, oddly enough, "stumped" them both.

"Can't you find it?" said our hero, forgetting for the moment what he had been about to say, as he contemplated the puzzled and almost despairing look on the face of his friend and fellow-student.

"Dashed if I can—it's not here," ejaculated Mr. Popham.

"Are you sure? Have you looked at all the places?"

"Perfectly certain," answered Mr. Popham, taking a voluminous gulp of the black coffee at his side.

"Then we must give it up," said Mr. Samuel, with that philosophic resignation to the force of circumstances which rarely deserted him.

" But we can't make head or tail of the sentence without it," said his friend, diving into the repertory of Riddell and White again.

" One—two—three," exclaimed Mr. Golightly, giving a deep-drawn sigh of relief, as he ran his fingers up their sentences of Livy, " four—five—six." Then, after a pause, " Seven."

" Well ?"

" Why, if Smith's there, it must come to him, and he is certain to know all about it."

" But if he isn't, it's mine, you know ! " replied Mr. Percy Popham, having, at the same time, the terror of Porson Plunkett, M.A., before his eyes.

" Ah, but Smith is sure to be there," returned Mr. Samuel, thereby clinching the argument.

" Well, we will knock off, then, if you like," said Mr. Popham, giving way before the force of his friend's reasoning. He closed the dictionary, and threw himself on the sofa, in an attitude of easy but inelegant repose.

" After Plunky's lecture," said Mr. Samuel, actually venturing to speak of that reverend Tartar by such a disrespectful, though commonly used, abbreviation—" after Plunky's lecture, and luncheon, I'm going out with Pokyr, and George, and Calipee, and all those fellows."

Naturally enough, Mr. Percy Popham inquired " Where?"

" The Drag," answered our hero, with quite a knowing nod, at the same time looking proudly at his friend. " I have joined—subscribed, I mean—you know."

" Where do they meet?"

" At Fulbourne."

" Bless me!" ejaculated Mr. Popham. "Are you a good rider—a *very* good rider—Golightly?"

" N-n-not *very* good, Popham," responded Mr. Samuel, who always told the truth, even when it was against him.

" Then you'll be thrown a dozen times at least, as sure as a gun. They go at an awful pace."

" If I am, Popham," said Mr. Samuel, in a quiet tone, and with a complacent smile, intended to convey the idea that falling off was out of the question—he certainly meant to pick a *very* quiet horse —"if I am, Popham, I certainly sha'n't get on again."

" After the twelfth time, do you mean?" inquired Percy, raising his eyebrows incredulously.

" After the first—or second," replied our hero. " I don't like falls, and, I may add, I don't often fall; though at home I often go out with the Loamshire."

But then, Dumple was the quietest of cobs.

"What I was going to propose, Popham," said Mr. Samuel, when his previous remarks had had time to make a due impression upon the mind of his friend—"what I was going to propose was—"

"Well?"

"Why, that you should join us, and come too."

"Nonsense!" said Mr. Percy Popham, abruptly turning round on the sofa.

"That," observed Mr. Samuel, in a slightly injured tone, "is neither here nor there."

"I'm not a member of the Drag," remarked Mr. Popham, turning round once more.

"That does not matter in the least; besides, we —that is, I—can easily propose you, and so you can be."

"Um," returned Mr. Popham, from the couch.

But in that "Um" there was indecision. This fact was not lost upon our hero.

"I will make another cup of coffee," he said, operating again with the tea-kettle and the percolator.

And the upshot of it all was, that, after two small cups of black coffee, with just the least little *soupçon* of Cognac in them, by way of qualification at that late—or rather, early—hour, Mr. Percy Popham announced to Mr. Samuel Golightly his intention of joining that gentleman—"after Plunky's lecture, and luncheon, and all that"—in an afternoon's sport with the "Drag."

Luckily for our two friends, Mr. Smith put in an appearance next morning at the Rev. Porson Plunkett's lecture; and the identical "bit" with the impracticable word in it fell to Mr. Smith's portion, as our hero had calculated it would; and, to the astonishment of Mr. Samuel and Mr. Popham, that gentleman cleared the obstacle without the slightest difficulty in the world.

"I told you it came from that," whispered our hero to Mr. Popham, who sat next him, as usual.

"Yes, but you did not know what part it was," Mr. Popham wrote on a slip of paper, and placed it on Mr. Samuel's open book.

After the lecture was satisfactorily disposed of, our friends hurried off to exchange their academical robes for the costume of the chase.

"Hallo—whoo-hoo-hoo-whoop!" cried Mr. Pokyr, as he somewhat unceremoniously entered our hero's bed-room, and there discovered Mr. Samuel, endued in a new pepper-and-salt coloured suit, all but the gaiters, over buttoning which he was getting very red in the face.

"Come—come along; we're waiting lunch for

you. You and the Nigger have a way of being always behindhand."

"I shall be ready in a minute," replied Mr. Samuel, looking up from the fatiguing occupation of buttoning the white pearl buttons of his gaiters over his manly calves.

"Don't you go in 'persuaders'—spurs, you know?" Mr. Pokyr explained, when he perceived Mr. Golightly's ignorance of the meaning of the term.

"Never wore spurs in my life," said Mr. Samuel.

"Well—perhaps you are better without 'em."

"I think it is cruel. I would not spur Dumple —that is, my horse at home; then why should I spur another horse, merely because it is hired? My Fa has often observed, when we were driving into Fuddleton, 'the merciful man has a care for his beast,' and told the coachman not to hurry."

"Do your carriage horses all the good in the world to hurry them a bit, and get some of the fat off them. Well, come along."

By this time Mr. Samuel's equipment was complete, and he accompanied Mr. Pokyr to his rooms, where his hospitable table was spread with a substantial luncheon, to which several members of the college, including our friend Mr. Popham, sat down; while Mr. Pokyr's man, assisted by the

obliging Sneck, did his best to minister to their
wants, carefully filling their glasses as often as occasion required.

After luncheon, Mr. Popham and our hero accompanied Mr. Pokyr to Spratt's stable, where the
two noble steeds owned by the last-named gentleman stood eating their heads off at livery. They
were met in the yard by Spratt himself—a wiry
little man, whose principal distinguishing features
were what are termed, I believe, a cock-eye and a
game leg. Touching his hat to Mr. Pokyr with
due respect, Spratt observed—

"The Whigs have had another thrashing, sir."

For Spratt was a very high Tory horse-dealer;
and liked, above all things, to combine politics with
business.

"Never mind the Whigs, Spratt," replied Mr.
Pokyr.

It is, of course, needless to mention that the
whole of the Shovelle family, from which Mr.
Pokyr sprang, are, and always have been, staunch
Conservatives.

"They'll come to ruin without us."

"Ha! ha! ha! sir. True! The house divided
against—" began the livery stable keeper.

"Drop houses, Spratt," said Mr. Pokyr, interrupting him. "Horses we have come about."

" Your gray hoss has been ready this half-hour, Mr. Pokyr."

" These gentlemen want a couple of ' tits.'"

" Where are they for—Newmarket?" asked the wary proprietor. For although old Hobson has long enough been dead, and the very Conduit designed to keep the good Carrier's memory green has been stuck away in an out-of-the-way place, still there is something of the principle of that Choice to which the old Cambridge horse-keeper gave a name yet hanging about Cambridge stable-yards.

In reply to Spratt's query, Mr. Samuel ingenuously replied—

" Out with the Drag."

" Then I've got two fust-raters—just the very thing, Mr. Pokyr. I'm glad I kep' 'em in. These gents being friends of yours, I should like to turn 'em out in Spratt's best style. I could have let them two hosses twice over; but somehow I kep' 'em back. Williim," shouted Spratt, at the top of his voice, at the same time giving a long, shrill whistle.

A head was poked out over a half-door at the top of the yard.

" Put the saddle and bridle on Prince and the gray mare."

In a few seconds, "Williim," Spratt's head man, led out Prince—a great, lumbering, brown horse, apparently about a dozen years old, very groggy on his legs all round, and shabby and charger-like about the tail; but groomed up, well fed, and made to look his best. And at the same time, another lad brought out the gray mare. A very skittish-looking lady she was, with a nasty way of laying back her ears, and a restless, fidgety manner of carrying herself; besides going very "dotty" on her near fore-leg—caused by standing so long doing nothing in the stable, her owner said.

"There!" said Spratt, sticking his Scotch cap on one side, and complacently scratching his head, as he looked on the Prince. "There's a hoss! He's a 'unter—that's what *he* is."

He had been in his youth, and loved the fun as well as any M. F. H. in England, as Mr. Golightly discovered to his cost.

"Groggy," said Mr. Pokyr, stepping up to his own animal.

"Jumps like a kitten. I'm told he clears a five-barred gate just as easy as he hops over one rail."

"That heel's cracked—by jingo!" said Mr. Pokyr.

"Best hoss I've got—a regular seasoned 'unter.

I never let him out 'ackney—do I, Williim?" with a wink.

"Never dew such a thing," of course was Williim's reply.

"Are they quiet?" asked Mr. Golightly. "I don't like going very fast myself. I like a quiet horse."

"So do I—quiet," chimed in Mr. Percy Popham.

"They're more lambs nor hosses, both of them—aint they, Williim?"

The ostler nodded assent.

The gray mare expressed her denial of this statement by giving one or two slight but uncommonly vicious-looking kicks.

"I don't—that is—*much* like the gray. Have you got any others?" asked Mr. Samuel—feeling that, after the character Mr. Spratt had given the pair, he was touching on delicate ground, and both the stable-keeper and "Williim" might take the observation in a personal light.

"They're the only two I've got," said Spratt, rubbing the end of his nose severely.

"Fit for the job," William put in.

"Ah! fit for the job," said the proprietor, catching at the idea. "They're Drag hosses, they are."

"Well known," said William.

" And the only two I've got as aint let," said
Spratt.

So it was Hobson's choice, after all.

By this time, Mr. Pokyr had ridden out at the
gate in the street, and the regular hunters expressed
a strong desire to follow his lead.

But both Mr. Samuel and Mr. Popham im-
mensely preferred Prince of the two animals before
them: at the same time that both were very shy of
the gray mare. An animated discussion followed,
which might have lasted some time but for a suggestion of William's.

" Don' know which to hev? Then torse up,
gemmen, and settle it that way."

" Ha!" said Spratt.

" I aint got no coin, or I'd do it for both on you
—which 'ould be the fairest way."

Mr. Samuel unbuttoned his coat, raised a shilling
from the depths of his breeches pocket, and placed
it in William's hand. Mr. Percy Popham agreed
to this mode of settling the question.

" Heads, the brown hoss—tails, the gray mare,"
said William, spinning the coin.

Our hero and his friend assented with a nod.

" Call, please, gemmen."

The excitement was intense.

" Head," said Mr. Samuel.

" 'Eads it is," said William, touching his hat, and very respectfully consigning the shilling to the deep-flapped pocket of his drab waistcoat.

"The brown hoss is yours, sir."

Mr. Samuel, not unobservant of the fate of his shilling, but affecting not to notice it, sprang with tolerable agility into the saddle, which turned round as he did so ; while it took two men to hold the gray lamb before Mr. Popham could effect a landing. All being right at last, the two gentlemen sallied forth into the street, in the wake of their friend and leader, Mr. Pokyr ;—farther in the wake of that gentleman than they cared for, as they had to trot through more streets than one, and were conscious of the impression they were creating upon the public in general: Prince, Mr. Golightly's animal, breathing high, and displaying symptoms of turning out a "bucketer;" while, on her part, Mr. Popham's gray mare edged and sidled along in a manner calculated to fill her rider with alarm as to what she might take it into her head to do when giving way to the excitement of the chase. Nor was the position of the two gentlemen rendered more agreeable by the audible remark of a person in the professional cricketing interest, who happened to be standing at the corner of Jesus-lane as they passed by—

"Two Freshmen," said he, in an unmistakably disparaging tone.

Almost immediately afterwards they overtook Mr. Pokyr, riding in company with several friends.

"How do they go?" asked that gentleman, referring to Prince and the gray mare.

"Not badly, at present," replied Mr. Samuel, wisely cloaking his apprehensions of the future.

"That is all right, then. Will you," said Mr. Pokyr, smiling benignly upon Mr. Popham, "oblige us by taking care of this?"

"What is it?" asked Mr. Popham, as he edged the gray up to Mr. Pokyr's side, and took from him a small and strong-smelling newspaper-covered packet.

"Only a spare bloater, in case we may require it," was Mr. Pokyr's answer.

And so they all trotted along towards the meet, speedily overtaking other parties of horsemen bent upon the same diversion.

Now, hunting the Drag, as practised at our two Universities and at other places, is so innocent, so health-promoting, and in every way so praiseworthy an amusement, that there seems nothing to be said to its discredit. A particular line of ground, not usually remarkable for its stiff fences, having been selected, and a red herring, rubbed with aniseed, having been carefully dragged over it some time previously, all is done that can be done; and the rest must be left to the hounds. The scent always lies, a run is a certainty, and you have the advantage of knowing beforehand pretty exactly where you are going, if you give your horse his head. Let it be understood, however, that these remarks are not written with any view to the disparagement of our noble sport of fox-hunting. The present writer is no sneaking vulpecide and hedgerow trapper of the " red rascal," but religiously believes that all foxes were providentially brought into this world to be preserved first, and hunted afterwards.

Having arrived at the meet, and the cap having been sent round to enable non-members to contribute their quota to the general expenses, no time was lost about the start; Mr. Pokyr, Mr. Fitzfoodel, and several other highflyers showing the way, which at first lay through a grass field. The Prince, with our hero on his back, at once bounded off like a deer, and also roaring so well that he might have played Lion instead of Snug the Joiner, in Shakspeare's play—pulling, besides, in a most unpleasant way.

" Woa, Princey—woa, my b-boy," exclaimed Mr. Samuel, in as soothing a tone as circumstances permitted him to employ.

But Prince wouldn't "woa;" and, on the contrary, tore along, soon placing his rider a long way in the van.

OUR HERO UNFORTUNATELY LOSES HIS STIRRUP AT A
CRITICAL MOMENT.

"Gently there, sir—you'll be on the dogs in a minute.

But Prince would not listen to reason or obey the rein.

"Good gracious—what a horse!" ejaculated Mr. Golightly, as he gave the Prince his head in a hilly turnip field. "This must quiet him."

Quite the reverse, however. Prince's roaring did not stop him in the least; and, topping the hill, he galloped down the slope on the other side, at a fearful pace.

"Woa," cried his rider, faintly—"here's a hedge."

They reached it in an instant, and over it they went—Mr. Golightly losing his off-stirrup in the scrimmage. On again—another fence—a tremendous drop, evidently.

"Oh, lor!" thought Mr. Samuel, "I dislike hunting the Drag, if this is it."

He landed—but on his horse's neck. The others were close at his heels. Prince heard them. Across a lane—another fence! Mr. Golightly precipitately deposited on the soft turf on one side—Prince left standing on the other.

"Look out there," cried Mr. Pokyr, "or we shall be on the top of you!"

And our hero just got out of the way in time to avoid the hoofs of his friend's horse.

During his short but sharp run, Mr. Samuel had almost forgotten his friend, Mr. Popham, and the gray mare. The question now arose in his mind, "What has become of Popham?"

"LOOK OUT THERE," CRIED MR. POKYR.

With characteristic determination, he scrambled through the hedge; and, luckily, found Prince within a hundred yards of the place where he had parted company with him a minute before.

"Ah!"—hearing cries from a neighbouring ditch—"Ah! who is that? Somebody hurt? I hope not," called out Mr. Samuel, ever ready to succour the distressed.

"Oh—o-h-h-h! what do they want? What is it? What is it?"

"What is what?" demanded Mr. Golightly, rapidly advancing to the rescue.

"Oh-h-h, they'll eat me! I'm sure they mean it."

"Popham!" said our hero, recognizing the voice of his friend, and conscience-smitten that he had neglected to look for him before—"what is the matter?"

"Golightly!" cried the distressed voice of Percy, "I shall be eaten, I'm sure I shall."

At that instant the speaker, turning the corner, came into sight, vigorously pursued by five or six stragglers from the pack, who kept jumping round the terrified little man in a horribly anthropophagous fashion. The hounds had followed the scent, found poor Percy in a ditch, where his gray had left him, and wanted the spare bloater he carried in his pocket.

"Down!" said Mr. Samuel to the dogs, raising

his hunting crop, while his friend took refuge behind him—" down!"

But five damp noses hovered round Mr. Popham's coat tails, in spite of Mr. Samuel's commanding " Downs!"

" What in the world is it?" asked Mr. Popham, in despair.

" Why you—you must have something in your pocket," suggested Mr. Golightly, with consummate sagacity.

" To—be—sure; the red herring—I forgot it. Here," said he, throwing it to the dogs, who speedily took the paper off.   " Good dog."

" What do you say," asked Mr. Samuel, who had never once, in all these trying circumstances, lost his coolness or presence of mind, and still held tight to Prince's bridle—" shall we go on again?"

"All right, just as you like," said Mr. Popham, ashamed to appear in any way deficient in mettle.

" But where's the gray?"

CHAPTER XV.

OUR HERO PAYS A VISIT TO MR. GALLAGHER'S
ESTABLISHMENT AT SKY SCRAPER LODGE.

E left our hero and his friend, Mr. Popham, busily engaged. The search for the gray at last proved successful. She was discovered by Mr. Samuel—who had in the mean time remounted Prince—peacefully cropping the herbage in a thicket in a remote corner of a very large field, nearly half a mile from the spot where he had left Mr. Popham.

Mr. Samuel, wisely considering that if he rode up to the skittish gray mare mounted on his own horse, she might take it as an encouragement to proceed farther on her wild career, dismounted, and tied Prince to a gate at some little distance from the thicket. Thence advancing stealthily behind a hedgerow, he seized the broken rein which was dangling on the ground, and secured Mr. Popham's spirited steed before she had time to reflect upon

s

the state of affairs, or offer any objection to being caught. Having thus strategically compassed his purpose, Mr. Golightly held the gray mare by the bridle until his friend, Mr. Popham, succeeded in reaching the thicket where he stood. Now, however, the two gentlemen found they had their work cut out for them; for it was apparent, the instant Mr. Popham attempted to put his foot into the stirrup, that mounting the gray mare in Spratt's stable-yard, with the assistance of William and his helpers, and getting on in the open field—where she stood, with fiery eye, panting flank, and distended nostril—amidst all the excitements of the chase, with only Mr. Golightly to hold her head, were two very different things. At length, after considerable trouble, and the display of great patience on all sides—except the gray mare's, who snorted and pawed the ground in a terribly fidgety manner—Mr. Percy Popham succeeded in taking his seat again.

"Bravo, Popham! Now you're all right again," said Mr. Samuel, in an encouraging tone, to his friend, who held his steed in with a very tight rein.

"Yes—thank you—all right now," replied the brave Percy—devoutly hoping in the depths of his manly breast that he might be permitted to continue so.

By this time they had reached the gate to which our hero had fastened his horse. It was the work of a moment for Mr. Samuel to vault nimbly into the saddle.

"Tally-ho! and away!" cried Mr. Samuel; and the two sportsmen proceeded to cross the field—in pursuit of those who, owing to unforeseen accidents, had gone before them—at a very pretty canter; the gray mare bestridden by Mr. Popham laying back her ears, and doing her best to get her head down; while the Prince announced his coming to all whom it might concern in a solo as loud, if not quite so melodious, as anything ever executed on the ophicleide or bassoon.

Their onward career was for a moment interrupted by an obstacle in the shape of some weather-beaten and rotten-looking railings, which constituted one of the jumps in the course, and had, to all appearance, been successfully cleared by everybody else—judging from the facts that the rails were still standing in their primitive integrity, and that there was nobody to be seen on the near side of them.

Having in childhood and youth often beguiled an hour in the perusal of the late Mr. Seymour's clever "Sketches"—which work, by the way, is always known at the Rectory by the name of the

"Mad Bull Book," from its celebrated picture of Walter on the Willow Stump, smiling in conscious security on the infuriated animal below: a plate which fascinated our hero at the early age of four —Mr. Samuel did not forget the advice the chimney sweep on the donkey gave to the gentleman on the horse—namely, never to jump when there was a "reg'lar gate" to ride safely through.

Accordingly, he looked around, with a view to discovering a way into the next field other than taking the rails. His thoughts were accurately divined by a rustic who was at work—or play: it was not easy to say which—on the other side of the hedge.

"You'll ha' to joomp it," remarked this smock-frocked individual, rather viciously, "for there aint no gate."

Our hero, with becoming dignity, thought fit to treat this remark with silent contempt; not choosing to admit that such an idea as that presented by the possible existence of a gate had ever crossed his mind. He boldly took his horse back some five and twenty yards from the fence, and rode him at the railings like a man. This headlong leap resulted in his taking the greater portion of the timber with him—attached to the Prince's hind legs—for some short distance into the next field.

This left a very wide opening for Mr. Popham, who was speedily by his side, making, jointly with our hero, a gallant effort to be in at the finish if possible yet.

The finish of the course was a haystack, about four miles from the starting point; and at the very time that Mr. Samuel and his friend were toiling hopelessly in the rear, all the other members of the club were within sight, at least, of the goal, with the exception of Mr. Calipee and Mr. Chutney, who had unfortunately got pounded in a close of Kohl Rabbi they had no business to have got into, and were making meritorious—but, as far as they had proceeded, unsuccessful—efforts to get out again. A few gentlemen had already pulled up their foaming steeds under the hayrick, and among these we may mention Mr. Pokyr—who had been the first to arrive—and Jockey Fitzfoodel, who was second in the race. These bold spirits and expert riders, who led the van, after giving their horses a few minutes' breathing time, set off to "lark" it home; choosing on the homeward journey to perform astounding feats of horsemanship, at a game of cross-country follow-my-leader, in preference to taking the turnpike road as the more eligible way into Cambridge. The fortunes of our hero and his friend were less favourable. They kept together for the length of a few fields in gallant style, alternately stimulating one another to deeds of valour. Mr. Golightly's horse, however, tiring under the weight of his rider, began to hang out the white flag, and require a little gentle assistance from the whip Mr. Samuel carried; the gray mare, on the other hand, was still, in proper sporting parlance, game as a pebble, and fresh as a daisy, pulling with all her might and main. In this state of affairs, Mr. Popham not only involuntarily obtained the lead, but kept it also against his will. The shades of the winter evening were fast closing around, and with them—blown from the direction of the Fens— came a thick and heavy fog. The two friends were separated by a field from each other. Mr. Samuel saw Mr. Popham's back as he popped over a hedge in fine style, and a few seconds afterwards rode at it in the same place himself; but here, also, for the second time, horse and rider came to decided grief. When our hero succeeded in getting the Prince out of the ditch into which they had both been precipitated, he discovered, to his alarm, that his horse was dead lame, that it was becoming dark in an unaccountable manner, and—a few minutes after— that he was in a field of vast extent, apparently without a gate on any of its four long sides.

" Well," he ejaculated—at the same time blowing on his fingers to warm them, and leading the Prince after him—" this is really dreadful. Popham!" he shouted, hallooing after his friend; but there was no answering call—not even an echo, in that flat country—to cheer and encourage him to make another effort.

"My word!" he could not help saying to himself many times, as he led his horse along the hedgerows, treading down the wet grass—" my word! I wish I was safely back. Why doesn't Popham come to look for me?"

In his circuitous wanderings, to add to his discomfiture and make his confusion worse confounded, Mr. Samuel unfortunately lost his reckoning, and forgot on which side he had come into the field; so that when at last he discovered a way out, through which he lugged his horse, he was at a loss to know which way led towards home and Popham.

" Oh, dear!" he exclaimed, turning up the collar of his coat, and sticking his hands in his pockets, "what a dreadful predicament to be in! I wonder which is the way to—anywhere!"

But morn follows the darkest night, and every cloud has its silver lining, the poets say; and so it proved in our hero's case, for after crossing a ploughed field—with what were, in his opinion the

deepest furrows he had ever had to stumble over—
he found himself at a gate which led into a lane.
Words were insufficient to express his delight, so
he was prudently silent.

On and on—for ever, almost, it seemed to Mr.
Golightly. Was there in the world a lane that led
nowhere? Was there a lane without an end at all?
This must be it, if such there were.

" It does not get much darker," said Mr. Samuel
to himself; " and I am sure the fog is clearing off
a little."

Suddenly, to his great joy—for he could not see
many yards ahead—he descried the end of the lane;
at the end of the lane an old finger-post, where three
ways met; and, curiously enough, close to the finger-post stood Mr. Popham and the gray mare.

" Popham!" cried our hero, cheering up at the
sight of his lost companion—all his expressive features absolutely beaming with delight.

"Oh! Golightly!" groaned his friend. " She's as
lame as a cat, and I've had to lead her no end of
a way."

"Mine is as lame as a cat too," said our hero,
pointing over his shoulder at the Prince—" and
I've had to lead him almost ever since I lost you.
How did we manage to miss each other? Where
in the world did you get to?"

"Goodness only knows!" sighed Mr. Popham. "I got into a field, and I thought I should never find my way out."

OUR HERO AND HIS FRIEND POPHAM SUDDENLY CONFRONT
EACH OTHER.

"How very curious," said Mr. Samuel, moralizing on the coincidence. "Why, I got into a field, and thought I should never be able to get out."

"Query—were we both in the same field?"

"Perhaps," said Mr. Samuel. "But what is to be done? Do you know the way?"

"I think so. I think this lane must lead towards Cambridge."

"Come along, then," cried Mr. Samuel, in his cheery way. "Let us lose no more time. Have you any cherry brandy left?" he added.

"Not a drop—and I have got a cigar; but my box of lights must have fallen out of my pocket."

At last they met a man.

"Is this the way to Cambridge?" they both asked in a breath, the instant they sighted him.

"Way to Ca-ambridge?" said the fellow, with a grin. "No—this is the road to Newmarket."

"Goodness!" said Mr. Samuel. "Are we—how far are we, now, from—"

"You're about half-way between 'em, sir."

"Oh, lawd!" exclaimed Mr. Popham, in a cold perspiration at the prospect before them. "Is there no village near? We can't lead our horses seven miles."

"Straight on—you're close to the village," said the rustic, and bade them good night.

"Close to," seemed a long way off; but at last they reached the village, and made their way to the only public-house of which the place could boast.

"Thank Heaven!" said Mr. Popham, as they mounted the baker's cart, the only vehicle in the village at their disposal, "we shall get back at last."

They had refreshed themselves with hot brandy and water; seen their horses safely bestowed for the night; and now—three on a seat, counting the driver—were fairly on their way back to Cambridge. In this inglorious way ended Mr. Golightly's first day with the Drag.

It was getting very near the end of the term, when, one fine December morning, as Mr. Golightly was wending his way in a leisurely manner through the narrow defiles of Trinity-street—that opposite the shop of that eminent bibliopole, Mr. Johnson— he came suddenly upon his friend, Mr. Popham.

"Hallo!" said Mr. Samuel, pleasantly.

"Hallo!" was the response of Mr. Percy Popham, who stood on the doorstep of the shop above mentioned, and from that coigne of vantage was carefully scrutinizing with his eyeglass three little dogs and two large ones, held respectively by an old man and a young one, of very disreputable appearance, whom our hero had on former occasions seen Mr. Pokyr speak to as the two Farrans—father and son.

"Require anything in the daug line, sir, this morning?" said the father.

"Sell you a little daug, sir?" said the son.

Both of them turning their attention from Mr. Popham to Mr. Golightly.

"N-no—not to-day," said Mr. Samuel. "Are you going to buy a dog, Popham?"

"I am, when I see one that takes my fancy, Golightly."

After hearing this announcement, the Messrs. Farran —*père et fils*—became perfectly frantic with delight. The prices of the five curs that formed their well-selected kennel went up cent. per cent., in their own minds, on the first blush of such news. First the old man picked up one of the animals out of the gutter, and thrust it immediately under Mr. Popham's nose. Then the youth seized one of the dogs—an old pointer—in his firm grip, and elevated him in a most playful manner.

"There, my lord, that's the daug for you. He's a beauty, and no mistake. Close to yer, an' all. No magnifying glass *nor* spectacles required to see fleas on him, for we washes all ourn twice a-day. Don't we, old un?"

The "old un," thus apostrophized, displayed his yellow teeth in a comic grin, meant to be eminently propitiatory.

" Wunst a-day we does, there now; and that's the truth, yer honour."

But the laudable exertions of the pair of rogues were destined to be of little avail; for, at that moment, Mr. Jamaica Blaydes strolled up, arm in arm with Mr. Calipee.

" Buying a daug, Golightly ? " said the former gentleman, with a smile.

" Popham is," answered our hero.

" Sell you a little daug ? A prime little ratter this is," said the younger Farran, putting a black and tan terrier before Mr. Blaydes.

" Take them away, Farran. They won't do for us. Here is old Gallagher with his cart, and all the stock-in-trade. He is the man for our money."

As Mr. Blaydes made the remark, a yellow cart, drawn by an elderly pony, with the legend, " R. Gallagher, Dog Fancier," emblazoned upon it, came round the corner. The cart in question was full of dogs of all sorts; three dogs ran underneath it, fastened by three chains ; in the midst sat Mr. Gallagher himself, holding a tame fox on his knee with one hand, and grasping the reins with the other.

" Mornin', gentlemen," he remarked, touching his hat, and bringing his travelling menagerie to a stand.

"My friend here is in want of a dog, Gallagher."

"Yes, sir. Now, what sort of a daug, sir?" dragging successively half a dozen specimens of different breeds from the bottom of his cart, and speaking in terms of the warmest commendation of them all.

"Stay—we'll come down this afternoon, and look at what you've got, Gallagher," said Mr. Blaydes.

"Certainly, sir. Which gentleman is it, now, as wants one?" asked the dog fancier, meaning to wait upon his customer, if the appointment should, from any unforeseen circumstance, fail to be kept.

Mr. Popham having intimated that he was desirous of becoming a purchaser, Mr. Gallagher said—

"Thank you, sir—thank you, gentlemen;" and with great alacrity produced from the pocket of his fur waistcoat a somewhat soiled piece of pasteboard. "I leave you this," he said, handing to Mr. Popham the card, on which was inscribed, in plain and ornamental typography—

R. GALLAGHER,

ROYAL RIFLE SALOON,

SKY SCRAPER LODGE,

(OPPOSITE SNOOKES'S BOAT HOUSE), CAMBRIDGE.

Every accommodation for keeping and training gentlemen's DOGS upon reasonable terms. A large quantity of PIGEONS, RABBITS, RATS, &c., always on hand. Orders for public or private matches punctually attended to. Gallagher's Fox Hounds meet daily at the Kennel (sure find). Foxes kept on the Premises.

GALLAGHER'S

ZOOLOGICAL GARDENS.

Admission 6d.

The Wonderful Bird, 7 feet high, no tongue, no wings, no tail; also the Golden Eagle, The Wonderful Porcupine, Jackalls, Monkeys, Racoons, and other Foreign Animals, to be seen at R. GALLAGHER'S.

The above are always on Sale.

N.B.—Persons having Pigeons, Rabbits, &c., to dispose of, can always obtain the best price by applying to R. GALLAGHER, as above.

In the afternoon they strolled down to the river side, to pay a visit to Mr. R. Gallagher, at Sky Scraper Lodge. They were accompanied by Mr. Jamaica Blaydes's celebrated bull terrier Jumbo, and by Mr. Calipee's little black and tan. On entering the yard of this menagerie, the proprietor advanced a few yards towards the doorway to meet them. Mr. Gallagher wore a sporting coat of velveteen, with large white mother-of-pearl buttons, on each of which was represented an engraving of a coach and four at its top pace, calling to mind good old times that have long since passed away. Mr. Gallagher's continuations were of Bedford cord, his waistcoat was made of some skin or other —whether it was the dressed hide of some wonderful animal deceased, or whether it was made from the skin of the *Vitulus Britannicus*, or British calf, is a matter of conjecture: certainly it strongly resembled the latter in marks and colour. His neckerchief was of blue kersey, spotted with yellow, of the sort known as "birds'-eyes;" and under one arm he carried a short, thick-knobbed stick, which served to preserve order among the various animals of the collection; while tucke under his other arm, a tiny dog nestled comfortably enough.

The entrance of our party within the space en-

closed within the four walls of the yard of Sky
Scraper Lodge was the signal for a general yelping
and barking from the numerous representatives of
the canine species, loose and chained, cribbed and
caged, that appeared in overpowering numbers in
every nook and corner.

"Lay down!—quiet!" said Gallagher to his
kennel. Then, turning with a captivating smile
upon Mr. Popham, winking and blinking all the
time in a half-awake sort of way, he asked—

"Is it a large daug, or a leetle daug?—a t'y
daug, or suffin' of this yere description?"—pointing
to a huge mastiff as he spoke.

Mr. Golightly, while this interrogation was proceeding, amused himself by looking round Mr.
Gallagher's establishment. Ranged round the
walls were tiers of cages, containing fowls, a few
pheasants, three or four ravens, a pair of owls,
groups of little dogs too small to take care of
themselves among their heavier brethren, tabby
cats, a monkey or two, several foxes; and, in a
tub set on end, was what, from the perfume and
refuse cabbage leaves diffused around, and from a
placard on the wall—"Drawing the Badger, One
Shilling"—might be presumed to be Gallagher's
famous badger.

Whilst our hero, with his customary quickness

T

of observation, was running his eagle eye over this curious collection, and striving in vain to discover the whereabouts of the " Wonderful Bird, seven feet high, that had neither tongue, wings, nor tail,"

MR. GALLAGHER AND HIS MENAGERIE.

he became aware that Mr. Popham had communicated to the dog fancier his views upon their immediate business; for he observed Gallagher leading the way into a sort of shed or stable, carrying in his arms a rough-haired terrier, and followed by our hero's three friends. Naturally enough, Mr. Samuel followed them—to the rat-pit, as it turned out.

"Now, sir, let him have a dozen o' these," said the fancier—"and if he don't kill 'em before you've time to tek out your ticker and tell us wot's the time o' day, I'll eat him up myself—T-h-e-r-e!"

Mr. Popham having consented to the expenditure of six shillings in rats, Gallagher opened the door of a wire cage, and let two or three into the pit. But the terrier, for some reason or other, declined to kill them, which made Gallagher affirm that it was because he had "that instant had his dinner, and gorn and blowed hisself out fit to bust."

On the proposition of Mr. Calipee, who was familiar with the resources of the establishment, they saw the ravens kill rats, and the cat kill rats, and the fox kill rats, and several sorts of terriers destroy the vermin, at a cost of only sixpence per rat.

"By Jove! Gallagher, everything you've got kills. I believe the old pony would rat, too, if you put him in the pit."

" I've no doubt he would, sir. I've trained 'em. I've trained 'em all to it."

Mr. Blaydes's dog, Jumbo, next drew the badger. The process was simpler than may be supposed. The tub having been overturned, and the unfortunate occupant well shaken up to liven him into a fit state of anger, Gallagher presented Jumbo to the badger—putting him a little way into the barrel, and pulling him out again a few times, till the enraged badger flew at him; when there was an angry tussle, a few yelps from the poor dog, and the draw was over : to be repeated as often as was desired, at one shilling per time.

" That old badger's no good, Gallagher. You've had him for years," said Mr. Calipee, who was quite a sportsman.

" Not more than six months—on my honour, I haven't," replied the fancier.

" How often is he drawn?" inquired Mr. Popham.

" Well, sir, that depends on the gentlemen's fancies a good deal. Sometimes oftener than others."

" Doesn't cost you much to keep, Gallagher," said Mr. Blaydes.

" Subsists on vegetables, sir."

" Cabbages, apparently."

"Is it not cruel—that is, unkind, I mean?" said Mr. Golightly, somewhat timidly.

"Cruel, sir?" said Gallagher. "Varmin's varmin —that's what varmin is. It's sport—all sport."

"But is it sport for the badger?"

"To be sure, sir. He loves it. No dog can't hurt him. He's as happy in that there tub as ever Dio-génous was—and happier; for he has as much as ever he can eat—that he do. Let your little daug run arter a rabbit, Mr. Calerpee—do him good."

Accordingly, Mr. Calipee assenting, they all sallied forth through the doorway on to the Common, where the rabbit, having had a few yards start allowed it, was chevied by half a dozen dogs —all the party, except our hero, crying "Loo."

After doubling and dodging for the space of three or four minutes, the poor little animal was surrounded by its pursuers; but Mr. Gallagher, whose agility was remarkable, soon arrived at the spot, and, rescuing the rabbit from the dogs, brought it back in his arms.

"Do again another time—eh, Gallagher?" said Mr. Blaydes.

"Cert'nly, sir—a fair run's a fair shillin's worth any day. Have one more, sir?"

But here our hero interposed, saying—

"Come, let us go. The rats I'm in doubt about —the badger may like it; but it is not fair to the poor little rabbit. Do not let us do it again."

"You aint no sportsman, sir, I'm afraid."

Mr. Samuel admitted that he was not.

"Well, sir, you'll hev this yere leetle daug, I s'pose?" said Gallagher to Mr. Popham.

And, after considerable haggling as to price, the rough-haired terrier became the property of Mr. Percy Popham for the moderate consideration of four pounds sterling and the promise of two old pairs of trousers, of which the fancier said he was badly in want; and the terrier was led off in triumph by his new master.

CHAPTER XVI.

MR. GOLIGHTLY QUITS ALMA MATER FOR OAKINGHAM RECTORY.

UR hero was so well pleased with his life at the University, that he found the end of the term approaching with feelings akin to regret. There was left, however, the comforting reflection that, although the Michaelmas term was nearly at an end, the Lent term would follow hard upon its heels. The vacation was heralded by the appearance of Mrs. Cribb daily in a clean apron, while Mr. Sneek persistently wore his Sunday necktie for a week. The cups and saucers were washed, and the crockery generally polished up, and arranged in order in the cupboards of the proprietors. All the jam pots that had been emptied in term time were scrubbed and displayed in the gyp-room. Articles of furniture that had been unvisited by the renovating influence of the domestic duster for weeks, received a few hasty touches.

The carpets were swept, and grates touched up with black-lead. New brushes and brooms made their appearance on the scene; and a much heavier stock of tea, coffee, and groceries in general was laid in than could possibly be consumed by the gentlemen in whose bills an account of the same would appear, in due course, next term.

The activity and zeal of Mr. Sneek, the civility and care of Mrs. Cribb, increased daily; also the propensity of both to enter into conversation on subjects relating to the loss they always sustained while "the gentlemen" were away; the advent of Christmas; high price of commodities; possible effect of severe weather in bringing either themselves or near and dear members of their families to an untimely grave, during the absence of their masters—for whose comfort they were always ready to do anything in the world. The meaning, intent, and purpose of all of which protestations are too manifest to require much explanation at our hands. Their common object was a liberal tip. After a grand farewell dinner of the Mutton Cutlet Club, to which many old Cutlets from many parts of the country came; after several festive evenings at the rooms of various friends; after a number of college meetings on as many different subjects, the morning of the Friday that was to witness our hero's re-

turn to Oakingham-cum-Pokeington arrived. Lectures and chapels being over for the term, he in-
dulged himself a little, and did not rise until
eleven o'clock. He found both Sneek and Cribb
officiously attentive at breakfast.

"Sausages?" was Mr. Samuel's first remark
"Why, George is coming to have some breakfast
with me, and I told you to get me some cutlets, *aux
tomates.*"

"The cutlets, sir—" answered Mrs. Cribb.

"And tomarters—" said Mr. Sneek, continuing
the sentence.

"Is in—"

"The fender, sir," said the gyp.

"If you please, sir," said Mrs. Cribb, smiling
very blandly, and lifting the cover off the dish,
"my sister, sir—she lives a few miles out of
Cambridge, at a village, sir—and she always kills
a pig, fed on the best of oatmeal, and nothing
else, a few weeks before Christmas; and, sir, I
have took the liberty—without giving offence,
I 'ope, sir—of offering you a few sossinges made
by her own hands, so I can warrant they don't
contain nothing but country pork and bread
crumbs!"

Our hero could do nothing else but graciously
accept Mrs. Cribb's present. Accordingly, he did

so; at the same time requesting her to call his cousin George up to breakfast.

"Which," said Mr. Sneek, with a knowing wink, as soon as ever Mr. Samuel's door had closed upon the bedmaker, "which I've often heard Mr. Pokyr say as them sausages every term's worth a guinea a pound to Betsy Cribb. I do believe she gets that for 'em out of the gentlemen—and no mistake!"

"Does she?" said our hero, looking at the bright tin cover which enshrined the precious delicacy.

"I," said Sneek, heaving a great sigh from the very bottom of his capacious chest, "aint—got—no sister now." Here the gyp took out a prodigiously holey yellow and green bandanna, and flourished it about in a heartrending manner. "I lost mine— two year ago come Whitsuntide. I have not got sausages—nor pork pies—like Cribb; but I do hope I do my duty, and leave it to gentlemen to—"

"Do theirs, I suppose you are going to say, Sneek."

"Beggin' pardon, no, sir—not at all. What I do and meant to say was, I leave it to gentlemen to behave in what way they think proper; but when gentlemen, for instance, is Freshmen, and now, for instance, just at the end of their first terms, they might not know the usual custom, and—"

" Very well—very well. I dare say, if you leave
the matter to me, you will have no reason to be
dissatisfied."

" That I'm sure on—and more than sure on,"
continued Sneek; adding, if possible, to the compliment by this further assurance, " for no more
liberal master nor Mr. George Golightly did I ever
want, and yourn's the same name, sir—so it is."

The gyp's further remarks were stopped by the
entrance of Mr. George.

" Well, I suppose you will be ready when we
are? The train leaves at three o'clock."

" I must be," said Mr. Samuel. " Oh, good gracious, George!" he exclaimed, putting his hand in
the pocket of his coat.

" Well, what now!" asked his cousin, who never
sympathized too much with Mr. Samuel in his little
troubles.

" Why," said our hero, excitedly, producing from
his pocket a letter duly addressed to his father,
" they won't know I am coming. I wrote this
letter last night, and I declare I quite forgot to
post it."

" Never mind; post it now. You'll be there before the letter, that's all; and you can tell them it's
coming, instead. Do you see?"

" Oh, dear, oh!" said our hero. " And I promised my Fa I would call on Mr. Smith; and, besides that, I've got all sorts of things to do."

Being thus pressed for time, Mr. Samuel hurriedly despatched his meal.

" You've had sausages from Mrs. Cribb, I see," said his cousin. "I have had a pie. I don't believe her sister makes them at all. I don't even believe she has got a sister!"

" Um!" said our hero. "I think they are all right—come from the country, I mean. There is a horrid little pie and sausage shop in a street near the Market-square. I would not for the world have touched one if I thought—"

" She got them there," said Mr. George. "Well, she does, I firmly believe. Pokyr swears he saw her come out of the shop last night with her basket crammed with things."

" Dear me!" said Mr. Samuel, in undisguised concern.

" Yes," continued his cousin; "and accordingly this morning, when the old girl made a speech and presented him with a pie, Pokyr threw up the window like a man, and chucked the abomination into the middle of the river."

" B—but," said our hero, musingly, "I don't think I could have done that. I should have been afraid of hurting Mrs. Cribb's feelings."

" Pokyr knows a sovereign remedy for wounds of that kind," replied Mr. George.

"Well," said Mr. George, an hour and a half after, when he met Mr. Samuel in Brown-street, " have you called on Mr. Smith, and got all your other things done?—because the train won't wait for you, as you know."

" I have," replied our hero. " I was lucky in finding Mr. Smith at home; and, George, I'm sure Fa will be quite delighted. You know how fond he is of science and scientific men."

" I know," said Mr. George, " that he is a contributing member of the Loamshire Archæological Association."

"Well," said Mr. Samuel, " Mr. Smith tells me that the next meeting of the Royal Geological Association will be held at Fuddleton, and that visits to all parts of Loamshire will be made. Mr. Smith is coming, and the—the great Dr. Fledgeby—Professor Fledgeby, you know—and, in fact, everybody. And Mr. Smith said, 'As an old friend of your Fa's'—' Father's,' he said, of course—' I shall ask him to put me up at Oakingham Rectory.' Fa will be delighted, I'm sure."

In the excitement consequent on making this important disclosure, Mr. Samuel had, without know-

ing it, come to a full stop at the very door of
the cigar shop kept by the Brown-street Venus's
mamma. As soon as he became aware of his
locality, he felt to a certain extent embarrassed, as
he had studiously avoided Miss Bellair since the
day when the practical joke had been played on
him in her name.

"I'm going in to get a canister of smoking mixture to take down with me," said his cousin.
"Come in!"

Mr. Samuel, with a greater show of coolness than
might have been expected, did so. On entering
the shop, they found Mrs. Bellair quite alone. She
at once commenced a long explanatory and apolo-
getic discourse, in which she assured Mr. Samuel
that both she and her daughter were wholly innocent of any complicity in the plot by which his
friends had hoaxed him; and, in a word, the moral
and pith of her remarks appeared, on a moment's
consideration, to amount to this—namely, that her
matronly feelings had been outraged in such a way
by the use to which her errand boy's services and
her daughter's name had been put, that nothing
but an assurance from our hero that he was satisfied of her innocence, and would give her his custom again in future, would restore her mental
equilibrium.

In the end, Mr. Samuel assured Mrs. Bellair that, in his opinion, she was the repository of all the virtues; and purchased a box of cigars of her accordingly.

Matters having been thus satisfactorily arranged, Mr. Samuel and Mr. George returned to St. Mary's —where they found Sneek had lost no time in what they termed " getting their traps together." Everything having been packed, and their *exeats* duly forwarded to the buttery, they were ready to start. Mr. Sneek and Mrs. Cribb received their tips with a profusion of thanks, expressing their heartfelt regret at the separation that was about to take place between themselves and such excellent masters. Mr. Pokyr and a friend, who were to accompany them as far as Bletchley, met them at the station; where, having secured a compartment to themselves and their dogs, they soon left Alma Mater behind. They beguiled the tedium of the journey with a game at cards, in which our hero, with his usual luck, came off worst man. Without either accident or delay, they arrived in due course at Fuddleton, where they found the carriage from the Hall in waiting to convey them to Oakingham.

CHAPTER XVII.

RECOUNTS AN INSTANCE OF CHARITY ILL-BESTOWED

UR hero's reception by the various members of his family was of the most enthusiastic description. When his uncle's carriage drew up at the door of the Rectory, Mr. Samuel found his father already on the steps, waiting to receive and embrace his son. The welcome he was destined to meet with at the hands of his mamma, and his aunts Harriet and Dorothea, was no less hearty. In a word, his family were delighted to see him at home again; and Mr. Samuel was equally happy and pleased to be there. The amount of news they had to tell him was only exceeded by the importance of that which he had to impart to them. He amused his family with descriptions of the various ways in which he had spent his time since he had left them; passing from grave to gay, and back again, in a manner at once vivacious and impressive.

On the other hand, when all the news of the country-side had been communicated to our hero by his aunts and his mamma, the worthy Rector began to dilate upon the topic just then most talked

THE WELCOME HOME.

about in that part of the world—the approaching visit of the great Geological Association to Fuddleton and the neighbourhood. The subject having

U

been thus introduced by his father, reminded our hero of his visit to Mr. Smith, and the announcement made by that scientific gentleman that he intended to avail himself of the hospitality of his friend, the Rev. Mr. Golightly, during the two days' excursion of the Association to Loamshire.

"I am sure," said Mrs. Golightly, who was a Loamshire lady, "I have lived in the country all my life, and I never knew there was anything particular in sand for people to come and see." •

"Some of the strata and fossil formations are of a very remarkable character, and well worthy of a visit," said Mr. Morgan, the curate.

"My dear," said the Rector, who by this time had placed himself in his favourite position and attitude on the hearth-rug, "it must always be left to Associations, consisting of men of science, to determine what such Associations think worthy of their important deliberations."

"Certainly, brother," said both the maiden ladies.

"I could almost have wished," continued their brother, "that their pursuits had been of an archæological rather than a geological nature; for, certainly, no church for ten miles round is better worth the attention of the curious and learned than our own interesting church of Oakingham-cum-Poke-ington."

"Certainly, dear," said all the three ladies, in chorus.

"The painted glass in the eastern window is most remarkable," continued the Rector—"that must be

MR. SAMUEL'S RECEPTION BY HIS MAMMA AND AUNTS.

admitted. The brasses are in more perfect preservation than any I ever saw."

"And Rackett, the sexton, takes beautiful copies

U 2

of them with cobbler's heelball," said Miss Harriet, interrupting her brother.

"The tombs of our own family are not altogether to be overlooked, I trust," remarked Miss Dorothea, with some show of asperity, tempered by a just pride, not unbecoming in a distant connection of the great Tredsofte family.

"You say so with justice, Dorothea," said the Rector. "But passing over all these minor points, in my opinion the piscina is the glory of Oakingham Church. It has long been a theory of mine—which I am prepared to maintain at all hazards—that that piscina is the finest and most perfect in the county."

"The sedilia are finely chiselled, and in wonderfully good preservation," said Mr. Morgan.

"They are, they are!" cried the Rector, with animation; "but, when all's said and done, commend me to the piscina."

However, as geological science has to deal rather with the material itself than with the carving and tooling thereof; and, further, thinks nothing of carrying back its speculations over a period of five thousand years or more, the antiquity of only a few centuries more or less, claimed by the Reverend Mr. Golightly for the stone curiosities of his church, would inevitably seem little in its eyes.

" Well," said he, at the conclusion of a discourse of some considerable length on the wonders of Oakingham parish generally—including, of course, his parishioner, Mrs. Vine, who has on two occasions received the sum of three sovereigns from her Most Gracious Majesty—" Well, I shall be only too happy to entertain my old friend Mr. Smith, and any friend of his who may accompany him."

" Professor Fledgeby is coming with the Association," said our hero.

" Is he really ? " said the Rector. " The illustrious and venerable author of ' The Elephant's True Place in Nature,' ' Talks on Tusks '—and—and—"

" ' Mornings with the Mammoth and the Mastodon,' " said Mr. Morgan, " if I am not mistaken."

" They will be more trouble than half a dozen ordinary visitors, Samuel, my dear," said Mrs. Golightly, in a tone of mild remonstrance. " Tuffley will have to take all the best silver out of the cases, and clean it ; and I'm sure the centre candelabrum is a day's work in itself, if it is done properly."

" But there is something in the honour of entertaining such guests," remarked Miss Dorothea, who was ambitious in her notions.

" Precisely my own view, Dorothea," said the

Rector; "and I shall beg of Mr. Smith to persuade the great Dr. Fledgeby to come."

The pending visit of the Royal Geological Association was an event calculated to set all Fuddleton in a commotion such as the oldest inhabitant of the town had never witnessed before. The mayor and corporation had several meetings among themselves, and two dinners at the expense of the Reverend Canon Playfair, Vicar of All Saints, Fuddleton—first, on the occasion of their graciously taking into consideration the propriety of permitting the Royal Geological Association to hold sittings in the Town Hall; and, secondly, on the occasion of their giving consent to the same. An order in council was made, on the proposition of Mr. Councillor Dasher, that the mayor's robe of state be trimmed with a border of real sable fur, in place of the imitation ditto now upon it; a new pair of plush inexpressibles for the town-crier were voted *nem. con.;* and the leading local brass-founder, Mr. Alderman Noysey, proposed a new bell for the same useful functionary of the corporation; but this expense was considered unnecessary, as the present bellman's voice was louder than any bell, and equal to all occasions. Nor was the county behindhand. The magistrates met in solemn form, as at quarter-sessions. Letters were sent by the lord-lieutenant of the county, the two members for North Loamshire, and the bishop of the diocese, expressing, with more or less perspicuity, their great and unspeakable regret that they were not able to be present on the auspicious occasion. Nobody thought the lord-lieutenant would come to welcome the Association, for his letter arrived twenty minutes after Sir Tattleton Pratt, who had already informed his brother J.P.s that Lord Shovelle had told him—when the hounds met the other day at Fendre Abbey—that "he had hunted the county for many years without seeing anything peculiar in the geological formation, except that in some parts it wasn't so sandy as in others; and he wondered what they wanted to come to Fuddleton for." His lordship added, also, that "if he went to their confabs he must ask them out to Fendre; and though, as everybody knew, he liked company, and saw as much as any man in the county, they weren't his sort, and he should not have anything to do with 'em—that was flat. Besides, it's Playfair that has asked 'em to come, and he's a Whig?" So, when his lordship's letter was read, stating he had got another fit of gout, it was not believed.

As for the bishop, he had only been asked out of compliment; for, being nearly blind, quite deaf, in his ninety-fourth year, and bedridden about nine months out of the twelve, he did not go out into society much. But the county members were subjected, in their absence, to much criticism of an angry kind; and old Squire Wombwell—who was very deaf, and came in late, with an imperfect knowledge of the business before the meeting—was so impressed by the heated debate going on, that he thought it was election time; and, solemnly rising from his seat, proposed the reading of the Riot Act—with him a panacea for the healing of all dissensions, civil or military. The result of the meeting was that the Shire Hall was placed at the disposal of the Association, and a resolution come to by the county to act in concert with the town authorities in giving the scientific gentlemen a fitting reception; though the chairman interposed an obstacle in the way of a united procession to the railway station, by saying he would never, so long as his name was Sir Tulse Hill, Bart., consent to walk behind any mayor of Fuddleton—past, present, or to come. The difficulty was got over by an arrangement in the nature of a compromise: Sir Tulse Hill was to ride in his own coach and pair, while the mayor and corporation—who had not got any coaches—preceded him on foot.

The eventful day arrived. Flags of an inexpensive but gaudy character floated from several houses

and shops. The Union Jack was displayed at the
Town Hall, and the Royal standard floated from
the roof of the Shire Hall. Red baize and laurels
in plenty decorated the platform of the railway station. The wind was very high; and, at a quarter
to ten, the triumphal arch in the High-street, with
the inscription, in yellow paper rosettes, "Welcome
to the R. G. A.," on it, was blown down. Time
did not admit of its re-erection on a firmer basis,
as the "special" with the distinguished visitors was
expected at eleven. At half-past ten, the Union
Jack was blown away; and a few minutes afterwards the flagstaff followed, carrying with it a portion of the stucco balustrade. Providentially, no
one was near at the time, so that was all the mischief done. Precisely at a quarter to eleven by All
Saints' clock, a heavy rain began to fall. The only
cheering feeling in the breasts of the corporation,
as they marched down to the station, was that it
was too heavy to last. The procession was most
imposing—or rather, it would have been so, had
the day been fine. It was marshalled in the following order:—Ragged boys and girls of Fuddleton, forming a very irregular vanguard; six county
policemen, with staves sheathed; six town ditto,
staves ditto; the chief constable of the county
police, mounted on his horse, well known with the

Loamshire hounds, and unquiet with music; the mayor of Fuddleton, Mr. Timothy Figgins, J.P.; the worshipful the mayor's mace-bearer, holding an umbrella over his worship's head; the town council, carrying their own umbrellas; Sir Tulse Hill, Bart., in his carriage, drawn by two gray horses; other carriages, intended for the conveyance of members of the Royal Geological Association's Loamshire excursion party; the town-crier, and other corporation servants; six policemen; townspeople of Fuddleton who had nothing better to occupy their time. In the station yard was placed a guard of honour of the First Fuddleton Volunteer Rifles, with their regimental band, at present sheltering themselves from the rain under the commodious goods shed.

The last detachment of the august procession had hardly taken up a position on the platform, when the "special" containing the excursion party of *savans* entered the station.

The men of science were evidently taken by surprise at the magnificent reception which awaited them. Loud cheers greeted them as the train drew up at the platform. The town-clerk advanced, and read a neat address, in which they were assured by that functionary that their visit to Fuddleton was an honour that would never be forgotten in the annals

of that ancient and loyal borough. This speech
having been acknowledged in fitting terms by the
members of the Association, they took their seats
in the carriages provided for their accommodation,
and were at once driven to the Town Hall; the
band appropriately playing " The Roast Beef of Old
England " as they left the station yard. Arrived at
the Town Hall, they found a cold collation spread
out in the council chamber for the refreshment of
the animal part of their nature; and although the
advancement of science was the sole object of their
visit, it is to be observed that they did full justice
to the liberal breakfast provided by the corporation.
This ceremony over, the party split of its own ac-
cord into two sections—one of which went to the
Shire Hall, the other remaining at the Town Hall;
at both of which places short papers were read, for
the edification of the party, by local magnates in
the scientific world.

By the time that the papers had been read, and
as much light thrown upon the geological wonders
of the neighbourhood as could conveniently be done
in half an hour, the rain had ceased; and the two
sections were ready to set out upon their explora-
tions. It was at this moment that our friend, the
Rector of Oakingham, had the felicity of renewing
his acquaintance with the learned and ingenious

Mr. Smith; and, at the same time, of making a friend of the distinguished author of the " Elephant's True Place in Nature," Professor Fledgeby. Mr. Smith was in appearance no more unusual than his name; but the Professor was more remarkable, being a fossil old gentleman, in threadbare snuff-coloured clothes, with a low-crowned hat of antique fashion. His face was the colour of parchment, and over his eyes he wore a huge green shade. Like the other members of the excursion party, he carried in his hand his geological hammer, which he had previously used to such good purpose in ascertaining the elephant's place in nature.

After an interchange of compliments on both sides, the Rector gave his friends a cordial invitation to make Oakingham Rectory their home during their two days' stay in Loamshire; which was willingly accepted. The programme for the day was an excursion to the fossil formation at Frampton Magna, thence to the coprolites being worked by a limited liability company at Whelpton-on-the-Hill; next, dinner at Oakingham Rectory; and lastly, a grand *finale* in the shape of a *conversazione* in the Shire Hall at Fuddleton—at which the rank and fashion, wit, learning, and beauty of Loamshire were to be abundantly represented.

The visit to Frampton Magna passed off without

any incident worthy of remark—except that the Professor missed his footing, and fell into a gravel pit, from which he was happily extricated without much damage, but with a good deal of mud sticking to his coat, which did not improve his appearance, if dress is to be taken as a rough test of respectability. He had likewise so far improved the occasion as to fill all his pockets with fossils and specimens of different kinds, which, for the most part, fell out in the course of his tumble, and took some little time for his friends to collect again, and restore to him. At the coprolite diggings at Whelpton, however, his friends lost him altogether for a while—whether with something of the perversity of genius, or from that absence of mind which not unfrequently accompanies absorbing study, it is not easy to say; but, for some reason or other, the Professor had succeeded in detaching himself from the main body of excursionists, and was quietly pursuing some investigations of his own by the side of the road which leads from Whelpton-on-the-Hill to Oakingham. Here, as luck would have it, the Misses Dorothea and Harriet Golightly found him seated on a huge stone, and pecking away diligently at a heap of smaller stones, placed there at the expense of the parish, for the purpose of mending the way.

"I really wonder where the Association has got to, Harriet," said Miss Dorothea, giving her pony a cut with the whip.

"Samuel said they would be here about half-past three," said Miss Harriet, pulling out her watch, "and it is that time now."

"Is it?" said her sister. "Really, it is quite provoking, when one feels such an interest in their doings, to be unable to find them. It reminds me of Samuel's directions to find the hounds, which we have often driven miles after without ever seeing once."

"I don't see anything of them," said Miss Harriet, turning round to the footman, who sat behind the two ladies. "Which is the coprolite place, Smith? You come from Whelpton, don't you?"

"Yes, ma'am. These is the diggin's, ma'am—leastways, this is where they wash 'em, ma'am."

"Servants never know anything," said Miss Dorothea, tartly.

"He knows this is the coprolite place, sister," said Miss Harriet, apologetically.

"It can't be. Where is the Association?"

To this question there seemed to be no answer.

"I wonder," said the younger lady, in a mild and propitiatory tone, as she caught sight of Professor Fledgeby—"I wonder if that old man has seen any-

thing of them," she continued, pointing at the un-
conscious *savant* with her umbrella.

"Perhaps he has. But, really, the people about
here are so stupid they never seem to me to be able
to see the length of their noses. Ahem!" said the
elder spinster, raising her voice. "Ahem!"

But as the Professor was deaf, the interjection
was lost upon him.

"Hi!" said Smith from behind.

The old gentleman heard this, and looked up vacantly from his stone heap; then pulled his green
shade farther over his eyes, and went quietly on
with his pecking.

"Did any one ever see such ignorant stupidity
and ill-manners?" said Miss Dorothea. "You see
what it is for the parish to be without a resident
clergyman: the people are like heathens."

"Quite awful," chimed in her sister.

"He is a Whelpton man, is he not, Smith?"

"He's out o' the Union, I think, ma'am. The
Union men break the stones on the roads."

Hereupon Miss Dorothea drove up close to
the Professor—who had so much of the scarecrow
about him that the pony became quite frightened
and restless, and fidgeted about in a most uneasy
manner.

"Get down, and hold the pony's head a minute,

Smith. Have you seen any gentlemen about here, my good man ?"

" I'm rather deaf—I beg your pardon," said the geologist, putting his hand to his ear.

" Have you been here all day ?" said the lady, in a louder voice.

" Not very long," replied the Professor.

" Have you seen any gentlemen about here?"

" The Association, you mean ?"

" There!" said Miss Harriet, with enthusiasm. " You see, he is more intelligent than you thought. He evidently has heard of the visit of the Association."

" Yes—where are they ?"

" They are in a field over there, I believe," said the man of science, pointing over the hedge.

A short conversation followed, in which the unfavourable impression Dr. Fledgeby had at first made on Miss Dorothea Golightly's mind was entirely removed. He stood close to the little four-wheel as Miss Dorothea reined up her pony to follow his directions concerning the whereabouts of the Association.

" Really, he is very intelligent and civil, Harriet," said the elder sister, fumbling in the pocket of her gown. " I've a great mind, if I've got one— yes, I have. There, my man."

The carriage drove on, leaving Dr. Fledgeby staring vacantly at a new shilling that lay shining in his astonished palm;— probably the first instance on record of a University Professor, and the senior fellow of St. Mary's, receiving out-door relief in such a fashion.

The Doctor was aghast—the sheer dishonesty of receiving a shilling under such false pretences!— but he could not run after the vehicle, being too old and shaky even to walk well. Luckily, he had a keen sense of humour, which stood him in good stead; so he laughed a dry, geological laugh, and pocketed the coin. He resumed his labours at the stone-heap.

"Oh, here you are!" exclaimed the Reverend Samuel Golightly and Mr. Smith, suddenly bursting through the hedge.

"Yes," said the author of "Mornings with the Mammoth," when he perceived his friends. He related the incident.

The Rector and Mr. Smith laughed at the joke until they held their sides; and the Professor joined them in their fun.

"Capital! I beg a thousand pardons, though, for the utter want of common penetration displayed by my neighbours. It reflects the highest credit on your philosophical principles, Dr. Fledgeby, to be able to take as a joke what a meaner and less enlightened mind might have construed into an insult."

"Oh, the Professor does not mind," said Mr. Smith.

"What am I to do with the shilling, though?" asked the geologist.

"I once found a fourpenny-piece," said the Rector, "and that I placed in the poor-box. That certainly was different—ah—somewhat."

"Restore it to the owner, Professor," said Mr. Smith.

"You'll never find— Stay, though," added the reverend gentleman, with his finger on his forehead, "I think—yes, I feel sure, I know who it was. There are two ignorant, affected—well, I won't be uncharitable—old women who live at Whelpton Hall, and I believe—yes, I may say I'm sure—it was Miss Sally or Miss Betty Harris; so as you, Professor Fledgeby, will never see either of them again, you must put the shilling in my poor-box when you honour me by looking over my church. But here is the carriage," said the Rector, pulling out his watch, "and we shall not do more than be in time for dinner; so, if I may presume to request so distinguished a man of science to lay aside the hammer for the knife—ah—and

fork," continued Mr. Golightly, " and to suspend
his benevolent studies for the good of humanity for
the present—permit me to assist you in getting
into the carriage, my dear Dr. Fledgeby."

In the drawing-room at the Rectory, a few minutes before dinner was announced, Dr. Fledgeby
made his appearance—quite an altered man—in
his black suit and white neckerchief.

" Dr. Fledgeby," said the Rector, in his blandest
tones, " may I present to you Mrs. Samuel Golightly?   Dorothea, my dear, I have the honour to
present you to one of the most distinguished men
of science in Europe.   Dr. Fledgeby—Miss Dorothea Golightly, my elder sister."

The old geologist bowed pleasantly, and a smile
twinkled in his eyes as he put his hand into his
waistcoat pocket, evidently feeling for something
he had there.

CHAPTER XVIII.

OUR HERO PURSUES SCIENCE.

" THINK I have had the pleasure of meeting you before," said Dr. Fledgeby, bowing graciously to Miss Dorothea Golightly, and still fumbling mysteriously in his waistcoat pocket.

The Rector nodded significantly behind the Professor's back, intending by the action to convey his belief that his sister and Dr. Fledgeby had met at Bath or Cheltenham, very likely.

" No; I think," replied Miss Dorothea — who was firmly persuaded, from what she had heard her brother say of him, that the Professor was one of the greatest personages in the world—" that if I may venture to correct Dr. Fledgeby's recollection upon such a point—I think I never had the honour of being presented to him before; and I am sure I am delighted."

" My sister adores genius, Dr. Fledgeby," said

Mrs. Golightly. "We are all delighted to receive you at Oakingham."

"Delighted," echoed the Rector; and our hero, and Mr. Morgan, and Miss Harriet circling round the Doctor and Aunt Dorothea.

"I have met Miss Golightly before," said the geologist, with his finger and thumb still in his pocket.

"I really venture to presume," began Aunt Dorothea.

There was considerable curiosity manifested among the little group of listeners to know where Dr. Fledgeby could possibly have met Miss Dorothea. It was visibly increased when the great man of science added—

"And Miss Harriet, too."

At this remark, Aunt Harriet uttered a faint exclamation of surprise.

There was evidently something amusing to be told, for the Professor was all smiles. This was catching, and communicated itself to the Rector and everybody else—Mr. Smith, the Professor's friend, included. The faces of all wore an expression of pleased and expectant curiosity. Everybody laughed in a well-bred way; and they all, by an almost involuntary movement, edged themselves a little closer to the two central figures.

"We must apologize—indeed, we can hardly express our regret sufficiently for the circumstance, Dr. Fledgeby," said Miss Dorothea, who could not make it out at all, but was all the while most innocently unembarrassed; "but we, I am sorry to say, cannot either of us call to mind when we had the distinguished honour of making the acquaintance of the eminent Dr. Fledgeby."

"Not very long ago, Miss Golightly," said the old gentleman, with an arch look at Aunt Dorothea.

"Not long ago!" said both sisters, in a cogitative tone.

"We have not been to Bath this year," said Miss Harriet.

"It was not at Bath," said the Doctor; "and our interview was very short. Now do you recollect?"

"Prodigious memory for faces the Professor has," said the Reverend Mr. Golightly to his curate, in an undertone. "I always thought Dorothea's was very good."

"Prodigious!" said Mr. Morgan, in a whisper.

"Could it possibly have been at Cheltenham, dear?" suggested Mrs. Golightly, blandly.

"It was at Whelpton," said the geologist.

"Whelpton!" cried everybody.

" At Whelpton, Dr. Fledgeby!—to-day?" said Miss Dorothea. " Why, unfortunately, we were too late to see anybody."

" You saw me, Miss Golightly," returned the Professor, holding up the shilling. " Don't you recollect, you gave me this?"

" Oh, Dorothea!—what could have possessed you?" groaned the Rector, looking very grave.

" Whatever for?" asked Mrs. Golightly of the company generally.

Miss Dorothea had never felt so confused and ashamed before in her life; while poor Miss Harriet fairly hid herself behind her brother's shoulders.

When she had had time to recover her self-possession, she joined her brother in offering the most profuse apologies for her terrible mistake.

" Pray take back the shilling, madam," said the Professor, in the most good-tempered manner possible. " When you give it away again, bestow it on a more worthy and deserving object; and—and think no more about this matter," added the old gentleman, who now pitied the poor spinster so much, that he wished he had suffered the shilling to remain in his pocket until the opportunity had occurred for him to drop it quietly into the Rector's poor-box.

" Oh, dear, Dorothea!" groaned her brother ; " if it had been Harriet, now—but you ! Oh, dear, you ought to have known better !"

" Dinner is served, ma'am," said Tuffley, the butler, at this moment opportunely throwing open the door of the drawing-room, and thrusting in his portly person.

But poor Miss Dorothea was snuffed out for the evening, and a damper thrown upon the spirits of the company which they did not get over until the dinner was nearly at an end ; although Dr. Fledgeby did all he could to restore their equanimity by the most affable and gracious behaviour he could assume. The Rector's dry Clicquot, however, together with the thoroughly good dinner which it accompanied, and the choice old Château Margaux that followed the dinner, and the curious Port, worked wonders ; and, by the time the carriage drove up to the door to take them over to the county *conversazione* at Fuddleton, everybody, with the solitary exception of poor Miss Dorothea, had entirely recovered from the shock her ill-timed and ill-judged benefaction had caused them.

When at last they arrived at the Shire Hall, at Fuddleton, they found a brilliant company already assembled. Everybody of scientific and antiquarian tastes, every hunter after *bric-à-brac*, every collector

of objects of art and *vertu*, had contributed something to the general fund of amusement. The Hall,
lighted with numerous wax candles, was crowded
with persons of the first importance in Loamshire;
and, altogether, the *réunion* may be described as a
complete success. Cases of preserved butterflies,
cabinets of minerals, pictures, antique armour and
articles of wearing apparel, astoundingly powerful
microscopes and electrical batteries, and apparatus
on a most magnificent scale, were brought together
to promote the enjoyment and happiness of the
general company—who, for the most part, knew
nothing at all about them, and cared less; but admired them very much. Our distinguished acquaintance, Dr. Fledgeby, who was decidedly the
lion of the evening, suffered himself to be marched
about by his friends, and introduced to everybody
worthy of his recognition as "the distinguished
author of 'Mornings with the Mammoth and the
Mastodon';" by which proceeding much *kudos*
was reflected upon the shining bald pate of the
Rev. Samuel Golightly, the hospitable entertainer
of the great man. The mayor, aldermen, and
town councillors of Fuddleton, who had it all their
own way in the morning at the Town Hall breakfast, were now most appropriately ignored and
snubbed by the county people, who were on their

own ground, and made the most of their undoubted advantage.

Adolphus Golightly, of Oakingham Hall, Esq., with his daughters, Arabella and Georgina, and

THE SQUIRE AND LADY TATTLETON PRATT.

their brother George, were amongst the last arrivals on the scene. Our hero at once made his way to the side of his cousin Arabella, by whom he was introduced to her dear friend and former schoolfellow, Miss Thomasine Jekyll, only daughter of Thomas Jekyll, of Jekyll Place, Esq., who was on a visit at the Hall. With these ladies on either side of him, Mr. Samuel followed in the wake of the Squire, who was behaving with the greatest gallantry imaginable to old Lady Tattleton Pratt, and listening with a courteous ear to her not too good-natured remarks concerning such of her acquaintance as she recognized—and she knew pretty well all the county.

"Figgings," said the Lady Mayoress to her spouse, " Figgings, we're nowhere here."

She had sat, by virtue of her own rank, next to Lady Tattleton Pratt at the breakfast in the morning, and now her ladyship passed her by with only the slighest inclination possible of her head of hair.

" Why not, Mariar?" asked his worship, angrily —for he was equally as cognizant as his wife of the unpleasant fact.

" If I was you, Mr. Figgings," continued the lady, without deigning to reply to the question, " I'd assert myself. Though you don't happen to have your gownd on, you're Mayor of Fuddleton, I suppose."

" Where shall I begin, my dear?" asked Mr. Timothy Figgins. A happy thought struck him. " Will you take anything, dear? Here, attendant —he's one of the sheriff's javelin men at the assizes, Mariar—waiter, coffee for Mrs. Alderman Figgins."

"*Caffee nore*, Figgings, *sans late*—for I never can take cream at night, and sleep after it."

" Do you hear, sir? *Caffee nore*," thundered his worship, in his most approved committing tone.

Our friend the Rector, in his triumphal progress with the author of the " Elephant's True Place in Nature," suddenly came face to face with the worshipful pair.

" Mr. Alderman—a—a—Mayor of Fuddleton— Dr. Fledgeby," said Mr. Golightly, politely, thinking it his duty to make these distinguished persons known to each other.

Their civic and scientific eminences bowed to each other.

" Mrs. Figgins, my wife—Dr. Fledgling," said his worship, pointing with extended hand to his lady, who was busy with her cup and saucer. "You have done us a great honour by visiting Fuddleton," said the Mayor.

" I hope you've all enjoyed yourselves, sir," said the Mayoress.

The geologist assured Mr. and Mrs. Figgins that the excursion party had been amply repaid for the trouble they had taken by the curious natural phenomena they had witnessed.

"We shall find my son Samuel somewhere about," said the Rector, as they walked on. "I've been looking for him all the while. He is at Cambridge now, Dr. Fledgeby."

"He could not be at a better place," observed the *savant.*

"He is a very observant, a very intellectual, and most studious young man; and—and—I'm proud of him," said his worthy father.

"You have every reason to be," said Dr. Fledgeby. "Such traits of character lead to distinction. We may predicate eminence—predicate eminence for him, my dear sir."

"I hope we may, **my dear doctor**," replied the Rector, willingly endorsing the remark of the man of science. "He is so observant, and so curious, that I am sure we shall discover him somewhere engrossed in the study of the many wonderful things displayed before us to-night; or—"

"In the pursuit of science, I hope," said Dr. Fledgeby, who loved to see about him young recruits.

At this instant they came upon our hero, seated comfortably on an ottoman, and occupied not so much in the pursuit of science as in a most charming conversation with Miss Thomasine Jekyll.

"I hope, my boy—and Dr. Fledgeby hopes—

you are availing yourself of the advantages around you," said the Rector.

"I am, my dear father," said Mr. Samuel, blush-

OUR HERO DISCOVERED IN THE PURSUIT OF SCIENCE.

ing slightly, and continuing his conversation with the lovely and accomplished lady at his side.

"Really, I enjoy it almost as much as the county ball," said Miss Jekyll.

"More—*I* do," said our hero, glancing at his fair friend with enraptured eyes.

"Are you fond of dancing?" she inquired.

"Not very—that is, not always. I am rather a clumsy partner, I believe."

"Oh, Mr. Golightly, I can't think that. You Cambridge men all know how to dance, I'm sure. Now, tell me, is Cambridge a very, very wicked place?"

"Oh, not at all," sighed our hero.

"I know you have some fine—larks, I think you call them," said the lady, timidly. "I have heard my cousin Tom say so. I don't know what it means, you know."

"Of course not. It means fun, Miss Jekyll. And I—I wish you'd come with Arabella and Georgy. I don't know whether they will come this next May; but if they don't, Uncle 'Dolph has promised they shall come the May after that; and that is not so very far off, you know."

Miss Jekyll protested she should like it above all things.

"You have dances there?'

"Yes; and there are the A. D. C., and the boats, and—and—all sorts of things; though I have not seen them myself, yet."

"It must be charming," said Miss Jekyll; "a

perfect paradise of novelty and surprises for those who have never seen all the old colleges and things."

"It is," replied our hero, with enthusiasm lighting his brow.

"I'm sure, you are very comfortable, and luxurious even, in your bachelor rooms. It makes me envy you, when I hear my cousin Tom talk about it. Men have everything worth having in the world. I always used to wish I was a boy."

"And do you now?" asked Mr. Samuel.

"Well, not quite so much, I think. But we must not talk any longer—here comes Arabella."

"You are forgetting the time altogether, I think," said Miss Arabella. "We have been looking everywhere for you."

"We have been here all the time," said our hero.

When the time for the return to Oakingham came, Mr. Samuel contrived to secure a seat in his uncle's carriage, suggesting to the worthy Squire that he might prefer the company of his brother, the parson, and the two men of science; whilst it must be confessed his nephew vastly preferred the society of his cousins, and their fair and fascinating visitor.

On his safe arrival at the Rectory, our hero confessed that he could not recollect when he had spent a more pleasant evening. He went to bed; and, in his dreams, science, shillings, and Miss Thomasine Jekyll were mingled in a strange, but not altogether unmeaning jumble.

CHAPTER XIX.

MR. SAMUEL ADOLPHUS GOLIGHTLY MAKES THE
ACQUAINTANCE OF THE WHOPPER.

SINCE we last had the pleasure of meeting our hero, the Lent and May terms have glided happily by; the hot suns of the long vacation have passed over his head, and we renew our acquaintance with him at the beginning of his second October term. No longer a Freshman proper, but in all the budding dignity of a Junior Soph, Mr. Samuel is quite looked up to as an old hand by various Freshmen of the year below him. He has improved his opportunities of acquiring a sound elementary knowledge of many manly sports and pastimes. His whist, though by no means good, shows a considerable advance on what it was when first he quitted Oakingham. At billiards, such is his improvement, he now rarely gives a miss; and he has acquired a knowledge of the theory and practice of pool, under the express tuition of Mr. Pokyr. This game he finds at present exciting but expensive, as his lives go very fast before the sure aim of such proficients as the Captain T. F. O'Higgins and Mr. Pokyr. But whilst as a sportsman generally our hero has made rapid strides, his scholarlike attainments have been rather on the decline. On a fine October morning, a few days after his arrival at St. Mary's, Mr. Sneek, meeting our hero on the staircase, intimated to him that his tutor wished to have a private interview with him. Naturally, on hearing this news, Mr. Samuel was thrown into a state of considerable trepidation, in wondering what he was about to be " hauled" for.

" He's had," observed Mr. Sneek, pointing in the direction of the tutor's rooms, " a good many on 'em up this mornin'. Mr. Popham was one."

" What is it for, Sneek?" said Mr. Samuel.

" That I do *not* know, sir. But," he added, after a moment's reflection, " it must be for something."

" Dear—oh, dear!" said Mr. Samuel, who had been out to a quiet little supper the night before. " My cap was changed for this disreputable thing by some one or other. I must borrow George's or Pokyr's."

" They're both on 'em out, sir," said Mr. Sneek.

2

"That cap 'll do, sir. Pull it off directly you go in, sir."

So, straightening the battered board to the best of his ability, Mr. Samuel proceeded at once to the august presence of his tutor.

"Oh, Mr. Golightly," said the Rev. Mr. Bloke, shaking hands with his pupil, "I wanted to see you. You don't do very well at the lectures, the lecturers tell me."

"No, sir," said Mr. Samuel, with much candour.

"Well, you know, you will have your examination here directly."

At the mere mention of this unpleasant fact, our hero grew more uncomfortable; and, forgetting that the cap he held was very slenderly attached to the tassel, swung it about nervously, and without in the least knowing what he was at.

"Yes, sir," he said.

"And don't you think you had better have a private tutor, or you will be—"

"Plucked," said Mr. Golightly, smiling painfully, and swinging his cap about by the tassel more excitedly than before.

"Well, plucked was not the word I was going to make· use of, Mr. Golightly, but it was what I meant. You know, it is a serious thing."

"Yes, sir," said Mr. Samuel, now making his

cap into a machine for illustrating the properties of the centrifugal force, and causing it to describe a complete circle in its revolutions round the tassel, which was feebly secured to the rotten cloth by a pin.

"And therefore, I think, everything considered, you had better have a private tutor at once. Now, you can go either to Mr. Major, or to some gentleman in the college. There are Mr. Brown, Mr. Jones, and Mr. Robinson—all very successful in getting their men through. Which should you prefer, do you think?"

In a moment of fatal hesitation, Mr. Samuel's cap parted from the tassel, and, unhappily, caught the Reverend Mr. Bloke a blow full under the left eye. Our hero's alarm at such a catastrophe may be more easily imagined than described.

"Dear me!" exclaimed the tutor, gasping, and holding the place where the sharp corner of the board had struck his soft and fleshy cheek, whilst our hero picked up the offending missile, and poured forth a profusion of apologies. "I'll see you again, Mr. Golightly—I'm afraid I must bathe it at once;" and with this mild reproof, the reverend gentleman disappeared into his bedroom.

"What do you think I have done?" said our

hero, bursting into his friend Popham's rooms, and relating his misadventure in a breath.

Mr. Popham cheered him as much as he could; and some other gentlemen dropping in, conversation turned on the subject of " coaches." Mr. Bloke had left Mr. Popham, like our hero, to choose between Messrs. Major, Brown, Jones, and Robinson.

Gentlemen at Cambridge who are described, in academical parlance, as those " *qui honores non ambiunt,*" are more commonly known as Poll men, for they are many. Mr. Major, from his coaching exclusively for the " Poll" degree, had acquired the *sobriquet* of Poll Major, by which name he was always known. Having made this necessary explanation, we will now chronicle the conversation which took place on this important subject.

" I strongly recommend you to go to Robinson," said one of Mr. Popham's friends, who himself was a " pup" of Mr. Robinson's. " He's a regular brick. You can do just as you like: smoke your pipe over your papers at his rooms—in fact, Robinson's a brick."

" Do his men all pass?" asked our hero.

" Very nearly all," replied Mr. Robinson's "pup,' with emphasis.

" He's not half such a man as the Whopper."

The " Whopper" was a favourite *alias* of Mr. Poll Major's.

" I'll back the Whopper against any of them—and I've coached with three or four. They've different ways of putting it into you; but old Poll is always clear--there's no doubt about him."

" How do you mean?" said Mr. Popham, much interested in the merits of the rival preceptors, who were all devoutly believed by their supporters to be in possession of a Royal road to passing.

" Well, I mean this, you know," said the Whopper's "coachee"—a heavy, stolid-looking young man from the shires. " Look here—you're doing your classical subject. You come across some darned thing or another you can't make out. What's the good of a dictionary? Turn the word up—what then? Buttmann says it may mean this, and Dindorff says it is supposed to mean that, and Spitzner the other thing; but," said he, bringing his fist down on the table with a crash, " give me the Whopper. *He tells you what it is!*"

The value of such an instructor could not be gainsaid; and, accordingly, both our hero and Mr. Popham determined to throw up Messrs. Brown. Jones, and Robinson, and enlist themselves under the standard of Poll Major.

" His tips are worth any money," said the gentleman who had just favoured the company with his views on disputed classical points. "I haven't got through myself, certainly; but that's my fault, not Poll's. His tips in arithmetic are something splendid. I can do anything now at it, and regularly stump the examiners. At my last Little Go, I had this:—'What ideas does the figure 7 convey to your mind?' Well, I stumped the beggars. The Whopper gave us the same question two days before. There, now!" said his enthusiastic "pup," "what do you think of that? But," he continued, with a melancholy pull at the pewter of beer by his side, "that infernal Paley always floors me."

"I wish Paley had never written his confounded 'Evidences,'" said another.

"Ah!" sighed the first speaker, "if that had not been done, somebody else would have written something worse for examiners to make you get up. I used to wish Euclid had never been born; but it's no good wishing such things—or you might wish there were no examinations at all."

"I hate Paley as I hate the doose," observed the young gentleman who had advocated the claims of Mr. Robinson as a coach. "I can't recollect the stuff at all. I always mix the chapters up with one another. I took the book in, but I'll be dashed if I could tell where the answers were; and so I got plucked in it, after getting through in everything else."

" Ah!" exclaimed Mr. Poll Major's admirer, "you should go to the Whopper. Needn't bother over long chapters, or analyses that are worse than the chapters themselves. Poll's got a system of his own for Paley: reduces a chapter of thirty pages to half a dozen lines. You can't forget, if you try."

" How ?" asked Mr. Samuel, with great interest.

" Why, here you are—here's the chapter all about miracles. You can answer all the questions out of this. The examiners always set some out of it. This is what I call compression," said he, triumphantly reciting the lines :—

> "'Posterior ages—distant climes;
> Transient rumours—naked rhymes;
> Particular—otiose assent,
> Affirmance of allowed event.
> False perception—some succeed,
> Some are doubtful—thousands feed.'

" Now," he continued, " I contend, if a fellow can't remember that, he's a fool. Fifty different questions can be answered with that verse."

" Astounding !" said our hero.

" We'll take another chapter," said the former speaker. " Don't they always ask, ' In what does the Christian differ from all other religions?' Well, here you are—whole chapter in a nutshell. Take you a week to get up a quarter of it—here you have it in a second :—

> 'No invisible world, no duties austere,
> No impassioned devotion, no forwardness here;
> No fashions depraved, no sophistical views,
> No narrow mind this, like intolerant Jews';
> This religion, and that from the hands apostolical,
> Has no views political or ecclesiastical.'

" Well, now," said the speaker, having glibly repeated the Whopper's rhymes, " what more can you have ?"

" How very clever !" said Mr. Samuel. " Popham and I have worked for days at that very chapter."

" Ah ! and the beauty of it is, all the chapters are just as easy. You can't forget the verses if you try. But the doose of it is, you may put the wrong ones to the questions, and you forget what it's all about. But a *memoria technica's* a fine thing."

That evening our hero — having previously waited upon the Reverend Mr. Bloke, and made fresh apologies for the wound he had inflicted in the morning, and also announced his decision in favour of Mr. Major—made his way to the Whopper's house. A great brick house, standing back a few yards from the street, with a great front door, and a bold brass knocker to it, was the abode of the renowned Poll coach. The door stood a little ajar, and our hero could see into the hall as he stood waiting for the appearance of a servant in answer to his knock. A strong odour of tobacco came through the opening as he stood there. As no one appeared, Mr. Samuel knocked again.

"Who's that knocking at the door?" demanded a basso profundo from within.

Now, as our hero was a perfect stranger, it seemed useless to reply "I," and equally improbable that the name of Golightly would be known.

Before he had time to act, however, the voice continued—

"You've all been told not to knock, times without number;" and, simultaneously with this remark, a trim servant-maid came, and ushered our hero into the presence of Mr. Poll Major.

When Mr. Golightly had stated his business to Mr. Major, he looked about him.

The Whopper was a tall man, a stout man, and a very jovial-looking man, and was seated in his arm-chair by his fireside, smoking his pipe, and drinking beer out of a flagon. Our hero had expected something more like his old tutor, Mr.

Morgan, than this Bacchanalian personage before
him.

The Whopper spoke in a mighty voice—

OUR HERO'S FIRST INTERVIEW WITH POLL MAJOR.

" I beg your pardon, I'm sure, but I did not
know you were a stranger ; and we've hundreds of
fellows coming in and out, and if they did not let
'emselves in, we should have nothing else to do.

Always walk straight in, and look about in the rooms till you find me. I'll set you to work."

The Whopper now passed the beer to our hero, and told him to sit down. Mr. Samuel, having taken a pull at the flagon, sat down opposite the great man.

" Now," said Poll Major, smiling, " what don't you know, Mr. Golightly ?"

Our hero did his best to tell his coach what he knew, and left him to infer what he did not know.

" I hope you will get me through, sir," said Mr. Samuel.

" Ah, there's the mistake that's made! You must get yourself through. I shall do the same for all of you. I think you will be all right."

Mr. Samuel asked why Mr. Poll Major came to this conclusion.

" Well, sir," said the Whopper, smiling, " they say "—puff—" that the Little Go "—puff, puff— " is an inane attempt to fathom the "—puff— " depths of human ignorance. It may be. Now, there are two sorts of ignorance. There's simple ignorance—that's where a man doesn't know anything in the world, and knows he doesn't know anything. That's curable. Then there's compound ignorance—that's when a man doesn't know anything, and doesn't know that he doesn't know anything. You follow me?"

"Perfectly," responded our hero.

"Well, Mr. Golightly, I'm in hopes your case belongs to the former category."

"I hope so, sir."

"Well—now begin at once, is my motto. So take this paper on Latin Accidence, and sit down in the next room, and see what you can make of it. By the time you haven't done it, a lot of men will have come; and we shall begin the Cicero and Paley for the Little Go."

In accordance with Mr. Major's instructions, our hero went into the room indicated, took his seat at the extreme end of the long table—covered with baize once green, but now black with years of ink-spots—and tried his hand at the Accidence paper.

In half an hour, numbers of gentlemen came trooping in, and the room was filled to overflowing. Mr. Major, planting himself against the wall, with one foot on a chair, and holding before him a folio volume of Cicero, commenced his disquisition. Having put the history of the period before his pupils in terms as brief as the Paley verses before enumerated, he proceeded to construe a chapter. This done, he said—

" Now, gentlemen—look at your books, there. Attention! Come, Mr. Green, you can talk presently. Now, we will pick out a few of what I call the hard words."

An instance illustrative of Mr. Major's theory of compound ignorance soon occurred.

" Parts of *edo*, Mr. Green."

" *Edidi-editum !*" in breathless haste.

" You know the meaning of *edo* here ?"

" Yes—*to eat*, of course."

" No—that's precisely what it isn't."

The next gentleman to Mr. Green having made a successful shot at *edo*, the Whopper proceeded.

" What part of the verb is *gerendum*, Mr. Noodel ?"

Mr. Noodel's gaze became riveted on his book. but he said nothing.

" Is it a gerund or a supine?"

" Supine."

" No."

" Gerund, then."

" Which? There are three—*di, do,* and *dum.* Now, which is this ?"

" Gerund in *di.*"

" What! geren*dum?*"

" In *do*, then," replied the pupil.

" No."

"Well, then, in *dum.*"

"Ah! now you're right.   You must be careful, old fellow, or you'll never do for the examiners."

Matters proceeded pleasantly enough, enlivened

MR. MAJOR BRIDGING OVER EIGHTEEN CENTURIES.

by such episodes, to the end of the chapter.   The Paley was then begun; and here, as it is not generally taught in public schools, the shots were much more wildly speculative than at the Cicero. The Whopper took up his post on the hearth-rug, and dictated the verse, to which he had reduced all that was likely to be required of the chapter in hand. Some of his illustrations were very original, and his proofs unique, of their kind. He connected his pupils with Apostolic times by stretching his legs wide apart, observing, as he did so—

"Now, here we are in the nineteenth century—right leg; left leg, first century, A.D. Well—now, then, you perceive the connection between 'em."

And then Mr. Major stepped off the space of eighteen centuries, twelve inches at a time, giving a succinct history of the same as he went along. His system was rapid, if not thorough. The Whopper was the very prince of crammers, and earned £2,000 a-year at it. Mr. Samuel found his lectures quite as amusing as they were edifying.

CHAPTER XX.

OUR HERO FINDS A SEAT IN THE SENATE HOUSE
PLACED AT HIS DISPOSAL.

IN the nineteenth chapter of this authentic history was laid before our readers a truthful and graphic sketch of an hour spent at a Poll Coach's lecture. Enough—it has been said by our great Tupper, and, indeed, by many smaller lights before him—is as good as a feast; therefore, we shall not ask our readers to accompany us again, with Mr. Popham, our hero, and others of their friends, to the *matinées* or *soirées* held *de die in diem* by the Whopper. Suffice it for our purpose to say that, all through that eventful term, our hero, Mr. Samuel Golightly, steadily regarded all the mundane objects which presented themselves to his gaze through a haze of Little Go. Did he quaff his college ale: it smacked of the Previous Exam. Did he smoke the pipe of solace, or puff the fragrant cigar: they were flavoured with

Little Go. For Mr. Samuel sagaciously reflected, that neither in his beer nor in his bacca would there be comfort for him—if he missed his Exam.

"George," he said to his cousin, employing unwonted slang, "if I'm ploughed for this infernal Exam., what will my Fa say? I can never look Aunt Dorothea full in the face again."

"Don't be in a funk about it, Sam!" said his cousin. "You're bound to do the examiners."

"Am I?" asked our hero, mopping a cold perspiration from his lofty brow. "I wish I felt sure of it. The papers I may do all right, if I have good luck; but the *viva voce* is safe to stump me. I shall be as n-nervous as a baby in arms, George," proceeded Mr. Samuel, in a sudden burst of perspiration. "Coolness I have tried to make a practice of; but I feel the courage that might serve to make a man march up to the cannon's mouth without fear is, in fact, nothing to what is wanted when one has to sit down at a small table opposite an Examiner."

Many men fail to attain the success which is within their reach through underrating the difficulties with which they have to contend. It will be seen, from the conversation quoted above, that this was not our hero's case. As, day after day, he drew his pen through one of the days that intervened between him and his Little Go, he grew more ardu-

ous in his application to the seven subjects of which
he would then have to display a competent knowledge.

During the last fortnight, he shut himself up like
an anchorite, and worked at his sums with the re-
gularity of one of Mr. Babbage's calculating ma-
chines.   He attended twice daily at the Whopper's,
and covered quires of paper in expressing the ideas
conveyed to his mind by every one of the nine nu-
meral signs; and even noughts were not neglected.
His mind became an arithmetical chaos, in which
vulgar and decimal fractions, compound practice,
and double rule of three heaved and tossed in vol-
canic eruption.   Perpetual attention to his Paley
had inseparably mixed all the famous nine first
chapters in hopeless medley.   It was only too plain
that his health was giving way.

Under these distressing circumstances, he told his
cousin George to write, in his next letter home, a
hint of his state of health; so that, in case of a
breakdown, he might at least have that excuse.

Mr. George's letter struck terror into the hearts
of the family at the Rectory.   It was the first impulse of the ladies to rush off to the rescue of their
dear knight, and snatch him from the clutches of
Vice-Chancellor and Dons.   But the Rector's wiser
counsel prevailed.   They remained at home.   And

now the peculiar temperament of all the members of the family circle exhibited itself in their methods of treating "poor dear Samuel's" case. The Rector wrote a letter full of fine thoughts, couched in finer language; Mrs. Golightly packed up and despatched a goodly hamper of jams, and other appetizing confections, for which she is justly celebrated; while the two maiden aunts did a still wiser thing. Miss Dorothea wrote a note to her nephew, in which she expressed her great regret at his invalid condition, and her admiration of the hard study that had brought it about; and, further, recommended him daily horse exercise. Such advice was kind, thoughtful, and eminently practical; but what was much more so was the cheque that accompanied it. At the same time, Miss Dorothea urged her nephew to bear up with spirit for the examination, and, after it was over, purchase the horse of his fancy.

These several marks of the affection of his family considerably reassured our hero; and on the eventful morning which ushered in the first day of the examination, he was quite as calm as could be expected. He awoke in a state of feverish expectation For him, breakfast was a hollow sham. With cap awry, and gown half on, half off, and rapidly turning over the pages of his Euclid, Mr. Samuel made his way along King's Parade, to the edifice at the end of it, wherein the inquisitors await their victims. Our hero was among the first to put in an appearance, and was conducted to the place prepared for him by the senior bull-dog in attendance. He now had time to look around him—for he had pocketed his book on the steps of the Senate House. His name, "Golightly, St. Mary's," was printed on a little label, and stuck on the long table before him. There were other Gs above him and below him. Messrs. Pokyr and Popham presently took their seats, almost close together, at another table. He saw many men he knew enter and take their seats ; but there was no friend near him. In a few minutes the great Hall was full. The Examiners, in their caps, gowns, and M.A. hoods, appeared on the scene with bundles of papers, which they distributed along the tables. Then began a tremendous scratching of pens, which never ceased till the clock struck twelve, and the three hours were up ; and—

> "Happy then the youth in Euclid's axioms tried,
> Though little versed in any art beside."

To his own great astonishment, out of the twelve questions on the paper, Mr. Samuel was able to write out eight "props." to his entire satisfaction.

The Whopper's "tip propositions" had all turned up trumps; and, as soon as the morning's work was over, he rushed off exultant to his Coach, whom he discovered surrounded by "pups," who were detailing, with appropriate animation or dejection, how little or how much they had been able to do of the morning papers; while others, whose turn was still to come, were busily getting up tips for the afternoon.

Our hero next met his friend Popham, who was exceedingly downcast in spirit. Although he had taken in a number of "props.," ready written out on Senate House paper, kindly supplied by friends who had bagged it in previous Exams., such was the exemplary vigilance of the Examiners and their attendant myrmidons, the bull-dogs, that poor little Percy Popham could never once "check it," as he expressed it, to pull the papers out of his trousers. He brought them out as he had taken them in—though rather more crumpled, from leaning heavily against them. As he put it, he "knew well enough he was a dead pluck already;" but Mr. Samuel encouraged him to go on, and not give up so soon.

Mr. Pokyr was more lucky. He had adopted a system of cribbing entirely his own—which, he said, had "come off like a book." It consisted of a series of scraps of paper, covered with microscopic signs and symbols, which the ingenious inventor, probably, alone could decipher. Next day, Paley came on for discussion. Again our hero wrote away for three hours with great rapidity; and, as he counted twenty sheets of paper scribbled over, felt sure he had " done enough." Mr. Pokyr took " Coward's Analysis " in—and used it, while the Examiner read the *Revue de Deux Mondes*. Mr. Popham answered six questions; but, unfortunately for him, the Examiner in this subject, Mr. Blunt, had not the least taste for poetry, and Percy's answers were metrical. They consisted entirely of the Whopper's *memoria technica* verses, a specimen of which we have already given. Arithmetic, the day after, passed off easily for everybody, as the gentleman who set the paper— the incumbent of a college living close to Cambridge—was a merciful man, deeply versed in classic lore, and possessing a natural dislike to figures. Accordingly, his questions were simple, and his standard low.

Then came the horrors of classics, Latin and Greek, the pitfalls of Greek Testament, and the ordeal of *viva voce* examination. Our hero felt afraid that his performances in translation were anything but up to the mark. Mr. Pokyr, who had employed a little boy to read the cribs through to him daily for a week before—and took the books in besides—admitted he had "got through everything slick," while Mr. Popham confessed to having done more than he expected.

When our hero saw man after man coming back from the terrible *viva voce*, when every minute brought him nearer the dreaded *vis-à-vis* with an omniscient M.A., he felt absolutely ill. His turn came. He marched into the middle of the hall, and seated himself opposite Savage, of Magdalen. Mr. Savage had the reputation of plucking nine shaky men out of ten. Our hero trembled; his cheeks flushed, and his tongue became dry. Opposite him sat a cadaverous and wholly unsympathetic personage, who positively leered with diabolical malice over his white choker at the prospect of another victim.

"Mr. Golightly, St. Mary's," said Mr. Savage, without looking up from his list of names.

"Y-yes, sir," gasped our hero, faintly.

"Look at the fifth verse — where the pencil mark is—and read four verses."

Mr. Golightly read four verses of the "Gospel according to St. Mark."

"Go on—translate," said the merciless voice of his tormentor.

Our hero stammered through the verses. No motion, no word, no sound came from the Examiner to say right or wrong to what he did.

Mr. Savage simply sat and stared. Presently he spoke. It was in a sepulchral tone.

" There is a reference here to Angels."

" Y-yes," gasped our hero, looking wildly for it in his book.

He had lost the place for the third time.

" Can you tell me how Angels are first mentioned by name ?"

Mr. Samuel pressed his brow, and thought.

Verses and texts, familiar friends, rose in his troubled mind ; but as yet he racked his memory in vain.

Suddenly his hand fell, his eye lighted. As if by inspiration, he had it.

" ' Legion,' " he gulped out, " ' for we are many.' "

Mr. Savage smiled—horribly.

Our hero felt his foot was in it.

" I will ask you another question referring to Scripture history," said the Examiner, awfully. " In verse seven, we read of a ' merciful man.' Whom do you recollect as the most merciful man mentioned in Old Testament history."

Again did our hero think—deeply, silently.

Seconds flew by, and Mr. Savage only read his list. He gave no hint—no sign.

" Og," at last timidly suggested Mr. Samuel.

" Who, sir?" demanded his questioner, angrily.

" Og, the King of Bashan, sir."

" Why, sir?"

" B-because—I mean, ' F-for his mercy endureth for ever.' "

" That will do, sir. Send up the gentleman who sits next you."

And our hero's Greek Testament *viva voce* was over.

He got through his two other similar ordeals in the same morning, and left the Senate House as full of fears and hopes as a maiden in her first love.

At Mr. Poll Major's, he found Mr. Pokyr and other friends assembled, talking in a jubilant key.

" I know I've floored the beggars this time," said Mr. Pokyr.

" That's all right," returned the Coach, who was not so satisfied of a successful result as his pupil. " Now you had better look up your Mechanics, as you mean to go in for the next General."

" No more work this term, sir," said Mr. Pokyr, quite affectionately ; " besides, I know my Mechanics better than anything."

"Now, here's the first question," said the Whopper, reading from a paper in his hand. "Tell us how you do that!"

"What is it? Gravitation? 'If a pin be placed perpendicularly, with the thinner extremity, commonly called the point, downwards, on a horizontal plane surface—as, for instance, a mirror'—it won't stand. Why does it fall, and all that? Well, now, look here! I should deal with that in this way. If a pin were placed on a mirror with the thicker extremity, commonly called the head, downwards, it would not stand. Therefore, *a fortiori*, it won't stand on its thinner extremity, commonly called the point!"

"That'll never do," said the Whopper, laughing.

"I know the Examiners like the light of nature. Look here—in my Greek Test. paper they asked me to make a map tracing the course of the river Jordan. I couldn't do that, you know. Went on to the next. 'What is the modern name of the country on the other side of the Jordan?' Well, my answer was, 'It all depends upon which side of the river you stand, you know.' So it does, of course. Scored there, I think. Tickle the Examiner's fancy. 'Clever fellow that Pokyr, of St. Mary's—let him through.'"

"Well, good-bye, old fellow," said the Coach, shaking his precocious pupil by the hand. "See you again next term, I suppose? I hope you're all through."

"Now, Golightly," said Mr. Pokyr, linking his arm through that of his friend, "we will go down to old Wallop's stables, and look at what he has got."

"Very well, Pokyr," returned Mr. Samuel. "I rely on your judgment, mind, for I never bought a horse before in my life."

So they strolled down to Mr. Wallop's together.

"What sort of a hoss is it, Mr. Pokyr, as your friend wants?" asked the dealer, who had been roused from his after-dinner nap to see his customers.

"Let us see what you have got, Wallop," said Mr. Pokyr, warily.

An ancient charger, that had seen service in the yeomanry, was forthwith led out for inspection.

"Won't do, Wallop," was Mr. Pokyr's remark.

"He aint much to look at, but he's all over quality," remarked the dealer. "Look at the way he carries his head—and his tail an' all, for the matter of that. Don't like him! Well, bring out that little Irish cob I gave such a price for the other day."

Mr. Pokyr mounted the cob.

"Quiet—like a lamb," said the dealer.

"Not much in front of you," said the connoisseur.

"WHAT, DON'T YOU LIKE HIM?"

"No; and there aint much behind you either, is there?—and that's a balance."

"Goes rather dotty?"

"Sound as a roach."

The gray's merits having been disposed of, a groggy bay horse was produced.

"HE CARRIES YOU BEAUTIFUL!"

"What! don't you like *him?*" asked Mr. Wallop, in a marvelling tone of voice. "Why, that hoss can jump like a kitten; clever at his fences; never stumbled in his life. He's the best roadster

in the county. Meant to keep him for myself.
Never was sick nor sorry in his life. 'Appy 'orse
'e is—never off his feed. Sound as a bell of
brass."

These remarks were jerked out, one at a time,
in reply to remarks of Mr. Pokyr's.

Our hero, at Mr. Wallop's wish, mounted this
unique specimen of horseflesh. The animal resented the liberty by refusing to go one step forwards, and by backing, at a great pace, against the
stable wall, and nearly jerking Mr. Golightly out
of the saddle.

"Only his play—just at starting," observed Mr.
Wallop. "He carries you beautiful! Look at his
head—always up in the air, showing hisself off! I
call him a gentleman's horse—that's what I call
him."

Probably our hero's innocent and unsuspecting
appearance had made Mr. Wallop parade these
"crocks"—as Pokyr termed them—for his inspection; for the wily dealer soon found "metal more
attractive" in a showy little bay cob, rising six, and
very taking in all his paces.

"That will do," said our hero, giving his friend
a nudge.

After some half an hour or so spent in trying the
animal, discussing his various merits, and haggling

over the price, the bay cob became the property of Mr. Golightly at the moderate figure of forty-five pounds.

" And now, I ask, where is he a-going to stan' at livery, sir?" said Mr. Wallop, addressing our hero; "for that cob, he's so sweet on his quarters here, that he'll never be easy in his mind nowhere else in Cambridge."

With a promise that, when his master was up, his horse should inhabit the box so necessary to his happiness and tranquillity, our hero and his Mentor left the establishment of Mr. Isaac Wallop, licensed dealer in horses.

CHAPTER XXI.

MR SAMUEL GOLIGHTLY and his new purchase arrived safely at Oakingham, on the day after the events recorded in our last chapter. Miss Dorothea expressed herself perfectly satisfied with the use that had been made of her cheque; and all the family were astonished to see our hero looking so well, after the trying circumstances in which he had, for some time past, been placed.

It was on the neat little bay cob he had purchased of Mr. Wallop that Mr. Samuel trotted over to the market town of Fuddleton, on the third day after his arrival at home. An intelligent observer might have noticed a considerable amount of excitement in his demeanour; and it must be confessed that, as they splashed along over the soft country roads, the bay got more cuts from our

hero's whip than he either desired or deserved.
Mr. Samuel rode boldly into the yard of the principal inn, where the family were in the habit of
" putting up," as it is termed, when they made a
stay of an hour or so in the town of Fuddleton
—which event commonly happened once a-week,
usually on a Saturday, that being market day.
Having dismounted, and refreshed himself with a
glass of bitter beer, our hero made his way to the
new telegraph office—which is situate in the
Market-square—and, with as much confidence of
manner as he could assume, demanded of the clerk
in attendance there, if there was any telegram for
Mr. Samuel Adolphus Golightly. The official at
first did not condescend to make any reply—after
the manner of his class—being disposed to treat
the public generally in the light of impertinent in-
truders upon his particular privacy and retirement.
The personage whom we have called the official
was a sallow-faced and grimy youth of about nine-
teen or twenty. He was engaged—it being just
about twelve o'clock—in the engrossing occupation
of eating bread and cheese out of a piece of news-
paper, and was evidently amused with something
he was reading as he ate ; while his junior—the
little boy who carried out the messages—eyed him
with envious gaze.

Mr. Samuel, who was never impatient or domineering, waited until the clerk thought proper to notice his remarks.

"No, there aint." was the answer he received.

"Well, I expect a message this morning," said our hero.

"If it's sent, it'll come," remarked the official, in the intervals at which the bread and cheese allowed him to speak. "It aint come yet."

As there was no seat in the office, and no particular encouragement to remain leaning on the counter, Mr. Samuel returned to his inn, and there partook of a second glass of bitter beer, and performed an exploit which he would have been quite incapable of before he went up to the University—namely, addressed some highly complimentary observations to the pretty and affable barmaid at the Stag. Half an hour after his first visit, he made a second journey to the office, and repeated his former question.

The machine was clicking away, and the needle rapidly spelling out its message.

"It's now come," said the clerk, who had finished his bread and cheese.

Mr. Samuel seized the piece of yellow paper on which the clerk had transcribed the message, and read—

" *Sneek, Cambridge, to S. A. Golightly, Esq., Fuddleton.*

" *Golightly, first class; Pokyr, second; Popham, plucked.*"

" Good gracious!" said our hero, as he folded the paper, and put it away in his pocket for further perusal. " This is better news than I expected." And then, thinking of his friend, who had not been so successful, he added—" What will poor Popham do when he hears the news?"

He returned to the Stag, mounted his cob, and rode as gaily into Oakingham as ever he had done in his life. The good news that our hero was through his Little Go was received at the Rectory with manifest symptoms of delight on all sides; and everybody coincided in regarding Mr. Samuel in the light of a prodigy of learning and steadiness. Our friend, the Rector, was perfectly satisfied; and testified his contentedness — when the *Standard*, containing the list, arrived at Oakingham next day —by making his son the object of an appropriate complimentary speech.

The vacation passed rapidly away, and our hero soon found himself back again at Alma Mater. Here he met all his old friends; congratulated Mr. Pokyr, and condoled with Mr. Popham.

The latter was reading hard for a second attempt; while the former, out of play-hours, was busily engaged upon an elaborate series of cribs for his General, constructed upon an improved system.

One day, as our hero was quietly sitting at lunch, he heard an excited rap at his door, and in rushed Mr. Eustace Jones, his neighbour overhead, making profuse apologies for the intrusion—the reason of which our hero could not quite comprehend. Simultaneously, Mr. Sneck appeared on the leads outside the window, and something buff kept flapping blindly against the panes of glass.

Then our hero learnt that Mr. Jones's owl had escaped, and was the cause of all the commotion. When the bird had been secured by Sneck, Mr. Jones entered into some particulars of the origin and growth of his great affection for British birds, which had led him to try to tame an owl. A few days after, the sly old bird—taking advantage of an open window, after dusk—bade its master adieu, with a loud " Too-whit, too-whoo!" which echoed through the silence of the great quad. The mathematician's next venture was a hawk, properly secured against nocturnal flights by having had one of its wings operated upon by our old acquaintance Mr. Gallagher, who supplied him.

" If you please, sir," said the garrulous Mrs.

Cribb to our hero, " you rec'lec' Mr. Jones's bird bein' caught in your room?"

" Yes, Mrs. Cribb," said our hero.

" He's got another now," said the old lady, putting her finger in her mouth, and sucking it affectionately. " Which, 'xcuse me, sir, a Howl I did *not* mind, but a Nawk I *can't* abear."

" Oh," said our hero, " you don't like the hawk, Mrs. Cribb! Perhaps you don't like birds? Why, I was very nearly being tempted to buy a parrot myself, the other day."

" I do not dislike no gentleman's pets, sir, but birds of prey bites horrible, and parrits is inclined to peck when your eye aint on 'em. But, I beg your pardon—here's this note the Master's servant just gev me, and asked me to give to you."

Our hero found that Dr. and Mrs. Oldman requested the pleasure of his company on Thursday evening, at half-past eight o'clock. This was the first occasion on which he had been honoured with an invitation to a Perpendicular, as such entertainments are styled.

Punctually at a quarter past nine on the evening in question, with his arm linked in that of Mr. Pokyr, our hero rapped at the door of the Master's Lodge. It was a curious, rambling old building, of all dates and styles—a long succession of Masters

of St. Mary's having lived in it, and added to it, or
taken from it, according to their particular notions.
Our friends were conducted by Dr. Oldman's portly
butler up a fine old oak staircase, into a very long
and charming antique picture gallery, hung with
many portraits of interest, from the Founder of the
College downwards.   Here Mrs. Oldman—a lady
of the most prepossessing appearance and manners,
many years younger than her husband—was receiving her guests.   Presently, a string of a dozen
gentlemen marched up from dinner in Indian file,
the stout person of the Master of St. Mary's bringing up the rear.

There were among them a bishop, a great poet,
our old friend Dr. Fledgeby, and other University
magnates.

A move was now made for the drawing-room,
which communicated with the gallery.   Here, our
hero had an opportunity of discovering the meaning of the title by which these entertainments are
known among the undergraduates, as he remained
in a perpendicular attitude, with nobody to talk to,
for an hour and a half.

At last, Mrs. Oldman presented him to an old-
looking young lady, in amber silk, who occupied a
prominent position on an ottoman in the centre of
the room.

This lady at once asked our hero if he was a mathematical man, intimating that her name was Hart, and that her father was the astronomer of that name, and had been Senior Wrangler in his year; and that she would have been Second Wrangler herself if she had been permitted to go in for the examination, as her father made her work all the Senate House papers in "her year," as she termed it.

When she discovered that Mr. Samuel knew nothing of those high branches of mathematics in which she delighted, Miss Hart's interest in him was gone, and conversation flagged accordingly; while, on his part, our hero could not form a very favourable opinion of mathematical ladies.

Music, vocal and instrumental, having been given in abundance, the great poet, at half-past eleven, made a move for bed. Dr. Fledgeby wished his old colleague, the Master, and his lady, good night, and a general move was made into the picture gallery again, where a cold "stand up" supper was laid out—the table being decorated with numerous decanters of the worthy doctor's curious old wine. Our hero had the pleasure of seeing the poet eat a sandwich, and of pouring out a glass of water for Mrs. Bishop. Her right reverend husband partook of the same light refreshment; and the general company having retired, nobody was left but the undergraduates of the college who had been honoured with the doctor's invitation.

They settled down upon the viands and the claret with laudable determination; while the Master of St. Mary's and Mrs. Oldman stood by the huge open fireplace, and looked benignly on, and talked at intervals about the college boat. The fifteen vigorous young gentlemen who represented the undergraduate interest on the occasion, having eaten their supper, shook hands with the doctor and Mrs. Oldman; and, as they fought in the hall for their caps and gowns, declared "Old Tubbs"— as the Master of St. Mary's was affectionately styled in the collegiate corporation over which he reigned —"was a jolly old brick, and his wife the nicest lady in the 'Varsity."

CHAPTER XXII.

OUR HERO HAS DEALINGS WITH A JEW.

THE present historian and biographer cannot help perceiving that it is something of an anomaly to call his hero a Freshman at this advanced stage of his academical career. The same notion may have crossed the minds of some of his readers; and it is only doing justice to that amiable and appreciative body to inform them that the author is painfully aware of his shortcomings in this and other matters. However, to resume our history.

It was May, with all its associations of grass lamb and spinach, buttercups and daisies; more than that, it was late in the month—nigh on the Derby Day, in fact—and Cambridge at the end of May is seen at its best. The Carnival is kept then. Then the ancient town wears its gayest colours; and the men run up astounding tailors' bills for plumage where-with to dazzle the lovely girls who come to see them, with sedate and ponderous Pas and Mas in their train.

The windows of our friend Mr. Fitzfoodel's rooms opened on to the Parade. His *habitat* was on the first floor, and the window of his sitting-room afforded a lounge at once comfortable and amusing. His numerous friends availed themselves freely of the advantages of this seat of an afternoon, idly drinking iced Cup, and gazing at the various personages who strolled along the pavement in the sun.

Friends and acquaintances passing along came in for a kindly nod; little eccentricities of *personnel* were received with a wild halloo, worthy of a troop of Mohocks; objectionable cads were playfully pelted with the *débris* of the luncheon table; while favourites in the money-lending and cricketing interests were invited upstairs, to refresh themselves with a "swig" at the beer tankard.

"Most confounded baw," remarked Mr. Fitzfoodel in his drawling way, holding out a note penned by the fair fingers of his sister.

"What's that, Jockey?" asked Mr. Chutney—who, in a morning coat, with gorgeous monogram buttons down it, which coat encased a gorgeous blue and pink shirt, with startling studs in the front, lounged in a charming *negligé* attitude in the window seat. "What's a baw, old boy?"

" Everything baws me, Tommy," replied his friend. " I declare, no matter what I do to protect myself, I'm always being victimized."

On the tragic stage, Mr. Chutney would have pulled a face as long as a well-known stringed instrument, and ejaculated, in orotund voice, "Alas!" In real life, of course, he laughed at his friend's misery. But Mr. Calipee, who was one of the company, readily sympathized with poor Mr. Fitzfoodel's troubles.

" Just my case, Fitz," he sighed.

" What's the row, then—in the note, I mean?" asked Mr. Pokyr, bluntly coming to the point.

" Well, I never was a family sort of fellow, Jack," replied their host. " I mean, some fellows are intimate, you know, at their homes, and all that. I never was—"

" Poor devvle!"

" When I was a boy at Harrow, I always hated going home for the ' vacs.' Feeling's grown on me. Got a prodigal father, you see—try to be a forgiving son, and all that; but there are things human nature can't stand."

Mr. Pokyr playfully snatched the note from his friend's hand at this stage of his homily.

" Oh — people coming up, that's all. Sisters coming?"

" Father—mother—brother—sisters—all at one fell swoop," gasped Mr. Fitzfoodel. " Calipee, support me. What was that broke the thingamy's back ?"

" The—a—a—l-last straw," said our hero, ever ready with his apt quotation.

" Ah, Golightly, minor—as we should have called you at school if we had known you then—my back is broken now."

Perceiving at once that this was pleasantry on Fitzfoodel's part, Mr. Samuel laughed ; and as his laugh was very good-natured and very hearty, everybody caught it, and laughed too—till Mr. Fitzfoodel, their entertainer, began to feel himself a wit.

" Curiously enough," said our hero, " my people are coming up too, this term ; for my Fa and Ma, and both my aunts, are very anxious to come to Cambridge in the race week."

" Miss Jekyll is staying at your house, I think? I suppose she'll come to complete the party," observed Mr. Pokyr.

At this remark, our hero was observed to blush deeply.

" I only thought she might be, you know," added his friend.

Two London costers, with a cart-load of plants

in bloom, uttering their familiar cry in an unfamiliar place, next engaged the attention of our party.

"All a-blowin', a-growin'—a-blowin', a-growin'—
a-growin', a-blowin'! There, gentlemen, buy a few
pots o' nice flowers."

"How much for the lot?"

"These here three pots four shillin's, sir. There
—a old pair o' bags, your honour, sir."

As it was evident, after some further parleying,
that no business was likely to be done—the older
coster of the two remarking to his partner that
"These gents wor too full of chaff to be up to anything;" and further, as it was evident the flowers in
the cart would be watered gratuitously—the contents of one jug had already wetted the road—the
flower cart drove slowly on.

Our hero was leaning a little way out of the window, when a greasy voice struck his ear.

"I knows a real genelman when I sees one. Beg
pardon, sir—how do, sir—you rec'lects me? I sold
you a beautiful parrot last term, sir."

It was true. The Jew, who, on his last visit, had
brought with him an aviary on wheels, now appeared stocked with real fur rugs and noble pairs
of horns. Our hero fought rather shy of a renewal
of business relations with this child of the favoured
race, the last transaction having been against him

—for he bought a bird one day, described as " the best talker in the world, but a leetle shy afore strangers," for three pounds and a heap of old clothes ; and was glad to change him a day or two after, on payment of three pounds more, for a bird that really could talk.

" Who's your friend, Golightly?" asked Mr. Pokyr.

" It's only the man I bought my parrot of last term," replied our hero.

" Buy a nice pair o' horns, sir, to-day? Do, sir —take anything for 'em. Old clothes, sir—old boots—anything. Looks 'andsome in a room, or over a door, they do."

" Not to-day — future occasion, perhaps," said Pokyr. " Be off!"

As fate would have it, the Jew vendor of buffalo horns met our hero close to St. Mary's, and offered his tempting wares in his most seductive manner.

" Not to-day," said Mr. Samuel, hurrying along.

But who ever could shake off a merchant of the seed of Israel, whose keen eye to profit urged him on? In a moment of weakness our hero listened— hesitated—was lost !

" Well, come up to my rooms; perhaps I might buy a pair—that is, if they're very cheap."

"Cheap as dirt, sir; but I dursen't go into the college, sir, with you. I've been put out afore—often."

"Well, then, never mind," said Mr. Golightly.

"'Xcuse me, sir—is one o' them your windows?" said the Israelite, pointing to a row of windows within easy reach of the ground, in St. Mary's-lane.

"That *is* my window."

"I aint a-going to try for to get through, bein' narrow—though I dessay I've got pals as could," said the Jew, eyeing our hero's lattice in a business-like manner. "But just come and talk to us out o' the vinder, your honour."

Our hero did so.

"I never brought such horns and skins up here afore, sir. These are the real thing this time. They're the sort that always used to be kept on purpose for the London market; but now we gets some of them for the country," observed the itinerant vendor of natural curiosities.

"How much do you want for that pair?" asked Mr. Samuel, leaning out of his window.

"This here pair of beauties, sir?"

"No, the other pair—those under your arm, I mean."

"O—h," said the Jew, winking with each eye, and smiling in his most captivating way. "I

like to deal with you, sir—now that I do. You
know a good article when you see it, sir. Now,
that pair of horns as you've picked out is the finest
I ever see in my life. What a eye you've got

"HOW MUCH DO YOU WANT FOR THAT PAIR?"

Our hero's firmness began to give way under
this fire of delicate flattery.

"How much do you ask for them?" he demanded, trying to hide a smile, lest the Jew should put on something extra on the strength of his being in a good humour.

" I am giving them away at anything under thirty shillings, sir—there!" said the dealer, striking an imposing attitude, and putting the horns under his arm.

The intention obviously was to convey to our hero's mind the impression that any attempt at abatement on his side would be rejected by the Jew, who would march off to find a better market for his wares.

Mr. Golightly, however, had profited by his experience over the parrot bargain.

" Ten bob, I think, is what they're worth. I don't care about them at all."

At this the Jew put up one of his shoulders, ducked his head, and laughed a long laugh of derision.

At last, however, after some chaffering, a bargain was struck for the best pair of horns, at ten shillings and three pairs of trousers.

First, Mr. Moses put the half-sovereign into his pocket, and then stowed away the three pairs of trousers in his capacious sack.

Our hero demanded his pair of horns, and was much surprised to find that his own way of count-

ing and that of Mr. Moses differed considerably
—the latter gentleman calling Greens to witness
that " all he'd had was half a quid and two pair o'
bags."

A SPIRITED GAME OF PULL JEW, PULL GENTLEMAN.

Having both horns and "bags," he had the
best of the argument; and our hero reluctantly
found him another pair of trousers—keeping hold

of the upper extremity, while the Jew seized the lower. Having now the horns and half the "bags," our hero—to play the merchant a trick—began to haul them up; and, for a second or two, a spirited game of "Pull Jew, pull Gentleman" was played between them.

It terminated in favour of the Oriental, owing to the ill-timed advent of the tutor of St. Mary's round the corner.

"Mis-ter Go-light-ly," exclaimed the Reverend Mr. Bloke—"this is shocking indeed!"

Instantly recognizing his tutor's measured accents, our hero relinquished the "bags," and drew in his horns at the window; and waited in breathless expectation for a message that he felt certain would soon arrive.

Mr. Sneek put in his head at the door.

"If you please, sir, Mr. Bloke wishes to see you immediate, sir—if you please."

CHAPTER XXIII.

MR. GOLIGHTLY RECEIVES FRIENDS.

MR. SAMUEL ADOLPHUS GOLIGHTLY responded at once to the summons of his tutor. Hastily donning his cap and gown, he visited the angry Don—who declared, in forcible though strictly tutorial language, that, in the whole course of his experience as the friend and guide of the youth of St. Mary's, it had never been his lot to witness anything half so shocking. Our hero was prudently silent—remembering the well-worn adage, "*qui s'excuse s'accuse;*" so he sat on the extreme edge of the chair, and looked as penitent as he could.

"Had it been an after-dinner freak, Mr. Golightly, I should not have been so much surprised. But in broad daylight, and before the whole town —if they chose to be spectators of such a scene!— Shocking! Really, I am surprised."

Here came a pause of a quarter of a minute.

But our hero could think of no defence—having been caught *in flagrante delicto*, by the Reverend Mr. Bloke himself.

"And such a clever evasion of rules I have so stringently laid down. I have ordered the porter at the gate never to admit any one of those itinerant characters within the college walls. I never thought of the possibility of a gentleman handing his discarded garments out of the window."

"That was the Jew, sir," faintly remarked Mr. Samuel.

"Doubtless," said his tutor. "It is not the suggestion so much as the compliance with it that I complain of. I hope I shall never have to speak of such a breach of all rules of decorum again."

Mr. Golightly heartily promised that he would never hold dealings with Jew or Gentile from out his window again; and having made this promise, was dismissed with the customary tutorial blessing.

"I hope you aint gorn and gort gated, nor nothing for it, sir," said Mr. Sneek. "Not that I ever wear coloured bags myself, and Mr. Slater's things—which fit me to a T—is always kindly given; but I hate to see a gentleman dealing with a Jew. It's odds on 'em, sir. Do you think they'll be be't by gentlemen? No!" exclaimed the gyp, with a proper degree of conviction in his tone.

" 'aud bless me!" he continued, " three pair of bags!"

Our hero had said nothing of the fourth pair, surreptitiously obtained.

" —Three pair and ten shillings for them horns! I could have bought you as good a pair for seven and sixpence, and no bags at all."

Mrs. Cribb—who particularly disliked allowing Sneek to have a private audience of any of their half-dozen masters—now came in on the pretence of having some trifling thing to do. The conversation that was going on interested her so much, that she felt it her duty to remain.

" I expect my people up," said our hero.

" Certainly, sir."

" I should like to give a large wine or something the first night, just for my father to come to, and see how we do it, and whether there has been any improvement made since he was an undergraduate."

" To be sure, sir," said Sneek.

" Or a supper, sir," suggested Mrs. Cribb, with an eye to larger perquisites. " Poor Polly, then— Poll Parrot like a supper? Pretty Poll!"—the old lady stood by the cage. " Scratch a Polly's poll, then. Oh! my goodness me, how you do bite!"

It was indeed extraordinary how clear was Polly's perception of Mrs. Cribb's hypocrisy, and with what settled determination he waited for the moment when her finger was timidly put inside his cage.

"Naughty bird!" said the bedmaker, shaking her head, while the parrot gave a shout of triumphant satisfaction, shrill and loud, which rang through the room.

"Oh, dear!" exclaimed Mrs. Cribb. "I never shall get poor Polly to take to me."

"Take to her, indeed!" said Mr. Sneck, with scornfully indignant emphasis, when she had left the room. "I wonder if Cribb would take to anybody herself as was always giving of her pokes in the ribs with a paper knife."

"You don't mean to tell me that Mrs. Cribb thrashes my bird!" cried our hero.

"I do though, indeed, sir; and orfen I've thought to myself, 'Sneck,' I've thought, 'it's your dooty to tell Mr. Samwell Adawlphus Golightly of this here misconduct of Betsy Cribb's.'"

"Certainly it was, Sneck."

"And then, sir, I've thought to myself, 'John Sneck,' I've thought, 'ought you, as a man, to tell of a woman? And what should you do if a bird took and pecked you awful? John Sneck,'" continued the hypocritical gyp, with his notes of deepest solemnity, such as he used in his responses to the Litany on Sunday mornings, "'I hope you would have the Christian fortitude and resignation to turn the other finger also, and not go, like Betsy Cribb, and strike a pore dumb animal with a paper knife.' But, sir," he added suddenly, in his ordinary tone, standing, his head on one side and his arm behind him, "you won't breathe a word of this as I've felt it my dooty to tell you, to Cribb, sir?"

"Indeed, Sneck," replied his master, who could not help laughing at his servant's transparent hypocrisy, "I shall call Mrs. Cribb over the coals for this, now."

The trouble of looking for her was saved by the entrance of that individual.

"Talk of the devil," said Sneck, *sotto voce.* "Now there'll be a row—for Betsy's got a tongue in her 'ead, she has."

"Oh, my good gracious ha' mercy on me!" was the exclamation of the innocent bedmaker when she had heard the charge. "Oh! John Sneck, how dare you go and take away my character—which love all animals, keeping a little dog, two cats, and a canary myself—before a good master—"

"Now, now, Betsy Cribb," said Sneck, advanc-

ing to a favourable position on the battle field—
" that'll do ;" and he pointed significantly over his
left shoulder. "We know all about it ; and what
I told Mr. Golightly is gospel truth, every word on
it ; so the least said soonest mended, Betsy," he
added, being on his own account anxious to hush
the affair up.

"Least said, indeed!" said Mrs. Cribb, indignantly. "Least said—there, don't wink at me over
the master's shoulder, for I scorn to take no notice
of your winks."

"Oh! Betsy Cribb, how can you say such things!"
put in the gyp. " I was only a rubbing my eye,
sir. I think I've got one of them river flies in it.
But there, a woman 'll make mischief out of anythink! I suppose, Mrs. Cribb," continued the gyp,
with much sarcasm, "if I was to venture so far as
to blow my nose, it wouldn't be high treason."

And he took out his handkerchief, and applied
it to his eye—which, I fear, had winked with a
view to stopping Mrs. Cribb's anger.

" S-silence, sir!" said our hero. " Now, Mrs.
Cribb, is there any truth in what I have been
told?"

" Ah! tell the truth, do!" ejaculated the gyp,
in his religious tone of voice.

" Once, sir, after that bird had flown at me—"

" Once!" exclaimed Sneek, in a growling under-tone.   " Once every Hower or two."

" Will you be quiet, or leave the room, Sneek?"

" C'rt'nly, sir!"

" —Well, sir, once when he flew at me, and pecked my finger so—the mark's only just gone off, though it's weeks ago—I said to him, ' Polly,' I said, ' if ever you bite me again, I'll whip, whip, whip you, you naughty bird;' and I was just a-showing him the paper knife, which lay handy to my 'and, when Sneek came in; and this is what he's gone and made out of it."

" Oh!" cried Sneek, vigorously advancing to re-new the conflict—" oh! you old—old— There, I heven't got a word for you."

" And, sir," continued Mrs. Cribb, maintaining the advantage she had gained—" not that I tell tales, for it aint in my nature to do so—but one day, when I was a-feedin' the bird in the vacation, sir—which I waited on that bird hand and foot all the while you was away—Sneek says, ' Birds is very fond of Kyann pepper,' he says, holding up the pepper box. ' Kyann!' I said, ' Sneek; why, I never heard of such a thing. I'm sure, master never gev him no Kyann.' ' Oh, yes,' he says; ' in their own countries, they live on capsicums and Chilies;' and he peppered that poor bird all of a moment, and before I could stop him, till I thought he'd sneeze his very beak off."

Mr. Sneek met this narrative with a flat contradiction, calling most of the slang saints in the Calendar to witness the truth of his assertions. At last, after administering a suitable reproof to his two servants, our hero dismissed them. He was, however, doomed to hear the battle raging in the gyp-room, out on the staircase, for a good hour afterwards—where, without the restraint imposed by his presence, the worthy pair went at it, as Mr. Sneek subsequently remarked, " hammer and tongs."

Our hero carried out his intention of giving an entertainment to his numerous friends in honour of his father's visit. A supper, on a substantial and entirely satisfactory scale, was furnished from the college kitchens, while the champagne was sent in to his rooms in great abundance from the grocer's; the stock of wine he had brought up from home for his use during the term having been consumed some time before.

The arrangements were very complete. Our hero was to meet his father and mother, his aunts, and Miss Jekyll at the station; and—having escorted the ladies to their hotel, and personally

seen that everything necessary for their comfort
had been attended to—he and his father were to
walk arm-in-arm to his rooms at St. Mary's, where
supper would at once be served; and Mr. Golightly, senior, would have the pleasure of making
the acquaintance of his son's set. It was, therefore, with considerable disappointment that our
hero mastered the contents of a telegram from
Tuffley, Fuddleton, to S. A. Golightly, Esq., St.
Mary's, Cambridge, which ran as follows:—

" Sir—The family will come by first train in the
morning instead of to-night, as arranged. All well.
Sorry for delay."

It was plain that, as the supper was nearly ready
to be dished up when the telegram arrived, the entertainment could not be put off. Determining,
therefore, to make the best of a bad job, our hero
apologized to his friends for the unavoidable absence of his respected father; and it is only fair to
them to say that they bore the unexpected absence
of the reverend gentleman very well indeed—Mr.
Pokyr remarking that he " would have the old boy
at his diggings instead, another night." All our
hero's friends—Messrs. Pokyr, Calipee, Blaydes,
Chutney, Fitzfoodel, and a host of other gentle-

men—were present, in the highest possible spirits, and with undeniably good appetites; the rear rank being whipped in by the portly person of The O'Higgins, who laid the lateness of his arrival to "pool;" observing, at the same time, that, as they had not commenced, there was no harm done.

The supper was eaten amid general festiveness and the popping of champagne corks, cigars were smoked, and songs were sung; and by the time the long tables were broken up, and packs of cards placed upon them by Mr. Sneck and competent assistants, our hero had almost forgotten that he had ever "put on the feed" in honour of his worthy father.

Whist, loo, and vingt-et-un were played with much spirit, and varying success. At the last-mentioned game, it was observed by persons more observant than our hero, that Mr. Timothy Fitzgerald O'Higgins turned up an ace very frequently indeed. Indeed, the descendant of kings was proverbially lucky at "Van."

At last, at a very late hour, the party separated. Mr. Samuel—whose gait was very slightly affected by the hot room and the smoke of the cigars—insisted upon seeing some out-college men as far as the gate.

"Wickens," he cried, kicking at the door of the

porter's lodge—"wake up, ol' f'llr! Le' these gen'elmen ou'."

Presently, when the porter appeared, grumbling, and muffled up in his nightgown, our hero gave "the old cock" a playful push. The friends left, and the gate was closed.

"Hallo, Golightly, you're not well. You shall never walk back to your rooms."

"Yes shall."

"No!" and eight strong arms closed round the feebly resisting person of our hero. "We'll carry you."

"No sha'n't."

In an instant, Mr. Samuel was borne aloft at a rapid pace towards a well-known piece of ornamental masonry in the middle of the great quad.

"Don't put him in the fountain," said somebody, paraphrasing the well-known piece of advice.

And nothing less than the stout arm of his friend Mr. Pokyr saved our hero from a regular ducking. As it was, he was splashed by the trickling water from the spout above, and taken off to bed, where he soon gave the natural evidence of sound sleep.

In the morning, he felt himself rudely shaken out of his slumber.

"I—I sha'n't get up yet, Sneek. No chapel

for me—not equal to it," he muttered, still half asleep.

The shaking being continued, and Mr. Samuel's nerves being also a little out of order, he became rather angry.

" C-confound it—go away, will you !"

" Samuel—Samuel, what is all this ?" said a well-known voice.

Our hero was wide awake in an instant.

" Oh, F-fa—how do you do ?" he said, extending his hand from under the bed-clothes.

" A panel kicked out of your door, broken chairs and glass in your rooms, and a horrid smell of stale tobacco and the fumes of punch ! Oh, dear !" continued the Rector, in a tone of mild reproof. " And your aunts will be here in an instant; and I would not have them see it for the world. If your aunt Dorothea takes it into her head that you are wild, she'll leave all her money to your cousin George. Oh, dear ! what is to be done ?"

Our hero sent his father off to stop the further advance of the ladies; reproved Mrs. Cribb and his devoted gyp for not getting the place into present-able order sooner—all in his long nightgown, with a travelling shawl hastily drawn round him—for the occasion was too urgent for him to stop to dress, before giving a few necessary directions. In this costume, he was assisting his servants to move his dining table into its proper place, when he heard the rustle of silks on the stairs, and Mr. Pokyr's voice exclaiming—

"Those are his rooms. I'll rap him up for you."

"Oh, goodness!" he exclaimed, as Mrs. Cribb shut him in his china closet, and stood firmly with her back to the door—"Fa must have missed them somehow, and here they are! What will Aunt Dorothea think when she sees the room?"

CHAPTER XXIV.

IN WHICH OUR HISTORY IS CONCLUDED.

E left our hero in his china closet. His situation was not a very pleasant one. The air of the place was decidedly stuffy —there being a powerful odour of emptied but unwashed jam and pickle pots. He could not unfold the full dimensions of his manly form, for the brass hooks sticking out from the shelves ran into the back of his head if he did. Add to these causes of disquietude that he was shivering in his nightgown, and Aunt Dorothea's awful voice was to be heard on the threshold of his disorderly room, and it is not difficult to imagine that Mr. Golightly felt supremely uncomfortable.

Mrs. Cribb stood with her back to the door of the china closet, with an air of firm determination to let no one approach within a yard of her master's place of concealment. Twice our hero tried softly to open the door of his hiding-place the least bit in the world, just to enable him to breathe; but this action on his side was answered by a resolute bunt from the person of his gaoler on the other. He gave it up as hopeless; and crouched down among the pots and pans, to be slowly poisoned by the odours of decaying scraps of pickle and mouldy jam.

"When I do get out," he resolved to himself, "I'll make old Mrs. Cribb wash these pots and bottles, or turn them out."

"I don't believe the lazy fellow's up yet," said the voice of Mr. Pokyr.

Our hero could unfortunately hear only too plainly all that was going on.

"What a very nice part of the college Samuel's rooms are in," said a rather masculine voice.

It was Aunt Dorothea's.

"Oh, goodness, how *did* Pa miss them?" groaned Mr. Samuel, in the darkness of the china closet.

Then he heard a sweet, musical voice, the sound of which he loved to hear, saying, in reply to his aunt's remark—

"Really, quite beautiful! And look at his name up over the door!"

This was Miss Jekyll, he knew.

"What will she think when she sees the room? Hang it—it's too bad of Pokyr."

There was a rustle of silks, and the half-closed door of his room was pushed open by Mr. Pokyr.

"Oh, what a horrid smell of tobacco!" said Miss Harriet.

"Samuel knows tobacco smoke always makes me feel faint," exclaimed Mrs. Golightly.

Sneek and Cribb stood making a dozen reverences, in their accustomed fashion.

Mr. Pokyr dashed into our hero's bed-room, crying—

"I'll wake him up."

But the bed was empty.

"And where is his father?" asked Mrs. Golightly.

"Golightly's somewhere about," said Mr. Pokyr, observing our hero's clothes on a chair in his bedroom.

"Golightly," he called out; but of course there was no answering "Here."

"Oh, dear me, what a very disreputable appearance his room presents. Look, the door even is broken!" continued Miss Harriet, pointing to the bed-room.

"Oh, dear!" sighed Mrs. Golightly, not knowing exactly whether to side with her son or not.

"Beg your pardon, ladies. Party last night," said Sneek.

"Mr. Golightly is always a most steady gentleman, ma'am," said Mrs. Cribb, addressing herself pointedly to Miss Harriet Golightly.

But there remained the inexorable logic of facts.

"I thought Samuel's habits were very different," exclaimed the last-mentioned lady, pointing about with her parasol.

"What do you mean, sister?" asked Miss Dorothea, sharply.

"I mean this room is a disgraceful scene, Dorothea. Look at all those packs of cards hastily tucked away, and look at the broken glasses!"

At this moment the Rector put his jovial face in at the door, exclaiming—

"Oh, you are here!"

And Mr. Pokyr discovered the whereabouts of the "landlord."

"Cribb," said he.

"Sir," said the bedmaker—while the gyp winked at least a thousand and one winks with his working eye, all intended for Mr. Pokyr.

"Golightly's in that closet."

"Nothink of the kind, sir—which it's full of his china and things," said Mrs. Cribb.

"In the china closet! Samuel in the china closet!" exclaimed all the ladies in a breath. "Why is Samuel in the china closet?"

"Come, show us your head, Golightly—we won't ask for anything more," said Mr. Pokyr, removing Mrs. Cribb from the door.

"OH, SAMUEL, THIS IS SHOCKING!"

Thus adjured, our hero put out his head, and smiled very feebly, speedily popping it back again.

"Oh, Samuel, this is shocking!" said Miss Harriet. "We are quite—quite shocked."

The Rector and our hero's mamma waited nervously for the verdict of Miss Dorothea. They feared the worst consequences; but the spirit of the Normans, her ancestors, was strong in their daughter.

"Who is shocked, sister?" asked Miss Dorothea, in her most contradictory manner. "Speak for yourself, if you please."

"Well, sister, I'm sure—" the younger lady began, apologetically.

"I'm sure of one thing," said Miss Dorothea, tartly taking her up—"Samuel is a Tredsofte all over. I had no idea the boy had half so much spirit. I hate a milksop; and Har-riet, *I love the smell of tobacco.*"

Miss Dorothea looked so warlike in her majesty, that nobody dared reply; but three persons in the room breathed freely again. The reversion to the dear old spinster's Consols was assured.

"Samuel, I'm proud of you," said the good lady, addressing herself to the crevice in the closet door —for our hero had prudently closed it again. "We shall wait breakfast for you at the hotel for half an hour. Brother, give me your arm. Mr. Pokyr, you will join us at breakfast, I hope."

And having thus spoken, Miss Dorothea sailed out of the room with the majesty of an empress, followed, at a respectful distance, by the rest of the party.

When they were gone, our hero made a rush from the china closet to his bed-room, and dressed himself in the highest glee. All had gone well.

"What a spirit Aunt Dorothea has!" he thought to himself more than once.

While Mr. Sneek pronounced her praises in the words—

"Well, the old lady's a out-an-outer—she is."

The sun shone brightly on the party as they walked with Mr. Pokyr round the college, seeing in turn the library, the chapel, the bridge, and everything there was to be seen. Good temper soon reigned supreme again.

"I really must call on Mr. Bloke—not now, you know—but before I go away," said the Rector to Mr. Pokyr. "You must show me where his rooms are."

"All right!—close here," said Mr. Pokyr, vaulting lightly over some iron hurdles placed in front of the tutor's windows for the protection of the grass plots. "Those are his wind—"

But before Mr. Pokyr had time to say the word, an angry visage appeared at the open window. It was the tutor himself.

"Dear me, Mr. Pokyr, whenever I look out of my window I see you jumping those rails," said the irate Don, who did not see the Rector's portly figure.

"And it is very curious, Mr. Bloke," said Mr. Pokyr, presuming on the situation, " that whenever I jump those rails I see you looking out of your window."

"Oh dear, dear, Mr. Golightly! I did not see you. Your son told me you were coming up. Pray come in."

The Rector, having pointed to the ladies and introduced them, excused himself from paying a visit to Mr. Bloke on their account.

Presently they all sat down to breakfast, having been joined by Mr. Samuel, who, at Miss Dorothea's request, sat next to her.

After breakfast, they commenced to do the lions of the place; and during their stay, of nearly a week, they were constantly occupied in the same agreeable pursuit. They went every night down to Grassy, to the boat races; they visited the A.D.C., and accepted invitations to three dances and as many dinners.

It was when the college ball, which is an annual affair at St. Mary's, was being celebrated with great *éclat*, that our hero led Miss Jekyll out of the heated ball-room into the moonlight softly falling on the cloistered court; and there, without half the hesitation that might have been expected of him, asked her that question which all men ought to ask once in their lives, and no man wishes to ask twice.

Her reply may be easily divined, when we say that our hero, as he walked back to the ball-room, after an absence of half an hour, with the beautiful girl on his arm, looked very proud and very happy.

"Now I know I shall get through my Degree Exam. all right," he said.

And he did.